TIM KIZER

I SAW WHAT YOU DID

A Novel

I SAW WHAT YOU DID

"I saw my husband kidnap a woman forty minutes ago."

Shortly after Emma says these words to a 911 operator, her husband, Paul, is arrested on suspicion of kidnapping and murder. His victim, Alison Bowles, is found raped and strangled to death hours later. The evidence against Paul is irrefutable: there are traces of his DNA on Alison's body, and her hair has been discovered in his trunk. The police believe he may be a serial killer.

Paul insists he's innocent and claims he was with his lover, Julie, at the time of the murder. A few days after talking to Paul's lawyer, Julie disappears without a trace. Emma is surprised to find out that all fingerprints in Julie's house have been wiped off.

Where is Julie? Why were the fingerprints wiped off?

In her search for answers Emma uncovers a diabolical conspiracy masterminded by a serial murderer. He has a long target list, and he knows who he'll kill next.

TIM KIZER

I SAW WHAT YOU DID

Also by Tim Kizer

Dead Girls
Abduction
The Girl Who Didn't Die
An Evil Mind
The Vanished
Spellbound
Mania
The Mindbender
Days of Vengeance
Deception

Copyright 2020 Tim Kizer

CONTENTS

I Saw What You Did   1

Sample chapters from Dead Girls   .   .   259

I SAW WHAT YOU DID

Chapter 1

1

Why is she doing this? Emma wondered as the woman climbed into the trunk of Paul's car.

What was going on?

Her skin broke out in goosebumps.

The woman was being forced to get into the trunk. Emma's husband was kidnapping her.

2

Forty minutes earlier

When Emma opened the passenger's door, Susan jerked her thumb toward the back seat and said, "Sit in the back."

That was a good idea: it would be hard for Paul to see her face if she sat in the back.

Emma slipped into the back seat, and the car pulled away.

"Who's babysitting Ollie?" Susan asked.

"He's at my parents'."

Emma had told Paul that she and their son, Ollie, would be at her parents' house until eight o'clock so he would have the option of meeting with his lover at their house.

She had found out that Paul was cheating on her thanks to Susan, who had seen him with an attractive young woman at the Galleria Dallas mall two weeks ago. It was Susan's idea that they follow Paul together in her car. Emma hoped she would catch Paul with his lover today and wouldn't have to tail him again.

Susan had come prepared: there were a twenty-four-pack of bottled water and three boxes of energy bars on the back seat.

"Did Paul tell you anything about his plans for today?" Susan asked.

"He said he was going to hang out with his friends."

Susan smiled. "I think he's going to hang out with that bitch."

She pulled over to the curb about seventy yards from Emma's place and turned off the car.

Paul was still home: his BMW was still parked in front of their house.

"I have water and energy bars," Susan said. "Too bad we can't pee in a bottle."

"We should have worn diapers."

Susan chuckled. "Yeah."

Paul's lover might be in the house right now.

They might be having sex in our bed.

The thought made Emma grimace.

Paul emerged from the house and walked to his car. He was wearing blue jeans and a brown jacket.

"He came out of the house," Susan said.

Paul got into his BMW and started a three-point turn.

Susan switched on the engine. "Don't take your eyes off him."

"Okay."

Paul drove for about twenty minutes before pulling over in front of a one-story house with a fence around it. Susan stopped at the curb and shifted into park.

Did Paul's lover live in one of these houses?

Paul did not get out of the car.

Was he waiting for her to come out?

Where were they going? A restaurant? A motel?

Susan turned off the ignition. "Is he waiting for her?"

Emma leaned forward between the front seats, her eyes glued to Paul's car. "Probably." She sighed.

There were no vehicles parked at the curb between Susan's Toyota and Paul's BMW. About a hundred yards separated them, so Emma was sure her husband couldn't see that the Toyota wasn't empty.

They were not far from the University of Texas at Dallas campus. Was Paul's lover a student there?

Paul sat in the car for about ten minutes before he finally got out. There was a woman walking down the sidewalk toward him. She had on a blue skirt and white shirt.

Is she the woman he's cheating on me with?

"He got out of the car," Susan said.

Paul opened the trunk and stepped onto the sidewalk. The woman in the blue skirt and white shirt stopped a few feet from him.

"Why did he open the trunk?" Susan asked.

Paul and the woman moved to the rear of the BMW. Then a strange thing happened: the woman started to climb into the trunk.

Why is she doing this? What's going on?

Emma's skin broke out in goosebumps.

She's being forced to climb into the trunk. Paul's kidnapping this poor woman.

Paul's right arm was bent at the elbow. As her husband leaned over the trunk, it dawned on Emma. Paul had a gun in his right hand and he had threatened the woman with it.

Paul closed the trunk, got behind the wheel, and pulled away from the curb.

"I think he kidnapped her." Emma was shivering with shock.

"I think you're right." Susan started the car. "Let's follow him."

They stayed about a hundred yards behind Paul. Emma kept her gaze fixed on her husband's car, her heart thumping hard in her chest, her mind reeling.

That woman could try to open the trunk. It was possible to open the trunk from the inside, wasn't it?

Paul might have cuffed her hands behind her back.

If the woman banged on the lid, someone might hear and rescue her, right?

At the next intersection, Paul turned left, and Susan sped up a little.

What was Paul going to do to the woman? Rape her?

Would he eventually let her go?

Emma wanted to believe that he would.

As they turned left, Emma was relieved to see that they hadn't lost Paul's BMW.

Maybe they should catch up to Paul and ask him to let the woman go?

Would he listen to me?

Paul turned left again.

"Let's catch up to him," Emma said. "I'll ask him to let her go."

"Okay."

Susan's Toyota picked up speed. When they made the turn, Emma felt a sinking in the pit of her stomach: Paul's car was nowhere in sight.

"Do you see him?" Susan asked.

"No."

Maybe he had kidnapped the woman for ransom?

Susan took the next right and then said, "We lost him."

Had Paul noticed that he was being followed?

Susan pulled over and put the car in park. "Is he going to kill her?" she said in a tense voice.

"No." Emma swallowed. "I don't think so."

Should she call Paul?

What was she going to say to him? Ask him to let the woman go? Would he listen to her?

She took out her phone and dialed Paul's number. Her call went straight to voice mail.

"Did you call Paul?" Susan asked.

"Yes. He's not answering."

"Do you want to go home?"

Emma nodded. "Yes."

As she punched Emma's address into the GPS, Susan said, "Do you want to pick up Ollie?"

Emma shook her head. "I'll pick him up later."

3

On the way home, Emma called Paul's cell every two minutes, but it went to voice mail each time. As they drove up to Emma's house, Susan asked, "Do you want me to stay with you? I have nothing else to do."

"Yes, please stay."

Where was Paul now? Was he still driving? Was he about to rape that poor woman?

As they entered the house, Emma thought: Paul might have brought the woman here. She needed to check the garage.

The house was silent. In the living room, Emma switched on the TV and asked Susan, "Would you like some coffee?"

"Yes."

Emma went into the kitchen, opened the door to the garage, and saw that it was empty. Paul and that woman weren't here.

She grabbed two cups from the cupboard, filled them with coffee, and returned to the living room.

Was that woman Paul's first victim?

"I forgot about your car," Susan said.

"It's okay. I'll get it later."

Her Nissan was parked only a mile from her house.

Emma put the cups on the coffee table and sat in an armchair. Her temples were throbbing.

How many women had Paul killed?

She imagined Paul grabbing the woman by the hair and slitting her throat. Was he going to kill her with a knife?

"Are you okay?" Susan asked.

"Yes."

Was Paul raping the woman now?

Emma picked up her cup and took a swig.

Hopefully, the woman would manage to escape from Paul or someone would rescue her.

Hopefully, Paul would spare her life.

"I think that woman wasn't his first victim," Susan said.

"Maybe."

Emma dialed Paul's number again, but again got voice mail.

Paul would turn on his phone when he was finished with the woman. He wasn't done with her yet.

"He's still not answering?" Susan asked.

Emma shook her head.

"You think he'll rape her?"

Emma nodded.

Susan sighed heavily. Emma got up and began to pace around the room. When she sat down, Susan said, "Everything will be all right, Emma."

They were silent for a while, then Susan said, "We should do something,"

What would she do if it had been a stranger and not her husband who had kidnapped that woman?

She would immediately report the abduction to the police.

"What can we do?" Emma said.

"I think we should call the police."

Emma nodded. "Yes."

Did Susan expect her to try to dissuade her from contacting the police?

"Are you sure? We can wait, if you want," Susan said.

Was the woman still alive?

"Let's call now."

If the police found Paul before he killed that woman, he would be charged only with kidnapping and avoid the death penalty.

Why do you care if Paul avoids the death penalty or not?

Paul was a monster. She shouldn't care about his well-being.

Emma dialed 911 on her cellphone and when the operator answered, she said, "I want to report an abduction."

"Who was abducted?"

"I don't know her name. I saw... I saw my husband kidnap a woman about forty minutes ago. He forced her into the trunk of his car."

"Did you say the kidnapper is your husband?"

"Yes. His name's Paul Marston. He's driving a gray BMW seven-forty."

"What's your name, ma'am?"

"Emma Marston."

"Do you know where your husband is now?"

"No."

"Where are you?"

"I'm home."

"What's your address?"

Emma told the operator her address.

"Please help her," she said.

"Where did the abduction take place?"

"Not far from the University of Texas."

"Is Paul driving his own car?"

"Yes."

"What's his cellphone number?"

Emma gave the operator Paul's number. The police would try to track down his cell, but they couldn't track down a phone that was turned off, could they?

"Are you calling from your cellphone?"

"Yes."

When Emma hung up, Susan said, "I hope the police find them before he ..."

Before he kills her.

"They're going to track down his phone." Emma rubbed her temples.

She had lived with Paul for twelve years and had no idea he was a violent pervert.

Had Paul taken the woman to a secluded place or a dungeon? Emma hoped it was the latter, because then Paul wouldn't have to kill her today. She supposed that if one took a woman to a dungeon, he intended to keep her alive for at least a couple of days.

There must be hundreds of cars like Paul's in Dallas. It would probably take the police hours to find him.

"Has he ever hurt you?" Susan asked.

"No."

Should she confront Paul when he came home?

He might try to kill her to keep her silent.

He would surely be furious if she told him that she had reported him to the police.

"He looks harmless," Susan said. "You'd never think he was a rapist. You really can't judge a book by its cover."

Emma nodded.

"I wonder if he raped the woman I saw him with at the mall."

Had Paul killed her?

Emma asked, "Should I tell Paul I called the police?"

"Hell no. He'll kill you if you tell him that. Call the police as soon as he comes home."

At half past five Susan said she was going home.

"Are you going to be okay?" she asked Emma.

"Yes."

Chapter 2

1

Fifteen minutes after Susan left, the doorbell rang. Was it Paul?

Emma looked through the peephole before opening the door and saw that it was some guy in a dark suit.

Was he a police detective?

"What can I do for you?" Emma asked the man.

He held up a police badge and said, "I'm Detective Adam Korbin from the Dallas Police Department. I'd like to talk to Emma Marston."

Korbin was tall, deeply tanned, broad-shouldered, with close-cropped hair.

"I'm Emma Marston."

"Can I come in?"

"Sure." Emma stepped back, and Korbin entered the house.

"Is your husband home?" the detective asked when Emma closed the door.

"No."

As they went into the living room, Korbin said, "Did you call nine one one today to report an abduction?"

"Yes, I did."

Korbin sat down on the sofa and took out his notebook. "And you said the kidnapper was your husband, Paul Marston."

Emma nodded. "Yes."

"Do you know where your husband is now?"

"No. Are you looking for them?"

"Yes, we are. Do you know the name of the woman kidnapped by Paul?"

"No."

"Where did the abduction take place?"

"A mile or two from the University of Texas at Dallas."

"What time?"

"Around four o'clock."

What if he doesn't believe me? What if he thinks I made it all up out of spite?

Susan had witnessed the abduction, too. The police would believe her.

They might think I asked her to say that she'd seen Paul kidnap that woman.

"How did it happen?"

"That woman was walking down the street, and as she passed Paul's car, he forced her into the trunk."

"Was it a residential street?"

"Yes."

"Where were you when it happened?"

"I was in my car. I was following Paul."

"Why were you following him?"

"I thought Paul was cheating on me."

"Did you try to stop him?"

"I went after him but lost him. I called Paul several times, but his phone was off."

"Are you sure it was your husband?"

"Yes. I followed him from our house."

"What did the victim look like?"

"I was too far away to see her face. She wore a blue skirt and white shirt."

"How long have you and Paul been married?"

"Twelve years."

"Do you have children?"

"We have a son."

"What does Paul do for a living?"

"He's a lawyer."

"What kind?"

"A criminal lawyer."

"What do you do for a living?"

"I'm an accountant at Willowbrook Memorial Hospital. Did you try to track down Paul's phone?"

"We're doing everything we can. Can I see Paul's office?"

"Yes."

They went upstairs to Paul's office, where Korbin scanned the shelves and opened a few desk drawers.

"Where's your son?" the detective asked as they walked back to the living room.

"He's at my parents'."

Emma looked at the wall clock. It had been almost two hours since the abduction. Was that woman still alive?

"There's no one else in the house?"

"Yes. Are you going to arrest Paul when he gets home?"

"Yes. But I hope we'll find him before he gets here."

"Is it okay if I leave?"

"Yes. We'll try to arrest him before he enters the house."

If the police found no evidence of an abduction, they would release Paul, wouldn't they?

And when he comes home, he'll kill me for snitching on him.

"Are you going to tell Paul that I told you about the kidnapping?"

"You don't want him to know you called the police?"

She would have to testify against Paul in court, wouldn't she?

"I'd rather he didn't know that," Emma said.

"Are you afraid he'll hurt you?"

She would move out of the house before Paul was released from jail.

"Yes."

They might let Paul out on bail. How much could his bail be?

Probably at least a hundred thousand dollars.

"Do you have anyone you can stay with?" Korbin asked.

"Yes. Could you call me if you decide to release Paul?"

"Sure. Are you going to leave now?"

Should she leave?

She wanted to watch Paul get arrested. She wouldn't have to talk to him because they would arrest him before he went inside.

"Can I stay until he gets here?" Emma asked.

"Yes."

"Are you going to wait outside?"

"Yes."

Emma figured there were plainclothes cops watching the house.

"You can wait here," she said.

"Thank you."

Korbin took out his radio, pressed a button, and said, "This is Korbin. I'll wait for Marston inside."

If Paul was carrying the gun he had used to threaten that woman, he might try to shoot the cops during the arrest and would probably end up dead.

Paul might die tonight. She didn't know how to feel about it.

"He may have a gun," Emma said.

Korbin told the cops watching the house that Paul might be armed and then asked Emma, "Do you think your husband's going to kill the victim?"

"I don't know."

Had Paul turned on his phone?

Emma said, "Can I call him?"

"What are you going to say to him?"

"I'll ask him... I'll ask him if he wants to go to the movies."

"Okay. You can call him."

The call went straight to voice mail again. Paul wasn't done with the woman yet, and she might still be alive.

"His phone's still off," Emma said.

Twenty minutes later Korbin's cell beeped and he pulled it out. Emma wondered if it was a message saying that Paul had been arrested.

The detective said nothing after reading the text and remained on the sofa.

At ten past seven Emma's phone rang. It was Paul.

Emma felt a chill race up her spine: he was finished with the woman.

"It's Paul," she told Korbin. The detective stood up, went to the front door, and stepped outside.

Emma tapped the answer button and said, "Hi, honey."

"Is everything okay? Why did you call?"

"Do you want to go to the movies tonight? Ollie wants to see that cartoon about the dogs."

"Go without me. I have some work to do."

"Okay."

Had he killed that woman?

"Are you home?"

"Yes, but we're leaving soon."

"I'll be home in ten minutes."

"Okay."

Paul hung up.

Emma walked to the front door, opened it, and beckoned to Korbin, who was standing on the sidewalk near the Marstons' mailbox.

"He said he'll be home in ten minutes," she told the detective when he came in.

Korbin glanced at his watch. "Go upstairs and stay there until we arrest Paul."

"Okay."

"Stay away from the windows."

Heart pounding hard, Emma went upstairs to Paul's office.

In ten minutes, her husband, a kidnapper and probably a murderer, would be taken into custody or shot dead, and her life would change forever.

Actually, her life had changed forever three hours ago, when she saw Paul force that poor woman into his trunk.

2

At a quarter past seven, Emma stepped to the window, which faced the street, and opened the blinds. Two minutes later, she saw Paul's BMW pull into the driveway. She tensed up.

Paul got out, and as he walked to the porch, a man wearing jeans and a T-shirt climbed out of a gray Chrysler 300 parked across the street.

Had Paul left his gun in the car?

Emma went to the stairs and tiptoed to the landing between floors. She heard Korbin say, "I'm Detective Korbin with the Dallas Police Department. Are you Paul Marston?"

"Yes," Paul replied.

"Mr. Marston, you're under arrest."

"For what?"

"Please put your hands behind your back."

"How did you get into my house? Where's my wife?"

"Your wife is fine."

The front door closed and the voices became muffled. Emma ran down the last flight of stairs, rushed to the front door, and opened it a crack. Paul was walking down the driveway, his hands cuffed behind his back, escorted by Korbin, the guy in the jeans and T-shirt, and a man in khakis and a long-sleeved shirt.

Before he climbed into the back of the gray Chrysler 300, Paul looked toward the house and Emma hid behind the door and stayed there for a few moments. The cop in the jeans sat next to Paul and the cop in the khakis got behind the wheel. When the car drove off, Korbin went back to the house and told Emma that they were going to impound Paul's BMW.

"He was driving this car when he kidnapped that woman, right?" the detective said.

"Yes."

Korbin walked to the BMW and pushed a button on the key fob he held in his hand. As the trunk lid opened, gooseflesh broke out on Emma's arms.

What if her body's in the trunk?

Korbin glanced inside the trunk and then closed it. "She's not in there," he told Emma.

She swallowed.

What had Paul done with the body? What if it was never found? No body, no case.

"When is your tow truck going to be here?" she asked.

"In half an hour."

Emma needed some time alone, so she decided not to invite Korbin inside. She called her mother, Rosie, and told her that she would pick up Ollie in an hour.

Around eight o'clock, a police flatbed truck arrived and picked up Paul's car. Before he left, Korbin told Emma that he was headed to the police station and thanked her for her help.

"Are you going to interrogate Paul tonight?"

"Yes."

As Emma walked to her car, she called her mother and told her she was on her way to pick up Ollie.

"You sound tired, honey," Rosie said.

"I am tired."

Chapter 3

1

"Did they tell you why I was arrested?" Paul Marston looked exhausted and angry. He had on blue jeans and a tan long-sleeved shirt.

"They claim you kidnapped a young woman today," Jonah Wallach said.

They were in an interview room at Dallas Police Headquarters. Paul's right hand was cuffed to a metal bar on the table. He had done the smart thing and refused to talk to the detectives without his attorney. Wallach had been driving home from a restaurant when Paul called him. He knew Paul well—they had been friends for six years—and he was convinced Paul would never do what he was accused of.

Paul was forty-two, tall, fit, with thick brown hair. Wallach was forty-six, a bit shorter than Paul, lean, with a neatly trimmed mustache. He had been in private practice since graduating from law school, while Paul had worked for the government for eleven years before joining a law firm.

"Did they tell you who they think I kidnapped?" Paul said.

"No. Where were you this afternoon?"

"I was home until about three and then went to a friend's place. I stayed there until seven and then drove home. They arrested me when I opened the door to my house. One of them, Detective Korbin, was inside. I think they were searching the house when I got there."

"Did you give anyone a ride today?"

"No."

"Did you loan your car to anyone today?"

"No. Can you call Emma and tell her that I was arrested?"

"Sure."

Paul gave the lawyer Emma's number.

"Do you want me to tell her why you were arrested?"

"Yes."

Wallach got up, opened the door, and told the police officer standing outside, "Officer, we're done."

Five minutes later, Detectives Adam Korbin and Michael Heaney entered the room.

"Mr. Marston wants to know what he's charged with," Wallach said.

"We'll get to that in a minute," Korbin replied. Then he said to Paul, "Do you have a happy marriage, Paul?"

Wallach asked, "What does that have to do with Mr. Marston's arrest?"

"I'll explain later. Do you have a happy marriage, Mr. Marston?"

Paul said, "Yes, I have a happy marriage."

"Do you think your wife has a reason to lie about you?"

"No. Did you talk to Emma?"

"Yes."

"What were you doing in my house? Who let you in?"

"Your wife let me in."

"Were you searching the house?"

"No."

Heaney said, "Is she alive?"

"Who?"

"The woman you kidnapped this afternoon. Is she alive?"

"I didn't kidnap anyone."

Korbin said, "A witness saw you force a woman into the trunk of your car not far from the University of Texas at Dallas around four o'clock."

"The witness is wrong. I have an alibi. I was at a friend's place from three to seven."

Heaney said, "The witness is your wife. Emma saw you force that woman into the trunk of your car."

Paul's eyes widened. "Emma said that?"

"Yes."

Paul shook his head. "That's impossible. I didn't kidnap anyone."

Wallach said, "Emma must have seen someone who looked like Paul."

"She's sure it was Mr. Marston."

Wallach asked, "What's the victim's name?"

"We'll provide it later."

They don't know who was kidnapped, Wallach thought.

Korbin said, "Paul, tell us where she is and we'll make sure you get a good deal."

"I didn't kidnap anyone. I have an alibi."

Heaney asked, "Did you kill her?"

Wallach said, "Gentlemen, this interview is over."

"Okay," Korbin said.

The detectives stood up.

"I'd like to confer with my client in private," Wallach said.

"Sure," Korbin said.

When the detectives left the room and the camera was switched off, Wallach asked, "Is everything okay between you and Emma?"

"Yes."

"Do you have any idea why she told the police that you kidnapped someone?"

"Like you said, she probably saw someone who looked like me."

Or she had made it all up. The detectives seemed to think it was possible.

"I think they have no victim," the lawyer said.

Paul nodded.

"If they don't find any evidence in your car or house, they'll have no case."

"They'll find nothing. I didn't kidnap anyone."

"What's the name of the friend you were with this afternoon?"

"Julie."

Had Paul been alone with Julie? Was he having an affair with her?

"What's her phone number?"

Paul told Wallach Julie's number and then said, "Please call my father and tell him I was arrested."

"Do you want me to tell him about Emma?"

Paul nodded.

Chapter 4

1

Emma was sure now that Paul had murdered that woman: she had seen his face and could identify him. If her body was never found, the police would release Paul. What would she do if they let him go?

She could try to find out where he had hidden the body.

When she arrived at her parents' house, Emma told her mother that she needed to talk to her, and they went into a bedroom.

"Can Ollie and I stay here for a couple of days?" Emma said after closing the door.

"Sure." Rosie took her hand. "Sweetie, is everything okay?"

Should she tell her mother about the kidnapping?

Emma hesitated, then said, "I saw Paul abduct a woman today."

Rosie raised her eyebrows. "Oh my God. Paul abducted a woman?"

Emma nodded. "He forced her into the trunk of his car. I think he killed her."

"Did you call the police?"

"Yes. They arrested him an hour ago. I think he's done it before."

"Jesus." Rosie sat down on the bed.

"If they let him out on bail, I'll have to find another place to live."

"They're not going to tell him you called the police, are they?"

"I don't know."

Emma told Ollie that they would spend the night at his grandparents' house because there was something wrong with electric wires at their place. Her father, Phil, said that he knew a good electrician, and then Rosie asked him to help her with the computer and they moved into the office. Phil had a worried look on his face when he and his wife came back.

At ten o'clock Emma's phone rang. An unknown number.

"I'm sorry to call you so late, Mrs. Marston," a man said. "My name's Jonah Wallach. I'm your husband's attorney. Paul asked me to tell you that he was arrested. He's being held at the North Tower Detention Facility."

Had Korbin told Paul that she had reported him to the police?

"What was he arrested for?"

"The police claim he abducted someone. Did you let any police officers into your house today before seven p.m.?"

"Yes. A police detective. He asked me about Paul."

"Did he search the house?"

"No."

"Were you home when Paul was arrested?"

"Yes. Did they set bail?"

"The bail hearing is tomorrow."

"Please keep me posted."

"Sure."

When Emma hung up, Rosie asked, "Who was it?"

"Paul's lawyer."

"Do they know you called the police?"

"I don't know."

Half an hour later Emma's phone rang again. It was Nancy Marston, Paul's mother.

"Hi, Emma," Nancy said.

"Hi, Nancy. How are you?"

"Why are you doing this, Emma?"

"What do you mean?"

"You told the police Paul kidnapped someone. That's a lie. Paul's a good man. He wouldn't hurt a fly. He loves you, Emma."

Korbin had told Paul that she had reported him to the police.

He hadn't promised not to do that, had he?

Emma could tell Nancy was struggling to control her anger. She felt bad for her mother-in-law, but it wasn't her fault Paul had abducted that woman, was it?

"I know what I saw, Nancy. Paul kidnapped a woman. Let's hope she's still alive."

"It wasn't Paul. You saw someone who looked like him."

"I don't want to talk about it. Goodbye, Nancy." She hung up.

Emma waited for Nancy to call again, but it didn't happen.

Paul's family would try to get her to recant, but she wouldn't do it. Paul had to pay for what he had done to that woman.

She had gotten lucky today, hadn't she? She should thank the Universe for letting her find out that Paul was a rapist and possibly a murderer.

Thank you, Universe! Thank you so much!

At eleven Susan called.

I probably should have given her an update hours ago, Emma thought as she said, "Hi, Susan."

"Can you talk?" Susan asked.

"Yes."

"Are you alone?"

"Yes."

"Where's Paul?"

"In jail."

"He was arrested?"

"Yes."

"Are you okay? Do you want me to come over?"

"I'm fine."

"Did they find that woman?"

"No."

"Does Paul know I was with you when you saw him kidnap that woman?"

"No."

"Please don't tell him I was with you. I'd appreciate it if you kept me out of this. Can you do that for me?"

Was Susan afraid Paul would kill her?

"Sure," Emma said.

"Thank you." Susan paused. "I'm going to California in a couple of days to visit some friends. I don't know when I'll be back. Are you going to be okay?"

"Yes. I'll be fine."

"Great. Good luck."

Perhaps Susan thought that it would be safer to stay away from Emma for now. Who could blame her? She would probably wait until Paul had been convicted and gone to prison.

Was Susan really going to California, or did she make it up?

What does it matter? At least she was polite enough to explain why she'll no longer hang out with me.

Chapter 5

1

When she woke the next morning, Emma wondered why she was in her parents' house, then she remembered everything that had happened the day before and her head began to throb.

Her husband was a rapist and a murderer and her family had been destroyed.

As they ate breakfast, Ollie asked, "Where's Daddy?"

"He's on a business trip in Florida," Emma said.

"What city?"

"Miami."

"Is it far from Disney World?"

"Not very far."

"Will Daddy go to Disney World?"

"No."

"Are we going to Disney World this summer?"

"Yes."

What if Paul's parents call Ollie and tell him what happened to his dad?

Emma took Ollie's cellphone, opened his contacts, and blocked Paul's father's and mother's numbers.

After driving Ollie to school, Emma called her boss at the hospital and told him that she was sick. She kept thinking about Paul's bail hearing. Would the judge let him out on bail? Would Paul be able to post bail if it was set at, say, five hundred thousand dollars?

He could use their house, which was worth over five hundred thousand, as collateral.

Emma was afraid her phone would ring and it would be Paul calling to tell her he was on his way home. At noon, she took Detective Korbin's card from her purse and called him.

"This is Emma Marston," she said.

"How are you, Mrs. Marston?"

"I'm fine. Do you know if Paul got bail?"

"His request for bail was denied."

Emma breathed a sigh of relief. "Did you find the victim's body?"

"Let's talk about it later, okay?"

"Okay."

Hopefully, the police would find enough evidence to take the case to trial.

Emma called her mother and told her that Paul had been denied bail.

"Thank God," Rosie said.

Emma drove back home, ate a sandwich, and then searched Google News for "body found in Dallas." The most recent story was from two days ago.

Sooner or later, that woman would be reported missing. If the police found her DNA in the trunk of Paul's car, he would likely go to prison, wouldn't he? You didn't need a body to secure a conviction in Paul's case.

As Emma went through Paul's desk drawers (she hoped to find souvenirs Paul might have taken from his previous victims), her phone rang. She didn't recognize the number.

"Hello," she said.

"Emma, it's Paul."

Her stomach turned over.

"Why are you calling?"

"I want to talk to you."

"Did you kill her?"

"I didn't kill anyone, Emma. And I didn't kidnap anyone, either. I swear!"

"I saw you kidnap that woman."

"What time?"

"Around four."

"I was at a friend's place from three to seven o'clock. Call her, she'll confirm that."

Emma was amazed at how sincere Paul sounded.

Well, he had sounded very convincing when he told her he loved her, all the while screwing another woman.

"What's her name?"

"Julie."

"Do you sleep with her?"

Paul hesitated. "Yes."

"I was there, Paul. I saw you kidnap that woman."

"You saw someone who looked like me."

"It was you, Paul. I followed you after you left the house. And I watched you force her into the trunk of your car."

"You followed me? Why did you follow me?"

"I thought you were cheating on me."

"I was at Julie's place from three to seven. I didn't kidnap anyone. I swear on my mother's name!"

"I hope you didn't kill her."

"You're lying, Emma! Why are you lying? Why are you doing this to me?"

"Did you ask your mother to call me?"

"No. She called you?"

"Goodbye, Paul."

Emma hung up.

Chapter 6

1

Two days after his arrest, Paul called Jonah Wallach at eleven in the morning and told him that the detectives wanted to question him again. Wallach arrived at the North Tower Detention Facility an hour later. Paul was alone in the interview room when the lawyer entered.

"I called Emma yesterday," Paul said. "She did tell the police I kidnapped a woman." He sighed heavily.

"You still have no idea why she did it?"

Paul shook his head.

"Are you sleeping with Julie?"

Paul nodded. "Did you call her?"

"Not yet."

If Emma knew or suspected that Paul was cheating on her, she would have reason to make up the kidnapping story.

Detectives Korbin and Heaney showed up a few minutes later.

"Good afternoon, Detectives," Wallach said.

"Good afternoon," Korbin replied.

Heaney pulled a photograph of a young dark-haired woman from his folder and put it in front of Paul. "Do you know this woman?"

Paul looked at the photo and shook his head. "No."

"Have you ever met her?"

"No."

"Her name's Alison Bowles. Does it ring a bell?"

"No."

"She was murdered last Sunday. We found your DNA on her body and underwear. How do you think it got here?"

Wallach asked, "What kind of DNA did you find?" He glanced at Paul. His client appeared genuinely shocked.

Korbin said, "It was Mr. Marston's semen."

"We'd like to conduct an independent test. Where on the victim's body did you find the semen?"

How had Paul's semen gotten on the body of a woman he didn't know?

"On the inner thighs."

Paul said, "How was she killed?"

"She was strangled."

Heaney said, "You raped and killed her, Paul."

"I didn't do it."

Korbin said, "We found her hair in the trunk of your car."

"That's impossible. I never met this woman."

Wallach asked, "Where did you find the body?"

"In an alley between Arvada and Carol Stream Drives in Richardson. About four miles from the University of Texas at Dallas."

Heaney said, "Your wife saw you kidnap a woman not far from the university. She said the victim had on a blue skirt and white shirt. When Alison was found, she was wearing a blue skirt and white shirt."

"I don't understand." Paul looked at Wallach. "I don't understand."

Wallach asked, "When did you find Alison's body?"

"On Sunday, around seven p.m."

"What's the estimated time of death?"

"Between four and five p.m."

Had Paul lied to him? Had Paul raped and strangled Alison Bowles?

Korbin asked Paul, "Were you in Dallas on March seventh?"

"Yes."

"What does that have to do with this case?" Wallach said.

"I'll explain in a moment," Korbin replied. "Were you in Dallas on March twenty-ninth?" he asked Paul.

"I don't remember," Paul said.

"A woman named Angela Flynn was raped and strangled on March seventh. On March twenty-ninth, Elvira Gonzalez was raped and stabbed to death. Did you kill them, Paul?"

Paul shook his head vigorously. "No, no, no! I didn't kill anyone!"

Wallach asked, "Do you have any evidence that Mr. Marston killed those two women?"

Heaney said, "Not yet."

"We're done here."

Paul asked, "Did you find Alison's fingerprints in my trunk?"

Korbin said, "We found no fingerprints in the trunk. You must have wiped them all off."

When the detectives left, Paul said to Wallach, "They must have made a mistake. It can't be my semen. I never met that woman."

"Let's think this over, Paul."

"Okay."

"We'll meet tomorrow morning."

Chapter 7

1

Emma didn't go to work on Tuesday: she had decided to take the whole week off. She drove Ollie to school and then searched Google News for reports about bodies found in the Dallas area. She found out that a woman's body had been discovered in the Dallas suburb of Richardson on the day Paul had kidnapped that woman. The body was identified as Alison Bowles. She was twenty-two years old at the time of her death. The news story didn't have her picture.

Was Alison Paul's victim?

When Emma brought Ollie home from school, she went into Paul's office, shut the door, and called Detective Korbin.

"Did you find the victim's body yet?" she asked.

"Yes," Korbin said. "Her name's Alison Bowles. Her body was found last Sunday in a back alley in Richardson, about four miles from the University of Texas. She was twenty-two."

"Did Paul rape her?"

"Yes. He raped and strangled her."

"Why do you think she's the one abducted by Paul?"

"We found Alison's hair in the trunk of Paul's car. We also found your husband's DNA on Alison's body."

Paul's DNA.

It must be his semen.

"Where did you find his DNA?"

"On the inner thighs."

"Was it his semen?"

"Yes."

"What time was Alison murdered?"

"The estimated time of death is between four and five p.m."

Paul had killed Alison less than an hour after he kidnapped her.

Emma figured he didn't have a dungeon.

"You think you have enough evidence to put Paul in prison?" she said.

"Yes. It's a slam-dunk case. We really appreciate you reporting him to the police. If not for you, we might never have solved this case."

"Is he going to be sentenced to death?"

"He probably is. We believe he might have killed two other women."

"Did you find his DNA on their bodies?"

"No."

"Why do you think Paul might have killed them?"

"They were raped before they were murdered, just like Alison Bowles. One of them was strangled."

"When were they killed?"

"On March seventh and twenty-ninth."

Emma walked to the desk and turned the calendar to March. "What are their names?"

March 7 was a Saturday and 27 a Sunday. Paul had been off work when the murders took place.

"Angela Flynn and Elvira Gonzalez. I heard that Paul used to work at the Dallas District Attorney's office."

"Yes. He was an assistant DA when he left."

"He's not going to get any special treatment."

"Good to hear."

"It's shocking, isn't it? Your husband used to be a prosecutor and now he's a killer."

Emma breathed a sigh of relief after Korbin hung up. She wouldn't have to hide from Paul. Her husband wasn't coming back. He would be convicted of Alison Bowles's murder and get a life sentence at the least.

When she went into the living room, Ollie was on the couch watching a cartoon on TV.

"When is Daddy coming back from Florida?" Ollie asked.

"He doesn't know. He has a lot of work to do in Miami."

What would she tell Ollie when Paul was sent to prison? Would she tell him the truth?

Chapter 8

1

"I know how Alison Bowles's hair got in my trunk," Paul said. His eyes were bloodshot and there were dark circles under them. Wallach figured he hadn't slept last night.

"How?" Wallach asked.

"Someone planted it."

"Who?"

"I don't know. Maybe the police."

"Why would they do that?"

"I don't know."

"Do you have any enemies in the Dallas PD?"

"Not that I know of."

"What about the semen? The police couldn't have planted it, could they?"

"We don't know for sure that it's mine. Are they going to let you do an independent test?"

"They haven't gotten back to me on that yet. Are you sure you never slept with Alison Bowles?"

"Yes. I never met her!"

"We need to come up with an explanation, Paul."

"We'll figure it out." Groaning softly, Paul began to rub his face with his hands. "I'm being framed, Jonah. I'm being framed."

"Do you have any enemies in the DA's office?"

"No."

"If you were framed, you have to figure out who's behind this."

"Did you call Julie?"

"Yes. Many times. She never answered or called back."

Wallach had called Julie four times yesterday and twice this morning, and each time his call had gone straight to voice mail.

Paul frowned. "Go to her house."

"Paul, even if she confirms your alibi, no one's going to believe her."

"I don't care."

"What's her address?"

Paul told the lawyer Julie's address, and then Wallach asked, "Does she have a landline?"

"No. Did you mention my name in the message you left her?"

"Yes."

"Maybe she's in the hospital."

Or maybe she didn't want to lie for him.

Or maybe she didn't exist.

Wallach hated thinking that Paul might have murdered Alison Bowles, but considering all the evidence against him, it was hard not to doubt his innocence.

"I'll go to her house today," Wallach said.

"Go after six o'clock."

"Okay."

Paul wiped his forehead. "I'm thinking of taking a lie detector test."

"I don't think it's a good idea."

"It won't hurt. Tell them I want to take a lie detector test."

Paul was right. His situation wouldn't get worse if he failed the test.

Passing the test would mean nothing to the police, but it might help Paul in the court of public opinion.

"They'll ask you about the other two women," Wallach said.

"I don't care. I didn't kill them."

"You think you'll pass the test?"

Paul nodded. "I'll pass it, Jonah. I'll pass it. Because I'm innocent."

"Okay."

"You believe me, right?" Paul looked at Wallach searchingly. "I didn't kill anyone."

"Of course I believe you, Paul."

"Thank you, Jonah."

Chapter 9

1

Korbin was pouring himself a cup of coffee in the break room when Paul Marston called him from jail.

"I want to meet you, Detective," Marston said.

"What for?"

"I have something important to tell you. Can we meet today?"

"Yes."

"Thank you."

Korbin dumped a packet of sweetener (he had stopped using sugar twenty years ago) into his coffee, then went to Heaney's cubicle and said to his partner, "Marston just called. He wants to meet me."

"What for?"

"He said he has something important to tell me."

What did Marston want to tell him? Was he going to confess to Alison Bowles's murder? That would be nice, wouldn't it?

Marston was probably going to ask for a plea bargain. Korbin couldn't imagine him going to trial; the evidence was just too strong.

Two hours later, Korbin was in an interview room at the North Tower Detention Facility. As the guard cuffed Marston to the table, the detective said, "Is your lawyer coming?"

"No."

If Marston planned to ask for a plea bargain, he would have invited his attorney, wouldn't he?

When the guard left the room, Korbin said, "So what do you have to tell me, Paul?"

"I have a question for you, Detective. You claim I raped Alison Bowles. Where do you think I raped her?"

"You could have done it in the back seat of your car."

"Did you find her fingerprints inside my car?"

"No. But that doesn't mean she wasn't raped in your car."

"You think I wiped off her fingerprints?"

"Where are you going with this?"

"Did you find my wife's fingerprints on the back seat or the inside of the rear doors of my car?"

"Yes."

"That means I didn't wipe off the back seat and the rear doors, doesn't it?"

Korbin shrugged. "I guess so."

"If I raped someone in my car, I'd make sure to wipe off every surface inside it."

"Maybe you have another house where you raped your victims. Maybe you raped Alison in your friend's house. Is that all you wanted to tell me?"

"I don't have another house."

Korbin crossed his arms over his chest. "Maybe you raped her in the alley where we found her body. It's possible, and that's all that matters."

"It would have been too risky."

"Maybe you're a risk-taker."

Korbin felt the frustration coming off Marston in waves.

"I have an alibi. I was at a friend's place when Alison Bowles was murdered. You need to talk to her. Her name's Julie."

Did Marston think that his friend's word could outweigh the DNA evidence in his case?

"Okay. I'll talk to her."

Marston told Korbin Julie's phone number and address and then said, "I want to take a lie detector test."

"Great."

"You can ask me any questions you want."

"Okay."

"I'm innocent, Detective." Marston looked at Korbin pleadingly. "I didn't kill Alison."

"How did your semen get on her body?"

"I don't know, but I'm trying to figure it out."

When he returned to Dallas Police Headquarters, Korbin called Julie and left a message asking her to call him. If she told him that Marston had been with her from three to seven p.m. last Sunday, he would try to get her to admit that Marston had asked her to lie for him.

"Did Marston confess?" Heaney asked Korbin.

Korbin shook his head. "He wants to take a lie detector test."

"Why?"

"I don't know. I guess he's just grasping at straws."

Marston had to realize that he was done regardless of whether he passed or failed the polygraph exam.

After Korbin arranged for Marston to undergo a lie detector test at the county jail tomorrow morning, Jonah Wallach called and said that Marston wanted to take a lie detector test.

"He already told me," Korbin said. "He's taking it tomorrow morning at ten."

"I'd appreciate it if you would provide me with a copy of the polygraph charts."

"I'll tell my boss."

Chapter 10

1

Emma walked into Ollie's room and kissed her son on the head. Ollie, who was at his desk doing homework, put his pen down and turned to her.

"We're having rice and turkey meatballs," she said.

"Can we order pizza?"

"We had pizza yesterday, sweetie."

"Why can't we have it today?"

"Too much pizza is bad for your health."

"Everything I like to eat is bad for my health."

"Broccoli is good for you."

"I don't like broccoli."

"You said you liked it."

"I never said that." Ollie smiled.

Emma laughed, kissed him on the forehead, and left the room.

She put the rice and water in the rice cooker, then went into the living room, sat on the couch, and opened a browser on her tablet. She searched for news about Alison Bowles, hoping that her photo had been released. The latest news story about Alison had been posted today and contained her picture. She had a narrow face framed by shoulder-length chestnut hair. She was smiling, showing perfect white teeth, her big green eyes sparkling. Emma's chest tightened as she pictured Alison's beautiful eyes grow dim when the life had left her.

The doorbell rang. Emma went to the front door, looked through the peephole, and saw a middle-aged woman in a beige jacket. Emma opened the door and said, "Hello."

"Hi." The woman looked to be in her early fifties, with curly brown hair. She seemed tired and dejected.

"How can I help you?"

There was something familiar about the woman's face. Had they met before?

"Are you Paul Marston's wife?"

"Yes."

Was she a journalist?

"I'm Connie Bowles. Your husband killed my daughter."

A pang of sorrow shot through Emma.

"I'm very sorry about your daughter," she said.

Why did she come here? To harass me and Ollie?

"I'm not here to break your windows or anything like that," Connie said.

"That's good to know."

"I just wanted to... to talk, I guess."

"Please come in."

Emma opened the door wider, and Connie entered.

"Would you like something to drink?"

"Yes."

"Coffee?"

"Yes."

As she poured coffee into a cup, a horrible thought struck Emma: what if Connie kills Ollie to avenge Alison's death? Her daughter had been murdered only three days ago, she wasn't thinking straight.

Emma put Connie's cup and saucer on the table and asked, "Sugar?"

"No. What's your name?"

"Emma. I'm very sorry about Alison. What my husband did was horrible."

"You don't think he's innocent?"

"No."

Connie looked at her phone. "Alison was our only child."

Emma felt her heart break. What could be worse than losing your only child?

"Did you see Alison's picture?"

"Yes."

Connie held her phone in front of Emma and said, "She was so beautiful."

There was Alison's picture on the screen, different from the one in the news story.

"Yes, she was."

"Your husband's a lawyer."

"Yes."

"How long have you been married?"

"Twelve years."

"I'm surprised you're not defending him."

"I know that he did it. I saw him kidnap Alison."

"Were you with him?"

"No. I was following him in my car. He didn't know that. I was far behind him."

"Why didn't you stop him?"

"I went after him but lost him. And then I called the police."

Emma hated lying to Connie, but she couldn't bring herself to tell her that she had waited an hour before calling the police.

"He was caught thanks to you?"

"Yes."

"I didn't know that."

Emma heard Ollie running down the stairs, and then the boy came into the room.

"Hello," Ollie said to Connie.

"Hi." Connie smiled faintly.

Emma asked, "Do you need anything, honey?"

"I'm going to the kitchen," Ollie said, and headed to the kitchen.

Connie asked Emma, "Is he your son?"

"Yes."

"What's his name?"

"Oliver."

"How old is he?"

"Ten."

"Do you have other children?"

Emma shook her head. "No."

Ollie went into the living room carrying a bottle of mango juice. Connie didn't pull out any weapons as the boy walked to the stairs; she sat still and stared into space.

Now that she knows I reported Paul to the police, she wouldn't hurt me or Ollie, would she?

"Did you tell him what your husband did?" Connie asked in a low voice when Ollie's footsteps faded.

"No."

"Don't tell him." Connie took a sip of her coffee. "Where did the kidnapping take place?"

"About a mile from the University of Texas."

"Do you remember the name of the street?"

"No."

"What time did it happen?"

"Around four."

Did Connie know that Emma had called the police at five o'clock?

"We were going to go to a seafood buffet that day. Ali was supposed to come to my house at one o'clock, but she didn't show up. I texted and called her, but she didn't answer." Connie sighed and wiped her eyes. "I wonder why she didn't come to my house at one, why she didn't answer. I called her several times before she was kidnapped."

"Maybe she had an emergency."

"Why didn't she let me know?"

"Maybe her phone battery was dead."

Connie took a sip of coffee. "I thought she'd been in a car accident and was unconscious." She set her cup down. "If Ali'd gone to the seafood buffet, she'd be alive now." Connie looked at Emma. "She'd be alive."

Emma nodded.

"He forced Ali into the trunk," Connie said. "It means that they didn't know each other."

"Yes."

"Why were you following your husband that day?"

"I thought he was cheating on me. I wanted to catch him in the act."

"We're lucky you were there and saw what he did. Thank you for calling the police, Emma." Connie paused. "Did you visit him in jail?"

"No."

"Are you going to?"

"No."

Connie stood up. "Thank you for talking to me. I hope everything goes well for you."

"You, too."

Twenty minutes after Connie Bowles left, Detective Korbin called.

"I have a question for you," he said. "Do you have another house or an apartment or a cabin?"

"No. Why?"

"We believe Paul might have a place where he raped his victims. Do his parents have another house?"

"I don't know. Do you think he held women prisoner in that place?"

"It's possible."

"Do you think someone might be held there right now?"

"It's possible."

Chapter 11

1

The guard unlocked Paul Marston's handcuffs, waited for him to sit down, and said, "I'm watching you." He took a chair to the wall behind Marston and dropped into it.

"My name is Peter Villarreal," said the polygraph examiner, who sat across the table from Marston. "I'm a polygraph examiner."

"Nice to meet you," Marston said.

After filling out the paperwork, Villarreal explained the procedure to Marston and then asked if he had any questions.

"No," Marston replied.

Villarreal placed two pneumograph tubes (which measured the subject's respiration) around Marston's chest and abdomen, wrapped a blood pressure cuff around his left arm, and then attached electrodes to his fingers.

"It will only take a few minutes." Villarreal sat down at his laptop. A chart window was open on the screen. "Are you ready?"

"Yes."

Villarreal clicked the Start button at the bottom of the chart window, and the system began recording data. "Answer only yes or no."

"Okay."

"Is your name Paul Marston?"

"Yes."

"Are you forty-two years old?"

"Yes."

"Did you abduct Alison Bowles on April nineteenth?"

"No."

"Did you murder Alison Bowles?"

"No."

"Is your wife's name Emma?"

"Yes."

"Did you rape Alison Bowles?"

"No."

"Did you murder Angela Flynn?"

"No."

"Have you ever murdered anyone?"

"No."

"Do you live on Crestway Drive in Dallas?"

"Yes."

"Did you murder Elvira Gonzalez?"

"No."

"Is today April twenty-third?"

"Yes."

"Do you know who murdered Alison Bowles?"

"No."

Villarreal clicked the Stop button. "Thank you, Mr. Marston. We're done."

The guard got up and walked to Marston.

"When will the results be ready?" Marston stood up.

"This afternoon," Villarreal said.

Marston put his hands behind his back, and the guard cuffed them.

Chapter 12

1

"Are the results of Mr. Marston's polygraph exam ready yet?" Wallach asked.

"No," Korbin said.

"When can we expect them?"

"I'll call you as soon as they're ready."

"Thank you. Goodbye, Detective." Wallach replaced the receiver and leaned back in his chair.

It had been four hours since Paul had taken a lie detector test. Had he passed it?

Paul was a smart man; he wouldn't have taken a lie detector test unless he believed he had a good chance of passing it.

Unfortunately, Paul passing a polygraph exam would be of no significance whatsoever as far as the case was concerned, since they were still unable to explain how Paul's semen had gotten on Alison Bowles's body.

His cellphone rang.

"Hello," Wallach said.

"Hi, can I talk to Jonah Wallach?" a woman said.

"Speaking."

"My name's Julie. You asked me to call you."

Paul's mistress finally returned his call. He had gone to her house yesterday after work, but no one had been home.

"Yes. Thank you for returning my call, Julie. I'm Paul Marston's attorney. You know Paul, don't you?"

"Yes."

"When did you see him last?"

"A week ago."

"Was it last Sunday?"

"No. Thursday."

"April the sixteenth?"

"Yes."

"Did you see him last Sunday?"

"No."

"Julie, this is very important. Paul says he was with you from three to seven p.m. last Sunday. Are you sure you didn't see him that day?"

"Yes. Is Paul okay?"

"No."

Had Paul lied about visiting Julie last Sunday?

"What happened to him?"

"He's in jail."

"Why? What did he do?"

"So you're sure you didn't see Paul last Sunday?"

"Yes. Why is he in jail?"

Paul must have asked Julie to give him a fake alibi, and she had decided to tell the truth.

"Paul told me he's having an affair with you. Is that true?"

"I'm sorry, Jonah, but I'd rather not answer this question."

Perhaps she thought he might work for Paul's wife.

"If you'd like to see Paul, he's being held at the North Tower Detention Facility in downtown Dallas."

"Can you tell me what he did?"

"He's accused of murder."

"Oh my God!"

"Paul told me he was with you last Sunday."

"No, he wasn't with me last Sunday."

"Okay. Have a nice day, Julie."

Paul had lied about his alibi. What else had he lied about?

Korbin called Wallach at four o'clock and said that the results of Paul's polygraph exam were ready.

"I'm emailing them to you now."

Chapter 13

1

"I've got good news and bad news," Wallach said when the guard left the room. "You passed the lie detector test."

During the test Paul had denied committing the crimes he was accused or suspected of, and the examiner had found his answers—every single one of them—to be truthful.

Paul smiled. "I told you I'd pass it. I'm innocent, Jonah."

"Julie called me yesterday."

A look of hope flickered across Paul's face.

"Did she tell you I was with her that day?"

Wallach shook his head. "She said she didn't see you last Sunday. That's the bad news."

Paul furrowed his brow. "What? She really said that?"

"Yes. I asked her three times. I told her it was very important."

"I don't understand." Paul lowered his eyes to the table and bit his lower lip. "Why did she say that?"

"I don't know."

"Maybe she doesn't want to get involved in this? Ask her to come visit me. I'll explain to her that this is a matter of life and death."

"Okay. But no one's going to believe her."

"I understand." Paul bit his lower lip. "I was with Julie last Sunday. Do you believe me? I want you to be honest with me, Jonah. Do you believe me?"

"Yes, I believe you."

"I passed the lie detector test because I told the truth."

"We have to figure out how your semen got on Alison Bowles's body. That's our number one priority.

Paul nodded. "Yeah."

"Do you have any ideas?"

"No." Paul sighed. "I think I was set up by Alison's killer."

"Probably."

"Can you ask Emma to come see me?"

"Sure."

"Tell her I passed a lie detector test."

"I will."

If Emma was lying, the fact that Paul had passed a polygraph exam wouldn't matter to her.

Wallach wondered if Emma would be willing to take a lie detector test.

Then a startling thought hit him. If Paul was innocent, maybe it was Emma who had set him up? She could have collected his semen after sex. She might have killed Alison Bowles herself or had someone else do it (her lover, for example).

Wallach said, "Has it ever occurred to you that it might have been Emma who framed you? She could obtain your semen without difficulty, couldn't she?"

"Why would she frame me?"

"Maybe she doesn't like you. You were cheating on her, weren't you?"

"If Emma set me up, then she's the one who killed Alison. I don't think she's capable of murder, Jonah."

"Maybe she had someone else kill Alison."

Paul frowned.

"She called the police," Wallach said. "She said she saw you kidnap a woman. She wants you to go to prison, Paul."

After a long silence, Paul said, "Maybe someone made her do it."

"Maybe."

Perhaps whoever masterminded the framing of Paul Marston had turned Emma against her husband by informing her that he was cheating on her. They might have showed Emma pictures of him with Julie.

"Have you threatened to expose any powerful people recently?" Wallach asked.

Maybe they had framed Paul to shut him up?

"No."

"You need to make a list of people who see you as a threat."

Paul nodded.

Chapter 14

1

"Man charged in murder of 22-year-old Dallas woman," the top headline read.

She finally summoned up the courage to check if the police had released Alison Bowles's killer's name. It appeared they had.

Emma clicked the link. The news story said that Paul Marston had been charged with murder in the slaying of Alison Bowles. Emma scanned the first two paragraphs and closed the page without reading the rest of the article.

Now the whole world would know that her husband was a murderer. It was only a matter of time before kids at school started picking on Ollie, calling him a killer's son.

Her friends and coworkers would feel sorry for her.

Paul's parents must hate her guts. Thankfully, they didn't harass her. Nancy Marston hadn't called her since last Sunday. Perhaps she had learned that Paul's semen had been found on the victim's body.

Despite all the evidence, Paul's parents probably believed he was innocent.

As Emma put her tablet on the coffee table, her phone rang. She checked the caller ID and saw it was Jonah Wallach.

"Hello," she said.

"Hi, Emma. This is Jonah Wallach. How are you doing?"

"I'm fine."

"Can I ask you a couple of questions?"

"Okay."

"You said you followed Paul from your house. What time did you see him leave the house?"

"Around three-thirty."

"Did you follow Paul in your car?"

"Yes."

"What time did the abduction take place?"

"Around four."

"Did you see the abductor's face clearly?"

"No. But I'm sure it was Paul. I followed him from our house."

"Did you take your eyes off Paul's car between the moment he drove away from the house and the kidnapping?"

"Yes."

"So you can't be sure that the abductor's car was the same car that drove away from your house? There are thousands of cars like Paul's in the city. Thousands. You can't be sure that the man you saw kidnap a woman was Paul, Emma."

"They found Alison Bowles's hair in Paul's trunk."

"Do you agree that you can't be sure that the man you saw abduct a woman last Sunday was Paul?"

"No."

"Do you know Paul's car's license plate number?"

"Yes."

"What is it?"

"It's K...GT...Four one... one... six."

"Actually it's HKT Six one one three. Did you see the license plate of the abductor's car?"

"Yes."

"Did you make out every letter and number?"

Was Wallach trying to keep her from testifying at Paul's trial? Why? The prosecution didn't need her testimony to win this case.

"They found Alison's hair in Paul's trunk. It was Paul, Jonah."

"The hair might have been planted. What I'm trying to say, Emma, is that you need to keep an open mind about this. What you think happened last Sunday may not be what actually happened."

"It doesn't matter what I think."

"Paul took a lie detector test yesterday and passed it."

"I don't care."

"You haven't visited Paul at the jail yet, have you?"

"No."

"He needs you, Emma. Could you visit him sometime soon?"

"I don't want to see him. Do you think Paul's innocent?"

"I believe he's entitled to a vigorous defense."

"If you think he's innocent, then you must think I'm lying."

"I think you might be mistaken."

"The police suspect that he killed two other women."

"There's no evidence Paul has anything to do with those murders."

"Do you have any other questions, Jonah? I need to go."

"You said the abduction took place around four o'clock. You called nine one one at five. Why didn't you call the police right away?"

"I was in shock. Bye, Jonah."

2

After talking to Emma, Wallach called Julie and left a message asking her to call him.

If they were able to convince the jury it was possible that Emma Marston had framed her husband, even a flimsy alibi could be helpful.

Julie called him two hours later.

"Hello, Mr. Wallach," she said. "This is Julie."

"Thank you for calling me, Julie. Paul needs to talk to you. Could you visit him in jail this weekend or next week?"

"I'll try. What does he want to talk about?"

"I don't know."

"Can you text me the jail's phone number and address?"

"Sure."

"I know why Paul's in jail. I googled his name. They say he killed a woman."

"Paul maintains his innocence, and I believe him. He took and passed a lie detector test."

"Paul's a good person. I don't think he did it."

"Yes, he's a good man."

"Does his wife know about me?"

"Yes."

"Will they drop the charges if I say that Paul was with me last Sunday?"

"Was he with you last Sunday?"

"Tell Paul I'll try to visit him soon. Goodbye, Mr. Wallach." Julie hung up.

Paul called Wallach at seven o'clock and asked if he had talked to Julie.

"Yes," Wallach replied. "She said she'd try to visit you soon."

Chapter 15

1

"His lawyer told me he took and passed a lie detector test," Emma said.

The sun was low on the horizon. She and Rosie were taking a walk around her parents' neighborhood. Ollie was playing Monopoly with his grandfather, who usually accompanied Rosie on her evening strolls.

"It just goes to show lie detectors aren't accurate," Rosie replied.

"Paul wants me to visit him in jail."

"Don't do it. Who's paying for his lawyers, by the way? Don't let him use your money to pay for his lawyers."

"Okay."

"I think you need to divorce Paul as soon as possible. I know a good divorce lawyer."

Emma nodded. "Yeah."

Talk about a fall from grace. Only a week ago, her parents had adored Paul, he had been the son they had never had.

"I'll give you his number when we get home."

They turned the corner.

"Did Paul's parents call you?" Emma asked.

"No. Did they call you?"

"No."

"If they start bothering you, call the police. Do you know when Paul's trial starts?"

Emma shook her head.

"I think he should just do a plea deal," her mother said. "Did they ask you to testify at his trial?"

"Not yet. Should I?"

"I think you should." Rosie pulled out her phone and started tapping on the screen.

"The mother of the woman Paul killed came to my house last Wednesday."

"What for?"

"She wanted to talk."

"Did you let her in?"

"Yes."

"You should be careful, honey. What if she hurt you or Ollie?"

"I told her I reported Paul to the police."

An old woman with blue hair, who was walking toward Emma and her mother, waved to them and said, "Hi, Rosie."

"Hi, Karen." Rosie waved back.

Karen passed them without stopping.

"Paul's trial date was set for October fifteenth." Rosie pocketed her phone. "What will his defense strategy be? His case is hopeless."

When they got back to Emma's parents' house, Rosie gave Emma the divorce lawyer's number (his name was Ken Daugherty) and told her to call him on Monday.

The next morning Emma told Ollie's babysitter, Savannah, that she was going back to work on Monday and asked her to pick Ollie up from school.

"Do you know what happened to my husband?" Emma asked.

"No."

"We're getting a divorce, but don't tell that to Ollie."

2

On Monday Emma called Ken Daugherty and made an appointment for four-thirty in the afternoon. Her coworkers didn't mention Paul or Alison Bowles's murder and didn't treat her differently. Perhaps they still didn't know what Paul had done. Emma didn't have to remove Paul's pictures from her desk because she didn't have any family photos there.

Daugherty's office was located in an eight-story building in western Plano. He was in his fifties, of medium height, with graying hair and a potbelly.

"You're Rosie Delaney's daughter, aren't you?" Daugherty said when Emma sat down.

"Yes."

"She called two hours ago. I told her we'll take good care of you." The lawyer smiled. "Would you like something to drink?"

"No."

"You said on the phone that you want to divorce your husband."

"Yes. My husband's name is Paul Marston. Did my mom tell you anything about him?"

"No."

Had he heard of Alison Bowles's murder? Did he remember her killer's name?

Because Paul was a lawyer, the news of his crime might have spread throughout the Dallas area legal community. The fact that he was a former assistant district attorney must have made the story especially juicy.

"Have you heard of my husband?" Emma asked.

"Is he famous?" Daugherty smiled.

"He's a lawyer."

"What firm is he with?"

"Akerman Bird and Farber."

"Is he a partner?"

"No."

"What kind of law does he practice?"

"He's a criminal defense attorney."

Daugherty nodded, making a note.

"He murdered a woman a week ago."

"Is he in custody?"

"Yes. I thought you might have heard about it."

"No, I haven't. I'm going to look it up. Do you have children?"

"Yes. We have a son. He's ten years old."

"Do you want to start the process now?"

"Yes."

"If your husband is convicted, you'll have no trouble having his parental rights terminated."

"I'm glad to hear that."

Daugherty came out from behind his desk, and then they stepped out into the reception area.

"Mimi, Emma Marston is our new client," the lawyer said to the receptionist. "Please prepare a client agreement and give Emma a divorce worksheet."

"Sure, Mr. Daugherty," Mimi replied.

To Emma, the lawyer said, "If you have any questions, let me know." He went back into the office and closed the door.

After Emma signed a client agreement, Mimi explained to her how to fill out a divorce worksheet and then emailed it to her.

"Just email it to me after you fill it out," Mimi said. "We'll start drafting the documents once we have this information."

When she got home, Emma filled out the divorce worksheet and sent it to Mimi. After dinner, she went on the Internet and looked up visitation information for the North Tower Detention Facility.

Chapter 16

1

Paul looked ten years older than the last time she had seen him, and for a moment Emma felt sorry for her husband. Only for a moment.

"I'm really glad to see you, Emma." Paul smiled weakly. "How's Ollie?"

"He's fine."

Emma glanced at Paul's left hand, which was holding the receiver, and pictured his hands strangling Alison Bowles. She was glad they were separated by a glass partition and Paul couldn't touch her.

"Jonah told you I passed a lie detector test, didn't he?"

"Yes."

"I didn't kill that woman. Her hair was planted in my trunk. And my semen was planted, too."

"Paul, I want a divorce."

Paul froze. "What?" Shaking his head, he said, "No. No. Please don't leave me, Emma. I need you. Don't leave me."

"I'm filing for divorce this week."

"This week? Why? I'm innocent until proven guilty."

"Nothing you say can change my mind, Paul."

"I'm not a murderer, Emma. I was framed. I was framed!"

"I'm going to petition to terminate your parental rights."

"You want to take Ollie away from me?"

"You're going to prison for the rest of your life. How do you plan to exercise your parental rights?"

"Please wait until after the trial."

Emma shook her head. "No."

Paul leaned closer to the partition. "I have a question for you," he said, looking into her eyes.

"What is it?"

After a pause, Paul said, "Did you set me up?"

Emma frowned. "What?"

"Did you set me up? Did you plant my semen on Alison Bowles's body?"

"You think I set you up?" Emma said in disbelief.

"You're the only person who could have given them my semen."

"Paul, I didn't set you up."

Was that Paul's defense strategy? Did he plan to claim that she had framed him?

Is he going to say I murdered Alison Bowles?

"Did they make you do it? Did they threaten you? Tell me who's behind this, please."

All Paul needed was one juror to think he might have been framed by his wife.

"I didn't set you up, Paul. I didn't give your semen to anyone."

"Emma, I'm begging you. Tell me who's behind this."

"No one framed you, Paul. You kidnapped and killed that woman."

"I didn't kidnap or kill anyone! You have to believe me."

"Goodbye, Paul." Emma hung up the phone, got up, and headed for the door.

2

As Emma walked her to the door, Ollie's babysitter turned to her and said in a low voice, "I read the news about your husband. I'm very sorry."

"Did you tell Ollie?"

"No."

"Good. I'm glad Paul was caught. He's a terrible man."

Emma locked the door behind Savannah, then went to the office and called Detective Korbin.

"I visited my husband in jail today," she said. "He accused me of framing him. Did he tell you I framed him?"

"No."

"I think that's his defense strategy. Do you think it might work?"

"No."

"I didn't frame him."

"I know that."

"Will I have to testify against Paul in court?"

"I don't think his case will go to trial. Chances are he'll cut a deal to avoid the death penalty."

"Are you going to offer him a life sentence?"

"Probably."

"Is it true that Paul passed a lie detector test?"

"Yes. I guess he's a good liar."

"By the way, did you find out if he has a cabin?"

"We checked the property records but found nothing."

Emma put a frozen lasagna in the microwave and called her mother.

"What an asshole," Rosie said when she heard that Paul had accused Emma of framing him. "He's going to drag your name through the mud."

As Emma cut the lasagna, her phone rang. It was Susan.

Did she want to hang out?

"Hi, Susan."

"Hi. How are you holding up?" Susan said.

"I'm okay."

"Is Paul still in jail?"

"Yes." Emma went into the master bedroom and closed the door. "He was denied bail."

She thought of asking Susan if she was in California and decided not to.

"Did they find out who he kidnapped?"

"Yes. Her name was Alison Bowles. Paul raped and strangled her."

"Oh my God!"

"They suspect he killed two other women."

"Jesus! He's a serial killer."

"Yeah."

"Did the police find any physical evidence?"

"Yes."

"What kind of evidence?"

"They found his DNA on Alison's body and her hair in the trunk of his car."

"I hope he doesn't get off on some technicality."

"He won't."

"I'm so sorry, Emma."

She should thank Susan for suggesting that they follow Paul. If it hadn't been for Susan, she would never have seen Paul abduct Alison Bowles.

"I visited Paul in jail today. He accused me of framing him."

"What? Son of a bitch! He's truly evil."

"He admitted to cheating on me."

"What's her name?"

"Julie."

"How old is she?"

"I didn't ask. I'm filing for divorce this week."

"Great. Just hang in there, Emma. This will all be over soon. Talk to you later, bye."

Chapter 17

1

The prosecution agreed to provide Wallach with a sample of the semen found on Alison Bowles's body. He took it to a testing lab on Tuesday and received the test results the next morning. There were no surprises. The semen belonged to Paul Marston.

Julie never came to visit Paul. On Tuesday, Wallach left her a message asking her to call him.

There was evidence that Paul might have visited Julie on April 19, the day of Alison Bowles's murder. Between 2:58 p.m. and 3.04 p.m. and between 7:02 p.m. and 7:05 p.m. on that day his phone had been connected to a cell tower two miles from Julie's house.

From 3:04 p.m. to 7:03 p.m. his cell had been off. The prosecution would claim that Paul had switched off his cellphone to prevent the police from retracing his movements.

The fact that Paul had been near Julie's place at 3:04 p.m. didn't help him: his mistress lived only three miles away, so he could have returned home fifteen minutes before Emma had seen him leave their house.

Even if the phone records showed that Paul's cell had been near Julie's house from three to seven o'clock on the day of the murder, that wouldn't prove his innocence: he could have left his phone at Julie's place to fake an alibi.

On the way to the county jail Facility Wallach stopped by Julie's house. No one answered the doorbell. He walked to the window to the left of the door and peered in between the slats of the blinds. There appeared to be no furniture in the room, at least on the left side.

Had Julie moved out? Had she done it because of Paul's situation?

He looked in the window to the right of the door and saw it belonged to the kitchen.

When Wallach told him that an independent test confirmed that the semen was his, Paul was silent for a few moments and then said, "Emma gave the killer my semen. There's no one else who could have done it."

"You still have no idea who might have orchestrated this?"

"I have one suspect. He's pissed off with me and he's ruthless."

"Who is it?"

"Matt Sawyers. I defended him at his trial last year. I lost the case, and he got a life sentence."

"What was he convicted of?"

"Murder. He killed a drug dealer."

"He's in prison, isn't it?"

"Yes. But he has a lot of people working for him. He's a gang leader."

Wallach wrote down Matt Sawyers's name. "What's his gang's name?"

"The Wolf Brigade."

"I'll look into him. When was he convicted?"

"Last October."

"How old is he?"

"Forty-six."

"What's the name of the guy he killed?"

"Ricardo Cervantes."

"Are there any other crime bosses pissed off with you?"

"No."

Wallach glanced at his notes and said, "On the day of the murder you turned off your phone at three o'clock. You were near Julie's house at the time. You turned your phone back on at seven. Why did you switch it off?"

"I always kept my phone switched off when I was at Julie's place." Paul sighed. "When is she going to come see me? Why hasn't she visited me?"

"Maybe she's busy."

"She told me she loved me."

"How long have you known her?"

"Three months."

"I stopped by her place today. It appears that she doesn't live there anymore. There's no furniture in the living room."

"You think she moved because of me?"

Wallach shrugged. "She probably doesn't want to get involved in this."

"We could have her subpoenaed."

"Perhaps that's why she moved."

Paul leaned back and looked down at the table. "She's not going to help me, is she?"

"I don't know."

"Maybe her parents told her to stay away from me."

"She may change her mind."

Paul cleared his throat. "Emma visited me yesterday. She said she was filing for divorce this week."

"I'm sorry, Paul. Don't let that distract you. You need to focus on your case."

"I know."

Chapter 18

1

On Thursday Emma went to Ken Daugherty's office and signed the divorce papers. The lawyer said he would file the documents with the district clerk tomorrow morning. A sheriff's department officer would serve Paul with the papers.

"Do you think it's possible your husband's innocent?" Daugherty asked.

"No. They have DNA evidence against him."

"What your husband did is terrible. You're probably still in shock."

"Yes."

"Did he abuse you?"

Emma shook her head. "No."

About half an hour after Emma got home, the doorbell rang. It was Paul's mother. Nancy Marston's usual vivacity was gone, replaced by weariness. Her face was drawn, her shoulders slumped.

"I need to talk to you, Emma," Nancy said.

"About what?"

"Paul. We could go to a coffee shop and talk there."

"Come in." Emma stepped back, and her mother-in-law entered.

If Nancy misbehaved, she would kick her out.

Nancy went into the living room and said to Ollie, "Hi, sweetie."

Ollie smiled. "Hi, Nana." He got up from the couch.

Nancy kissed him on the cheek, and then they hugged.

Emma took her mother-in-law to the office, and when Nancy closed the door, she said, "Are you going to accuse me of lying again?"

"Please help me save Paul. He's facing a death sentence, Emma."

"There's nothing I can do for him."

"He passed a lie detector test."

"I don't care."

"Will you take a lie detector test?"

"No."

"Did someone make you do this? You can tell me the truth. I'm not wearing a wire. I'm not recording this."

"What are you talking about?"

"Someone made you get them Paul's semen, which they planted on that woman's body. Who was it?"

"I didn't give Paul's semen to anyone, Nancy."

"Did they threaten to kill you if you talked?"

"I didn't give Paul's semen to anyone. Paul raped and killed that woman. He wasn't set up."

"Yes, he was. Someone set him up. And you're the only person who could have given them his semen."

"Nancy, this is ridiculous."

"No, it's not. The police will give you immunity if you tell them who framed Paul."

"Is there anything else you want to tell me?"

"Just think about it, okay? They'll give you immunity, they'll put you in the witness protection program, you have nothing to worry about."

"Go home, Nancy."

"Paul's sorry he cheated on you."

Emma opened the door and stepped out into the hallway.

"God sees everything, Emma." Nancy followed her.

They went downstairs, and Nancy said goodbye to Ollie.

"Are you leaving already?" the boy asked.

"Yes. I have to cook dinner."

As she opened the front door, Emma said, "Tell Ryan I said hello."

Ryan was Nancy's husband and Paul's father.

"Paul's life's in your hands," Nancy said in a low voice.

Chapter 19

1

Victor Hopper, the head of VH Investigations (VH stood for Victor Hopper), was six feet three, muscular, broad-shouldered, with short brown hair and a plain face. Like many private investigators, Victor was an ex-cop. Jonah Wallach's firm had been doing business with VH Investigations for four years and was one of its top clients.

"What can I do for you, Jonah?" Hopper asked.

"I need information on Matt Sawyers," Wallach said. "He was convicted of murder last October."

"Who is he?"

"The leader of a gang called the Wolf Brigade. I have a client named Paul Marston. He's a lawyer. He's accused of murder. Have you heard of him?"

"No."

"Paul believes he was framed. Sawyers was a client of his. Paul lost his case and he got life. Paul thinks Sawyers might be the one who framed him."

"Who is Paul accused of killing?"

"A woman named Alison Bowles. He says he never met her."

"What evidence do they have against him?"

"They found his semen on the victim's body. They also found the victim's hair in his trunk."

"That's a tough case, to put it mildly."

"Yeah."

"Do you think Paul was framed?"

Wallach shrugged.

"Do you think it's possible he was framed?"

"Anything's possible. He seems to believe what he's saying. Either he's a great liar, or he's telling the truth."

"Or maybe he lost his mind."

"He passed a lie detector test, you know."

"Did you know that you can beat a lie detector by clenching your sphincter?" Hopper grinned.

"I've known Paul for a long time. I don't think he's capable of murder."

"Sawyers is in prison, isn't it?"

"Yes."

"You want me to find out if he had someone frame Paul?"

"Yes."

"You think Sawyers's people killed Alison Bowles and planted Paul's semen on her body?"

Wallach nodded.

"How did they get his semen?"

"I think his wife gave it to them. Who else could have done it?"

"Why would she help them frame her husband?"

"Paul was cheating on her. Sawyers's people might have showed her pictures of him with his mistress."

"Maybe she killed Alison Bowles and planted the semen?"

"It's possible. You need to find out if Sawyers's people ever contacted Paul's wife."

"What's her name?"

"Emma Marston. Also, find out if Sawyers's people ever contacted Alison Bowles."

Hopper made a note. "If Sawyers was mad at Paul, he would have simply had him killed, don't you think?"

"Perhaps he wants to make Paul suffer."

"How old is Sawyers?"

"Forty-six."

"Who did he murder?"

"A drug dealer named Ricardo Cervantes."

"Ask Paul if Sawyers is married and if he has any adult children or siblings."

"Okay."

Hopper sat back and steepled his fingers. "Emma isn't the only one who could have given Sawyers's people Paul's sperm."

Wallach looked at him questioningly.

"His mistress could have done it."

Hopper was right. Julie could have easily obtained Paul's semen. Why hadn't he thought of it?

Wallach nodded. "You're right. Dig up everything you can on her. Her name's Julie. I don't know her last name, so do a reverse lookup on her number." He told Hopper Julie's phone number.

"Do you have Julie's picture?"

"I'll ask Paul for it."

Maybe Sawyers's people had made Julie say that Paul hadn't been with her on the day of Alison Bowles's murder.

Wallach told Hooper Julie's address and said, "It appears she doesn't live there anymore. There's no furniture in the living room."

"Was Paul ever in Julie's house?"

"Many times.

2

Half an hour later Hopper called Wallach and told him that Julie was using a prepaid phone and her number had no name associated with it. Was that cell the only one she had, or did she use it only to call the men she slept with?

Or maybe she had bought it solely to communicate with Paul? Had she given him a fake name? Had she been afraid Paul might turn against her someday?

Maybe Julie had been planning to set Paul up when they first met?

Maybe she was part of the Wolf Brigade gang?

If Emma wasn't involved in framing Paul, then she had really witnessed Alison Bowles's abduction. The kidnapper was pretending to be Paul; they had wanted Emma to think that her husband had abducted a woman.

Emma had seen the fake Paul come out of their house. The guy might have picked the lock to get inside. Did the Marstons have a security system?

Wallach liked the fake Paul theory, but there was one thing that bothered him: How had those who had framed Paul known that Emma would follow him that day?

Chapter 20

1

"Do you know Julie's last name?" Wallach asked Paul when they were alone.

"No," Paul said. "Why?"

"I think it's possible that she provided your semen to those who framed you."

Paul frowned. "You think Julie did it?"

"It's certainly possible, wouldn't you agree?"

Paul nodded.

"Did you use a condom when you had sex with her?"

"Yes."

"Did you know she was using a burner phone to talk to you?"

"No." Paul shook his head. "What do you make of that?"

"I find it suspicious."

"She didn't want me to find out her real name," Paul said thoughtfully. "Maybe... Maybe she was sent by the people who framed me?"

"I suppose it's within the realm of possibility."

"Oh my God!" Paul ran a hand through his hair. "She played me. How could I be such a fool?"

"They killed Alison Bowles while you were with Julie so you wouldn't have an alibi."

"Yes." Paul nodded. "She told you I wasn't with her that day because she was in on this."

"They tricked Emma into thinking you abducted Alison. They somehow knew she was going to follow you that day. Alison's kidnapper got into your house after you left for Julie's place. Do you have a security system?"

"No. So Emma wasn't lying. She just didn't know the guy who kidnapped Alison wasn't me."

"That's right. Do you know where Julie works?"

"No."

"Do you know any of her friends?"

"No."

"Do you have her picture?"

Paul shook his head.

"Does she have a Facebook account?"

"I don't know."

"Did she give you an email address?"

"Yes. I think it's ladybug thirty-seven at gmail dot com."

It was probably a throwaway email address.

"Did she ever email you?"

"A few times."

"Did you delete her emails?"

"No."

"I want to look at them. I need your email username and password."

After Paul told him his email username and password, Wallach said, "How old is Julie?"

"Twenty-seven. How did they know Emma was going to follow me?"

"I don't know."

"Maybe they called Emma anonymously and told her that I was going to meet my mistress that day."

That seemed the most likely explanation.

Wallach asked, "Does Matt Sawyers have children?"

"He has a daughter. Her name's Pamela."

"How old is she?"

"I think she's twenty."

"Is she involved with Sawyers's gang?"

"I don't know. Sawyers might have arranged this through his brother, Rod."

"Is Rod involved with his gang?"

"I think so."

"Is Sawyers married?"

"No."

"Is he close with his daughter's mother?"

"I don't know."

"Do you remember who the lead detective on Sawyers's case was?"

"I think it was Luke Mathis."

"Is he with the Dallas PD?"

"Yes."

"The guy Sawyers killed, was he a small-time dealer?"

"Yes."

"Was he a gang member?"

"He worked for Sawyers." Paul lowered his head. "I was such a fool. I thought Julie loved me." He looked at Wallach. "When Emma visited me, I accused her of setting me up. Please tell her I'm sorry. I'd call her myself, but I'm afraid she won't talk to me."

2

When he returned to the office, Wallach asked the firm's IT guys to find out the IP addresses Julie's emails had been sent from. Half an hour later, they reported that all of Julie's five messages originated from IP addresses belonging to various Dallas-area Target stores. Wallach figured Julie had used public WiFi to send emails to Paul in order to conceal her identity. She had probably only used public WiFi to access that email account.

Chapter 21

1

On Friday Ken Daugherty called Emma and told her that he had filed her divorce papers. If Paul didn't contest, the divorce would be final in sixty days; if he did, the process might take a year or more.

When Emma came home from work, Ollie suggested that they go to the movies.

"Sure," Emma said.

As she checked the showtimes, Jonah Wallach called. She thought of letting the call go to voice mail but decided to take it.

"How are you doing, Emma?" Wallach asked.

"I'm fine. What do you want?"

"Paul apologizes for accusing you of setting him up."

"Okay."

"We believe it was Julie who provided Paul's semen to those who framed him. You know who Julie is, don't you?"

"No one framed him, Jonah."

"I don't expect you to believe Paul."

"Do you believe him?"

"Yes."

"He's manipulating you."

"Paul thinks one of his former clients might be behind this. His name's Matt Sawyers. Paul lost his case last year and the guy went to prison for life. Sawyers had a motive to destroy him."

Matt Sawyers. Emma didn't remember Paul ever mentioning this name.

"What did he go to prison for?" Emma asked.

"He killed some drug dealer. Sawyers is a powerful man. He was the head of a large gang in Dallas when he was sent to prison."

"I saw Paul kidnap Alison Bowles."

"The man you saw kidnap Alison wasn't Paul. How did you know Paul was going to meet his mistress that day? Did someone tell you?"

"No."

"Then why did you follow him that day?"

"It was a Sunday. I thought Paul might meet his mistress on his day off."

"Did you follow Paul before that day?"

"No."

"Did you tell anyone you were going to follow him?"

"No. Why do you ask?"

"I'm trying to figure out how the people who framed Paul knew that you'd follow him that day. The man you saw abduct Alison Bowles pretended to be Paul."

"Is that what you're going to tell the jury?"

"They wanted to trick you into thinking that Paul kidnapped a woman, and it worked."

"Jonah, this is ridiculous."

"Did anyone know you were going to follow Paul?"

"No."

"Emma, these people are murderers. Please help us find out who framed Paul. Are you sure no one knew you were going to follow Paul that day?"

"Yes. The man who abducted Alison didn't pretend to be Paul. He was Paul. I know that because I saw him come out of our house."

"That man got into your house after Paul left for Julie's place. He probably picked the lock. He wanted you to see him come out of your house so you'd think he was Paul."

It was a crazy theory, but Emma had to admit it wasn't outside the realm of possibility. She hadn't seen Alison's kidnapper's face clearly, had she?

"Did you talk to Julie about this?" Emma asked.

"We can't find her. She moved and she's not returning my calls. The number she gave Paul belongs to a burner phone. I believe she seduced Paul to get his semen."

"I hope you find her. Goodbye, Jonah."

Why had she lied to Wallach? Why hadn't she told him that Susan had known she was going to tail Paul that day?

I told Susan I'd keep her out of this, and it would be wrong to break that promise.

She wouldn't put it past Wallach to accuse Susan of being involved in framing Paul.

What if Paul is telling the truth? What if he really was framed?

She hadn't seen the face of Alison Bowles's abductor.

Julie could have obtained Paul's semen.

Susan could have told someone that they were planning to follow Paul.

Emma, stop! Don't let them manipulate you.

Was Matt Sawyers even a real person?

Emma googled "Matt Sawyers trial" and found that last October a Dallas-area man named Matt Sawyers had been found guilty of killing Ricardo Cervantes and sentenced to life in prison. Paul had been one of Sawyers's lawyers.

She put her tablet on the coffee table.

It was possible Paul had been set up, she couldn't deny that. She had to help him. She would not go out of her way, though.

She would call Susan and ask if she had told anyone they were going to follow Paul. It would only take five minutes. She would do it when she got home from the movie theater.

Chapter 22

1

Wallach called Victor Hopper after talking to Marston and relayed the information he had received from his client.

"Paul thinks Sawyers's brother might have been in charge of setting him up," Wallach said.

Marston was probably right.

"Today, I'm going to talk to the owners of the house where Julie lived," Hopper said. "Hopefully, they know her real name."

"Okay. Do you know Detective Luke Mathis?"

"Yes."

"Excellent."

According to the county records, the house Julie had lived in was owned by the living trust of Alfredo and Barbara Mendoza. It had taken Hopper only a few minutes to find the Mendozas' address: they resided in the Lakewood neighborhood of Dallas.

On the way to the Mendozas' place Hopper stopped by Julie's house and looked in the windows. There was no furniture in the living room and both bedrooms. He rang the bell, just in case. No one answered.

The Mendozas lived in a two-story house with a long front porch and dormer windows. Before ringing the bell, Hopper opened the voice recorder app on his phone and tapped Record.

A plump woman in her fifties opened the door.

"Hello," she said.

"Hi." Hopper smiled. "I'm looking for Barbara Mendoza."

"How can I help you?"

"My name's Victor Hopper. I'm a private investigator." Hopper took out his business card and handed it to Barbara. "Does the house at Eight Two Five Five Oberlin Drive belong to you?"

"Yes. Why?"

"I'm looking for the woman that rents it from you. Do you have her contact information?"

"Our tenant's a man. His name's Edward Zheng."

Was Edward Zheng involved in the framing of Paul Marston?

"Is he the only person on the lease?"

"Yes. Does a woman live there with him?"

"I believe so. Does Mr. Zheng pay rent by check?"

"He paid for six months in advance by money order. Why are you looking for that woman? Did she do something illegal?"

"She's a witness in a case I'm working on. Do you have Mr. Zheng's contact information?"

"Yes. I have his phone number."

It was probably a burner phone.

"Can you please give it to me?"

Barbara hesitated. "What kind of case are you working on?"

"A murder case. Julie's a very important witness. I have to find her."

"Her name's Julie?"

"Yes."

"Who was murdered?"

"A young woman named Alison Bowles."

"Do you work for her family?"

"Yes."

"Is Mr. Zheng involved in the murder?"

"I don't know."

Barbara folded her arms across her chest and thought for a long moment. "Okay, I'll give you his number," she finally said. "But don't tell him you got it from me."

"Sure. Do you have a copy of Zheng's ID?"

"Yes."

"Can you make me a copy?"

"I don't think I'm allowed to do that."

"Can I at least look at it?"

"Let me think."

Barbara went inside and came back a minute later with a cellphone and a sheet of paper. "Are you going to write it down?"

"Yes." Hopper pulled out his phone, opened his contacts, and tapped the plus sign button.

Barbara told him Edward Zheng's number and he saved it in his contacts.

"Here's a copy of his driver's license." Barbara handed the sheet of paper to Hopper.

Edward Zheng looked Asian (Hopper figured Zheng was a Chinese surname) and was thirty-seven years old. The address on his driver's license was 4311 Reid Street, Houston, Texas 77026.

Was it a real driver's license?

Was Edward Zheng the guy's real name?

Hopper memorized the address and the driver's license number and gave the sheet of paper back to Barbara. "Thank you very much, Barbara."

"Don't tell him I showed this to you," she said.

"Sure. When does his lease expire?"

What if Julie never lived in that house? What if Julie didn't exist?

"June thirtieth."

Maybe Marston had told Wallach some random address?

"When did he move in?"

Maybe Marston had given Wallach the wrong address by mistake?

"January fifth."

"When was the last time you talked to Zheng?"

"Last January, when he signed the lease."

When he got home, Hopper called Alan Rycroft, his former colleague at the Dallas Police Department, and asked him to look up Edward Zheng's driver's license in the DMV database and find out who Zheng's phone number was registered to. Then he called Luke Mathis and asked if the name Matt Sawyers rang a bell.

"Yes," Mathis said.

Hopper knew Mathis fairly well: they had worked in the same division for four years.

"He murdered a drug dealer last year. You were the lead on that case, weren't you?"

"Yep."

"I have some questions about him. Can we meet for coffee tomorrow? I'm buying."

"Sure."

They agreed to meet at Henry's Bar and Grill in northwest Dallas at noon.

Hopper looked up the address on Edward Zheng's driver's license and found that it was real. He would check out the address tomorrow unless the driver's license turned out to be fake.

Hopper was doing research on Matt Sawyers's brother and daughter when Rycroft called. He informed Hopper that there was an Edward Zheng in the DMV database and his driver's license number matched the number on the driver's license of the Edward Zheng in question. Rycroft emailed Hopper Zheng's picture, and when he opened the file, the private investigator saw that it wasn't the guy renting the house on Oberlin Drive.

Julie's friend's driver's license was fake.

Rycroft told Hopper that Zheng's phone number belonged to a disposable cell, just as he suspected.

Hopper sent Wallach an email with an update and then called him.

"I just emailed you an update," he said.

"Let me check."

"Are you sure Paul didn't make this Julie up?"

"Yes. I talked to her. Why?"

"What if she never lived in that house on Oberlin Drive? There are no women on the lease."

"Are you saying Paul lied? Why would he lie about that?"

"Maybe he gave you the wrong address by mistake. I'll take a picture of the house tomorrow morning and send it to you. Show it to Paul and ask if it's the right place."

"Okay."

"Ask Paul if he knows anyone named Edward Zheng."

"Okay."

"Julie and Sawyers's daughter are close in age. What if Sawyers's daughter is Julie?"

"I'll ask Paul if he knows what Sawyers's daughter looks like."

"When did Paul first meet Julie?"

"In January."

"Zheng signed the lease in January. Julie's in on this. I'm sure of it."

Chapter 23

1

They watched a comedy about middle schoolers, and they both enjoyed it. When they got home, Emma called Susan and left a message asking her to call back.

Ollie went to his room and began playing video games. Emma told him not to stay up too late, and as she kissed the boy, he said, "When is Daddy coming back?"

"I don't know. And he doesn't know, either."

"He's not answering my texts."

"He's very busy, honey."

"Will he come back?"

"Of course."

"You're not getting divorced, are you?"

"No."

Susan called at half past nine.

"How are you doing, Emma?" she said. "Is everything all right?"

"Yes. Did you tell anyone that we were going to follow Paul?"

"Yes."

"Who?"

"A friend of mine. Why?"

"What's her name?"

"Sharon. Why do you ask?"

"Paul claims that he was framed. He said that whoever framed him knew I was going to follow him that day. He said the man I followed wasn't him."

"Of course it was him. That man came out of your house."

"Paul said that guy got into our house after he left for his mistress's place."

"Oh."

"He said they wanted to trick me into thinking he kidnapped that woman. His lawyer asked me if I told anyone I was going to follow him."

"What did you tell him?"

"I told him I didn't tell anyone."

"Does he really think anyone will believe him?"

"He's desperate."

"Do you think it's possible?"

"That he was framed?"

"Yes."

"No."

"How does he explain his DNA on that woman's body?"

"He claims that his mistress gave his semen to the guy who set him up."

"He says his mistress is involved in this? Wow!"

"How well do you know Sharon?"

"We've been friends for about a year."

"Did she ever mention the name Matt Sawyers to you?"

"No. Who is he?"

"Paul's former client. Paul thinks Sawyers is the one who framed him."

"Why would this guy frame Paul?"

"Paul lost his case, and he got a life sentence."

"Did he kill someone?"

"Yes. He killed some drug dealer. He was the leader of a large gang in Dallas."

"He was a gangster?"

"Yes."

"I don't think Sharon's in a gang."

But she might know someone in Sawyers's gang.

Susan said, "You think Sharon told this Sawyers guy that we were going to follow Paul?"

"I don't know."

"Emma... What if Paul *was* framed? By this Sawyers guy?"

"I think Paul's just trying to manipulate me."

"I could ask Sharon if she knows Sawyers. Do you want me to do that?"

"I don't know. You'd have to be very subtle."

"I'll be subtle. You should confront Paul's mistress. Ask her if she gave Paul's semen to anyone. Do you know where she lives?"

"Paul's lawyer said that she moved to another place and they don't know where she lives now."

"She moved? That's suspicious."

"Maybe she's scared of Paul."

"Maybe. I'll talk to Sharon and call you back."

"Okay."

Suddenly Emma realized she was hoping that Paul would contest the divorce.

Chapter 24

1

On Saturday, Hopper took a picture of Julie's place and emailed it to Wallach. The night before, he had come to the conclusion that it was the right house and Marston hadn't lied about Julie's address. Zheng had signed the lease under a fake name and moved out two months before it expired. This sort of thing rarely happened and was awfully suspicious, and the chances of that address being random were very slim.

As Hopper looked through the transcript of his conversation with Barbara Mendoza, an idea occurred to him. Julie must have left a lot of fingerprints in the house on Oberlin Drive. He could lift them and have them run through the system.

Hopper wasn't going to break into the house, so he hoped the Mendozas would let him lift the prints.

He called Barbara Mendoza and told her that he needed a favor.

"What is it?" Barbara asked.

"I need to lift the fingerprints Mr. Zheng's roommate left in the house on Oberlin Drive."

"Why?"

"I'm going to run them through the system and see if there's a match."

"You want me to let you into the house?"

"Yes."

"I don't think we're allowed to do that."

"You have nothing to worry about, Barbara. Mr. Zheng and his roommate aren't going to complain because they moved out and are not coming back."

"How do you know that?"

"I watched the house for a week. No one lives there."

There was a long pause.

"Let me talk to my husband," Barbara said at last. "I'll give you a call tomorrow."

"I could ask the police to do it, but they'd take the place apart, and I'm sure you'd rather avoid that."

"If my husband doesn't object, I'll let you into the house."

"Thank you, Barbara."

2

Hopper arrived at Henry's Bar and Grill at ten minutes before noon and ordered an iced tea. When Mathis walked through the door, Hopper waved to him and the detective waved back.

"How's it hanging, Vic?" Mathis slid into the booth across from Hopper.

"Long and low. How about you?"

"Not bad."

Mathis ordered a crab cake, a prime rib sandwich, and a beer, and Hopper a cheeseburger.

"So what do you want to know about Matt Sawyers?" Mathis asked.

"What kind of activities is his gang involved in?"

"Drugs, prostitution, burglaries, the usual."

"How big is it?"

"About one hundred and fifty people."

"Do you remember Sawyers's lawyer, Paul Marston?"

"Yeah. He raped and murdered a woman two weeks ago. Did you know that?"

Hopper nodded. "Yes. I believe that Sawyers is planning to harm Marston for losing his case."

"Harm? Is he planning to kill Marston?"

"It's a possibility."

From his pocket Hopper pulled a sheet of paper with Julie's and Edward Zheng's phone numbers, unfolded it, and put it in front of Mathis.

"These phone numbers belong to the people hired to harm Marston," Hopper said. "I'm asking you to see if Sawyers's men ever communicated with either of them."

Mathis picked up the sheet of paper. "Are these burner phones?"

"Yes."

The waitress brought Mathis's beer. The detective took a sip and asked, "Do you know these people's names?"

"I know the name of one of them, but it's an alias—Edward Zheng."

"Which number belongs to him?"

Hopper took out his pen and scribbled Zheng's name next to his number. "I know that the other number belongs to a woman. She calls herself Julie, but I'm sure it's a fake name."

"Is Marston your client?"

"Yes. Maybe you could ask informants at Sawyers's prison to find out if he's after Marston."

Mathis sat back and folded his arms. "Marston raped and murdered a woman. Tell me why I should help him."

"He's innocent until proven guilty. Besides, Sawyers may be after his family, too. Marston has a wife and a young son."

Mathis took a long sip of his beer and said, "All right. I'll see what I can do."

"Thank you, man." Hopper bit into his cheeseburger. "Who's in charge of the Wolf Brigade now?"

"Matt Sawyers's brother, Rod."

"Is he under surveillance?"

"I don't know."

"Do you know where he lives?"

"I could find out."

"Do you have his picture?"

"Yes."

"Could you send it to me?"

"Yes. You should be careful, Vic. These guys are mean. They'll kill you in a heartbeat."

"I know. Do you know where Sawyers's daughter lives?"

"I could find out."

"Is she involved with her daddy's gang?"

Mathis shrugged. "I don't know. Do you want her picture, too?"

"Yes."

"I'll send it to you."

"Thank you."

"You should talk to the guys in the gang unit. Do you know anyone there?"

"Yes."

Hopper left the restaurant at half past noon. As he pulled into his driveway, his phone rang. It was Barbara Mendoza.

"Hi, Barbara."

"Hi. I talked to my husband and he said you can do that fingerprint thing you want to do."

"That's great. Thank you, Barbara."

"How long is it going to take?"

"About thirty minutes."

"Can you do it today?"

"Yes."

"Let's meet at the house on Oberlin Drive at four."

"Okay."

3

Hopper looked in the windows of Julie's house and was glad to see there was still no furniture in the living room and bedrooms. He rang the bell and no one answered. A minute later Barbara Mendoza called him and asked if he was on his way to the house.

"I'm already there," he said.

"We'll be there in fifteen minutes."

"Okay."

At four o'clock, a black Infiniti pulled to the curb in front of Julie's house. Barbara Mendoza sat in the passenger seat, the driver was a middle-aged man with a mustache (Hopper figured he was Barbara's husband).

"Hello," Hopper said when Barbara and the driver climbed out of the car.

Barbara said, "This is my husband, Alfredo."

"Nice to meet you." Hopper shook Alfredo's hand.

As they walked to the house, Alfredo said, "You're only going to lift the fingerprints, right?"

"Yes," Hopper replied. "Thank you for letting me do this, Alfredo."

Barbara rang the bell, waited about ten seconds, and unlocked the door. She and Alfredo went in first, and Hopper followed.

"I told you they moved out," Hopper said as the Mendozas looked around the empty living room. "Please don't touch anything."

He went into the hallway, scanned the doors, all of which were ajar, and set the fingerprint kit on the floor. Barbara and Alfred stood a few feet away watching him. Hopper took a pair of latex gloves from his pocket, put them on, then switched on the light and opened the fingerprint kit.

"Did you call Edward Zheng?" Barbara asked.

"Not yet. I'll call him tonight."

Hopper knelt in front of the bathroom door and dusted the knob with fingerprint powder. There were no fingerprints on the top or front of the knob or the rosette. Hopper carefully studied the underside of the knob and found no prints there, either.

Had Zheng and Julie wiped off their prints before leaving?

Hopper moved to the bedroom door across the hallway and dusted the knob. No fingerprints.

"Did you wipe off the doorknobs?" Hopper asked.

"No," Barbara said.

"You found no fingerprints?" Alfredo asked.

Hopped nodded.

"That's strange," Barbara said.

Alfredo walked over to the bathroom door and fixed his eyes on the knob. "Why would they wipe off the doorknobs?"

"That's a good question," the private investigator said.

He dusted both knobs of the second bedroom door and found no prints. The inside knobs of the doors to the other bedroom and the bathroom were fingerprint-free, too.

Both bedroom closets and the bathroom and kitchen cabinets were empty. Zheng and Julia had left nothing behind.

"Do you think Zheng and that woman are involved in that murder?" Barbara asked Hopper.

"I don't know."

Hoping Zheng and Julia had missed a print or two, Hopper dusted everything they might have touched in the house but found nothing.

"Did you find any fingerprints?" Barbara asked as Hopper stripped off his gloves.

"No."

It was clear that Julie didn't want to be found by the police. Hopper was convinced it had to do with Paul Marston: she had moved out of this house shortly after his arrest.

Hopper pocketed the gloves. "Did Zheng give you his Social Security number?"

"No," Alfredo replied. "He said he didn't have it. He said he was a Canadian citizen."

"Could you give me a copy of his driver's license?"

Alfredo nodded. "Okay."

"Could you let me know if Zheng contacts you?"

"Sure."

"Don't tell him I'm looking for Julie."

"Okay."

"He paid you a security deposit, didn't he?"

"Yes."

"Please give me a call before you return it."

"Okay. Do you want to track him down?"

"Yes."

Barbara said, "What if they come back and see that powder? Maybe I should wipe it off?"

"Yeah, you can wipe it off."

Hopper followed the Mendozas to their house, and Barbara gave him a copy of Zheng's driver's license.

"If you find them, please let me know," she said.

When he came home, Hopper scanned the copy of Zheng's driver's license and sent it to Mathis and Wallach. Then he called Wallach and told him that he had found no fingerprints in Julie's house.

"These people are cautious, aren't they?" Wallach said.

Hopper knew two detectives in the Dallas PD Gang Unit and decided to call Detective James Russo first. Russo told the private investigator he was still with the gang unit and agreed to meet him tomorrow at the Red Rock Café in North Dallas.

4

Russo came to the Red Rock Café a few minutes after Hopper. He didn't know who Paul Marston was, and Hopper didn't mention that Marston had been charged with murder. Russo said that the Dallas PD didn't consider the Wolf Brigade gang a major threat, so they didn't monitor its activities closely.

"Can you check the reports and surveillance transcripts and see if there's any mention of Paul Marston after Sawyers's trial?" Hopper said.

"Sure."

Hopper took out an enlarged copy of Zheng's driver's license photo and put it in front of Russo. "This guy was hired to harm Marston. Please check if he's a member of the Wolf Brigade."

"Okay."

"He has a partner, a woman. Can you give me pictures of female members of the Wolf Brigade?"

"Yes."

When Russo left, Hopper called Edward Zheng from his disposable phone. He was going to pretend he had called the wrong number.

It went straight to voice mail. Zheng had probably gotten rid of the phone.

Chapter 25

1

Wallach pulled out a picture of the Mendozas' rental house on Oberlin Drive and put it on the table. "Is this Julie's house?"

Paul nodded. "Yes."

The lawyer placed the photograph back in the folder. "My investigator talked to the owners of the house. They said that it's rented by a man named Edward Zheng. He signed the lease last January. That's when you met Julie, isn't it?"

"Yes."

"There are no other people on the lease." Wallach took out Edward Zheng's driver's license picture and gave it to Paul. "Do you recognize him?"

"No. Who is he?"

"Edward Zheng, but that's not his real name. He used a fake driver's license to rent the house."

"Did he live there?"

"I don't know. You've never seen him?"

"I don't think so. I don't remember ever seeing him."

"My investigator found no fingerprints in the house. Zheng and Julie wiped off all their fingerprints before they left. I think that proves that Julie was involved in this."

"Yes. We have to find her."

"Are you sure you don't have any pictures of Julie?"

"Yes."

"Do you know what Matt Sawyers's daughter looks like?"

"No. Why?"

"She may be Julie."

Paul nodded. "We need to get her picture."

"I'll have it soon."

2

Detective Ryan DaSilva of the Dallas PD Gang Unit told Mathis that they had Rod Sawyers's address but didn't have Pamela Sawyers's. As far as they knew, Matt Sawyers's daughter was not involved with his gang. Mathis pulled Pamela's DMV record and found that she was still a permanent resident of Texas (which didn't mean that she currently lived in Texas). She had no criminal record. She had no out-of-state tickets.

Mathis emailed Victor Hopper Pamela and Rod Sawyers's pictures and their addresses (he noted that he had gotten Pamela's address from the DMV database) and then requested the phone records for the numbers Hopper had given him.

After leaving Dallas Police Headquarters for the day, Mathis drove to the strip mall at Ross and Henderson Avenues and used a payphone to call Clint Ritter, his informant in the Wolf Brigade gang.

"Can you talk?" Mathis asked when Ritter answered.

"Yes."

"Does the name Paul Marston ring a bell?"

"No."

"He was Matt Sawyers's lawyer. He defended Sawyers at his trial last year. Was there any talk among Rod's guys about Marston?"

"I don't know. I didn't hear anything."

"We suspect Matt Sawyers ordered a hit on Marston and his family. If you hear anything, let me know."

"Why would he want to take out his lawyer?"

"Marston lost his case."

"Oh. Okay. If I hear anything, I'll let you know."

Chapter 26

1

I should tell him about Sharon, Emma thought as Wallach entered the house.

The lawyer had called her half an hour ago and asked if he could stop by.

"How are you doing, Emma?"

Wallach was carrying a tablet.

"I'm fine."

"I'll be out of your hair in ten minutes." Wallach sat down in a chair. "We have proof that Julie was involved in framing Paul."

"What is it?"

"As I told you, she moved shortly after Paul's arrest. We discovered that she'd wiped off all her fingerprints before she left. Innocent people don't do that, do they?"

Julie had wiped off all her fingerprints? That was strange. *What if he's lying?*

"Did you break into her house?" Emma asked.

"No. The owners of the house let my investigator in."

"Why were you looking for her fingerprints?"

"We're trying to find her." Wallach pressed the tablet's power button to wake it and tapped the screen. "Have you ever seen this guy?" he said, handing the tablet to Emma.

On the screen was a black-and-white picture of an Asian man Emma didn't recognize.

"No." Emma put the tablet on the coffee table.

"The lease of the house where Julie lived is in his name. He used a fake driver's license to rent it. You have to admit, Emma, something fishy is going on here."

"Do you have Julie's picture?"

"No."

Wallach picked up the tablet.

"Last time, you asked me if I told anyone I was going to follow Paul that day. I said I didn't tell anyone. That wasn't true. Well, technically, it wasn't a lie."

"Who did you tell?"

"My friend Susan knew I was going to follow Paul. It was her idea. She told me she told one of her friends that we were going to follow Paul."

"She was with you in the car when you followed him?"

"Yes. It was her car."

"What's the friend's name?"

"Sharon."

"What's her last name?"

"I didn't ask."

"Can you give me Susan's number?"

"She doesn't want to get involved in this."

"Can you ask her for Sharon's contact information?"

"Yes."

"Also, ask her how old Sharon is."

Wallach tapped the tablet a few times and then held it up. There was a picture of a young woman with brown hair on the screen. "Do you recognize her?"

"No."

"She's Matt Sawyers's daughter, Pamela."

"By the way, what's the name of Sawyers's gang?"

"The Wolf Brigade."

"What's their signature tattoo?"

"I don't know. Probably a wolf."

When Wallach left, Emma called Susan, but the call went to voice mail. She sent Susan a text asking her to call her.

Was Sharon involved in framing Paul?

Did she still think the idea that Paul had been set up was far-fetched? In light of what Wallach had told her about Julie and the guy whose name was on the lease of Julie's house, Emma couldn't be sure that Paul had kidnapped and murdered Alison Bowles. Wallach was right: something fishy was going on here.

2

Susan called at nine p.m.

"Hi, Emma. What's up?"

"Did you ask Sharon about Sawyers?"

"No, not yet. I'm still trying to figure out how to do it."

"Can you give me her phone number?"

"Do you want to ask her about Sawyers yourself?"

"Yes."

"I can't give you her number without her permission. I hope you understand."

"How about her email address?"

Susan hesitated. "Okay. I'll give you her email address. Let me find it."

Half a minute later Susan told Emma that Sharon's email address was lunazz3@yahoo.com.

"If I were Paul's lawyer, I'd try to find Paul's mistress," Susan said. "Are they looking for her?"

"Yes. How old is Sharon?"

"Thirty-four."

"Does she live in Dallas?"

"Yes."

"Does she have any tattoos?"

"Not that I know of. Do you still want me to ask her about Sawyers?"

"Yes. Thank you, Susan. Goodbye."

"Goodbye."

Emma hung up and then called Hopper.

"Susan didn't give me Sharon's phone number, but she gave me her email address," she said.

She texted Hopper Sharon's email address and said, "Sharon's thirty-four years old. Why did you want to know her age?"

"I thought Sharon might be Pamela Sawyers."

Pamela Sawyers was no older than twenty-five; she couldn't be Sharon.

"Are you going to email Sharon?"

"Probably."

"Susan said she'll ask Sharon if she told anyone we were going to follow Paul."

"I'll wait a week."

Chapter 27

1

"I got Pamela Sawyers's picture." Wallach took out Matt Sawyers's daughter's photograph and put it in front of Paul. "Does she look like Julie?"

Paul shook his head. "No."

Wallach pulled a stack of photos of female members of the Wolf Brigade from his pocket and handed it to Paul. "These women are members of the Wolf Brigade."

Paul went through the photos and then said, "None of them looks like Julie."

Wallach pocketed the pictures and updated Paul on their investigation.

Detective Russo had told Hopper that Edward Zheng didn't look like any known member of the Wolf Brigade. There was no mention of Paul Marston in the gang unit's reports and surveillance transcripts, and no indication that the Wolf Brigade was plotting to harm or kill any lawyers.

Hopper's contacts in the gas and electric companies had told him that Julie's house's gas and electric services were in Edward Zheng's name and that he paid the bills with money orders.

Detective Mathis had told Hopper that none of the numbers in Edward Zheng's and Julie's phone records belonged to known members of the Wolf Brigade gang or any other criminal organization. Their burner phones had been activated last December, two months after Matt Sawyers's trial. Zheng had made three calls from his cell, all of which were to Alfredo Mendoza. He had made his last call on January 5. He had received three calls: two from Mendoza and one from Victor Hopper (it was the last call Zheng had ever received). Zheng had never sent or received any text messages.

Except for the calls to Wallach, all calls made from Julie's burner phone were to Paul Marston. Except for the calls from Wallach, all calls she had received were from Marston, too. All text messages sent from Julie's phone were to Marston, and he was the only person who had texted her. (Mathis had asked

Hopper if Paul was sleeping with Julie, and Hopper said he didn't know.)

Wallach told Paul about Susan and Sharon and said, "I'm thinking of meeting Sharon."

"Does Emma believe me now?"

"I don't know. I think she's no longer sure you killed Alison Bowles."

If she was sure Paul was a murderer, Emma wouldn't have asked her friend Susan if she had told anyone they were going to follow him.

Paul's face lit up. "That's great."

"Do you have any other suspects besides Matt Sawyers?"

"No."

Chapter 28

1

Monday, June 8

"Honey, I'm home," Robert Lochner announced as he locked the door behind him. There was no answer.

Robert slipped off his shoes and went upstairs to the master bedroom. Tamara wasn't there.

Robert changed out of his suit and into shorts and a T-shirt, got a can of Bud Light from the refrigerator, and switched on the TV. He watched a rerun episode of Criminal Minds, and when it was over, he texted Tamara, "Where are you?"

Was she out shopping? Was she hanging out with her friends?

Robert warmed up the leftover meatballs and rice in the microwave, placed the food on the kitchen island, and then checked his messages. No new texts. He dialed Tamara's number and got voice mail. Her phone was off or out of range.

His conscience was clear. When his wife asked him why he had eaten without her, he would say that he had called and texted her to ask when she was coming home, but she hadn't answered.

Robert was fifty, tall, fair-skinned, with thinning hair and a little paunch that he had been trying to lose for the last fifteen years.

As Robert shoved his second meatball into his mouth, his phone rang.

It wasn't Tamara.

"Hello," he said.

"Is this Robert Lochner?" a deep voice said.

Robert realized that the caller was using a voice changer.

"Yes."

"We have your wife. We'll let her go if you pay us five hundred thousand dollars. Do not call the police."

Robert's heart skipped a beat.

Tamara had been kidnapped.

"Five hundred thousand? I don't have that kind of money."

"You're a banker, Robert. I'm sure you'll figure it out."

"Can I talk to her?"

His heart was hammering and his forehead was beaded with cold sweat.

"No."

"How do I know she's still alive?"

"She's alive. You have three days, Robert. Three days."

"Let me talk to her!"

"Goodbye." The kidnapper hung up.

Robert swallowed. His mouth was dry.

He and Tamara had been together for twenty-seven years and now he could lose her. He might never see his amazing wife again.

He stared at his phone for a moment, then opened the call log. His hands were trembling.

The kidnapper's number had a Dallas area code. He had probably called from a disposable phone.

The kidnappers' information was correct: he was a banker. He managed the North Dallas branch of the Bank of Texas.

There was about a million dollars in his branch's vault, but he couldn't just go in there and take out five hundred grand.

He had about two hundred thousand dollars in liquid assets, and he could probably borrow fifty grand from his friends and family. Would the kidnappers agree to reduce the ransom to two hundred and fifty thousand dollars?

What if the kidnappers take the money and kill Tammy anyway?

What if she's already dead?

Robert clenched his fists. He wanted to break Tamara's kidnappers' necks, to strangle them, to tear their hearts out of their chests. His hatred for these pieces of shit was as hot as the core of the sun.

Robert went into his home office, logged into his stock trading account, and saw that the total account value at the moment was a little over one hundred and eighty thousand dollars. They had about thirteen grand in their bank account.

What if the woman they kidnapped isn't Tammy? What if they made a mistake?

Robert called Tamara, and it went to voice mail again.

Should he contact the police?

Would the kidnappers kill Tamara if he called the cops?

They must realize that he would demand proof of life before giving them the money. They would get nothing if they killed Tamara.

He could ask the police to stay away from his house and keep things quiet.

He needed to call the cops; he couldn't handle this alone.

Robert picked up his phone.

What if the kidnappers had placed listening devices in the house?

Robert called his friend Seth Sulkin and asked him if he was home.

"Yes," Sulkin replied. "What's up?"

They had known each other for sixteen years. Sulkin was a dentist and lived with his wife and a seventeen-year-old daughter in Plano, about eight miles from the Lochners.

"Are you home?"

"Yes."

"I need to see you, Seth. Can I come over?"

"Sure. Is everything okay?"

"Yes."

Without changing into street clothes, Robert got in the car and drove to Sulkin's house. He monitored the traffic behind him to see if he was being followed; he detected no tail.

Sulkin's wife, Helen, was watching TV in the living room and Robert asked his friend if they could talk in private. When they went into his office, Sulkin said, "Bob, you look like shit. What happened?"

Robert took a deep breath and said, "Tammy's been kidnapped."

"Kidnapped?"

"The kidnappers called me half an hour ago. They want five hundred thousand dollars."

"Jesus, that's horrible."

"I'm not here to ask for money. I think the kidnappers might be watching my house. Is it okay if I tell the police to come here?"

"Sure."

"Do you think I should call the police?"

Sulkin nodded. "Yes. I think you should."

Robert looked up the Richardson Police Department's phone number and dialed it. When the operator answered, he said, "I need your help. My wife's been kidnapped."

"What's your name, sir?"

"Robert Lochner. My wife's name's Tamara. The kidnappers called me half an hour ago and said they wanted five hundred thousand dollars."

"Can you spell your last name?"

"L-O-C-H-N-E-R."

"What's your address?"

"Are you sending someone?"

"Yes."

"I live in Richardson, but I'm at a friend's place in Plano right now. The kidnappers might be watching my house, so can you send them to my friend's place?"

"Yes."

Robert told the operator Sulkin's address.

When Robert hung up, Sulkin said, "If you need any help, let me know."

"Thank you."

"Do the kidnappers want you to steal the five hundred grand from your bank?"

"I think so."

The cops arrived forty minutes later. They introduced themselves as Detectives Beau Ferland and George Jovanovic of the Richardson Police Department and handed their business cards to Robert.

"What happened?" Helen whispered to her husband.

"I'll explain later," Sulkin replied, and she left the living room.

After Robert told the detectives about the ransom call, Ferland asked, "Did you see any signs of a break-in or struggle?"

"No."

"I'd like to have a look around your place later, if you don't mind."

"They might be watching it. They'll kill Tamara if they find out I called the police."

"Does your house have a built-in garage?"

"Yes."

"You'll drive me to your place in your car."

"Okay."

"Are you a wealthy man?"

"No."

Jovanovic asked, "What do you do for a living?"

"I'm the manager of the Bank of Texas branch in North Dallas."

"Did the kidnappers tell you to steal the money from your bank?"

"No, but they probably think I could do that."

Ferland asked, "Did they let you talk to Tamara?"

"No."

"Did they call your cellphone?"

"Yes."

"Tell me the number they called from."

Robert pulled out his phone, found the number the kidnappers had called from, and gave it to Ferland.

"I also need your wife's phone number," the detective said.

Robert told him Tamara's number, and Ferland asked, "Does your wife have a tracking app on her phone?"

"No."

Ferland asked his partner to get the locations of Tamara's and the kidnappers' cells and find out who the kidnappers' number was registered to.

"Does your wife work?" the detective asked Robert.

"She's a high school teacher. She's on summer break right now."

"Did she tell you what she planned to do this afternoon?"

"No."

"Do you know where her car is?"

"No."

"Is it equipped with a tracking device?"

"No."

"When did you last talk to Tamara?"

"This morning at half past seven."

"What time did you come home?"

"At half past six."

"Do you have children?"

"Yes. A son, Jim. He's twenty-five, lives in San Diego."

"Did you try to call Tamara after the kidnappers' call?"

"Yes. Her phone was off."

Jovanovic came into the room and said, "The kidnappers called from a burner phone. Its last known location is near Central Expressway and Park Boulevard in Plano. They turned it off right after they called Mr. Lochner. Tamara Lochner's phone's last known location is near Renner and Jupiter Roads in Richardson. It was turned off at half past two."

Had the kidnapping taken place shortly before half past two? The intersection of Renner and Jupiter Roads was less than a mile from the Lochners' home. Had Tamara been abducted from their house or shortly after she left it?

"How far from their house is the intersection of Renner and Jupiter Roads?" Ferland asked.

"About a mile."

"They probably kidnapped her from your house," Ferland told Robert. "Let's go to your place." The detective stood up.

Robert said to Sulkin, "Thank you, Seth."

"No problem. Good luck."

Robert and the cops went outside. Robert and Ferland got in Robert's Lexus and Jovanovic in the detectives' Chrysler 300.

As they drove away from Sulkin's house, Robert asked, "Should I prepare the ransom money?"

"You have five hundred thousand dollars in cash?" Ferland said.

"If I sell all my stocks, I'll have about two hundred grand."

"But they want five hundred."

"You're going to capture them when they pick up the money, aren't you?"

"Sometimes we arrest the kidnappers right after they pick up the ransom, sometimes we trail them for a while before capturing them."

"Have you done this before?"

"Yes."

"Maybe I should just pay them. I don't care about the money. I just want Tammy back."

"You don't have five hundred grand."

"I'll try to get them to lower the ransom to two hundred thousand."

"I wouldn't do it if I were you, Robert. Chances are they'll kill Tamara after they get the money."

Jovanovic parked half a block from the Lochners' house. When Robert pulled into his garage and closed the door, he asked Ferland, "Are you going to tap my phone?"

"Yes."

"Please keep things quiet. I don't want the kidnappers to find out I called you."

"Sure."

Ferland examined the front and back doors, checked out every room in the house, and then asked Robert for his wife's picture. Robert emailed the detective a photo of Tamara that he'd taken in Oak Point Park three weeks ago.

"Are you going to get the FBI involved?" Robert asked.

"We'll see."

Chapter 29

1

Emma called Jonah Wallach when Ollie's babysitter left.

"Hi, Emma," Wallach said. "How are you doing?"

"I'm fine. How's your search for Julie going?"

"No progress yet."

It had been seven weeks since Paul's arrest. They had been looking for Julie for over a month. Would they ever find her? Would they ever figure out who had framed Paul?

Would they be able to prove his innocence?

So far Wallach had found no evidence that the Wolf Brigade was involved in this. He had emailed Sharon asking for a meeting, and she had told him that she was out of the country and would return to the United States in November. Sharon had told Susan that she had never heard of Matt Sawyers or the Wolf Brigade gang.

"Did Zheng contact the owners of the house about the deposit?" Emma asked.

Edward Zheng's lease was going to expire in twenty-two days.

"No. I think he's going to let the owners keep it."

"I think so, too. Sorry I bothered you. Goodbye."

Emma hung up.

She had told Paul that she believed him when she visited him a month ago.

"You didn't kill that woman," she said. "You were framed."

"You believe me?" A hesitant smile touched Paul's lips.

Emma nodded. "Yes. I'll do everything I can to help you prove your innocence."

Paul's eyes welled up. "Thank you, honey. Thank you. You can't imagine how much this means to me." He wiped away his tears.

"I'm sorry I didn't believe you."

"It's all right. You were tricked."

A few days later she withdrew her divorce petition. When she visited Paul two weeks ago, she had brought Ollie with her. Tears flooded Paul's eyes as he said, "Hi, Ollie."

"I miss you, Daddy."

"I miss you, too, very much."

Ollie asked Paul why he was in jail, and he said, "Mommy will explain it to you."

On the way home, Emma told Ollie that Daddy had done nothing wrong and that he had been put in jail by mistake.

"Like Paddington?" her son asked.

He was referring to Paddington Bear, one of his favorite characters, who was framed for stealing a book and imprisoned in the movie Paddington 2.

"Yes, like Paddington."

"Will they let him out?"

"Of course."

"When?"

"Soon."

Emma visited Paul every week to give him moral support. She had realized that she had felt better when she had thought Paul was a murderer. She had hated him, found him repugnant, but it hadn't made her life miserable. Now she was sick with worry about Paul, who might be executed for a crime he hadn't committed. It was becoming impossible for her to stay positive: Paul would be convicted unless they proved he had been set up, and it seemed it would take a miracle to do that.

She could only imagine what Paul was going through, and she was frustrated by her inability to help him fight the charges against him.

Her phone rang. It was Connie Bowles.

"Hi, Connie. How are you?" Emma said.

"I'm okay. How are you doing?"

"I'm fine."

"I visited your husband in jail yesterday."

"Why?"

"I wanted to see him. I wanted to tell him I was glad that he was caught and that he'd spend the rest of his life in prison."

"Did you do it?"

"Yes. He told me that he was set up, that the real killer was still out there."

"He tells me that, too."

She could try to convince Connie that Paul had been framed, but what would be the point?

"Ali must have screamed for help while she was in the trunk. I wonder why no one helped her. Someone must have heard her, but they did nothing."

"Maybe she couldn't scream. Maybe Paul gagged her and cuffed her hands behind her back."

It was certainly risky to put Alison in the trunk. Someone could have heard her move inside it and tried to help her.

Perhaps Alison's killer loved risk.

"Maybe," Connie said. Emma could hear her sobbing.

Poor woman.

Emma sighed heavily.

Connie's daughter was dead, and her killer was at large.

"I'll let you go. Goodbye, Emma." Connie hung up.

Chapter 30

1

On Tuesday Robert sold all his investments and transferred the money to his bank account. He wondered if the police had informed the CEO of the Bank of Texas that Tammy had been kidnapped and if the bank's security department was watching him.

An FBI agent named Michael Pendergrass called him at one in the afternoon.

"I'd like to talk to you about your wife's kidnapping," Pendergrass said. "Can we meet in an hour?"

"Where? I'd rather you didn't come to my house. The kidnappers might be watching it."

"How about my office?"

"Okay."

Robert was glad the police had gotten the FBI involved.

Forty-five minutes later he stepped into Pendergrass's office on the third floor of the Dallas FBI building. The agent was in his forties, tall, square-jawed, with dark hair, wearing a white shirt, black tie, and black pants. His suit jacket hung over the back of his chair.

They shook hands, and Robert asked, "Are you in charge of the case now?"

"No. The Bureau is only assisting the Richardson Police Department. Rest assured we're doing everything we can to save your wife, Mr. Lochner."

"Thank you."

"Do you have any idea who might be behind this?"

"No."

"Did you see anyone suspicious near your house before or after the kidnapping?"

Robert shook his head. "No."

"Are you a wealthy man?"

"No."

"Do you have rich relatives?"

"No."

"Why do you think the kidnappers targeted your family?

"Probably because I'm a bank manager."

"Did the kidnappers order you to steal the money from the bank or its clients?"

"No."

"Are you able to open your branch vault alone?"

"No. It takes two people to open it—me and the assistant manager."

Pendergrass could have gotten this information from the bank's security department.

He probably did.

"What's the assistant manager's name?"

"Sanjay Ashtekar."

"How long has he worked for the Bank of Texas?"

"Seven years."

"How much is the ransom?"

"Five hundred thousand dollars."

"How much money is in your branch vault?"

"Usually about a million dollars."

"Have you been able to find the money?"

"I'm three hundred thousand short." Robert hesitated. "Could the Bureau help me with that?"

"Three hundred thousand dollars is a lot of money. Let me talk to my boss."

"Thank you."

The government would have provided the ransom money without hesitation if Tammy were a high-ranking official or some other important person. Unfortunately, Tammy was a nobody.

"Have you asked your bank for a loan?" Pendergrass asked.

"No. I'll try that. Are you tracking the kidnappers' phone?"

"Yes. And your wife's phone, too. They've been off since yesterday." Pendergrass put his pen down. "Thank you for coming, Mr. Lochner."

Chapter 31

1

Emma was eating lunch at her desk when Wallach called her. She wondered if they had caught a break.

"How long have you known Susan?" Wallach asked.

"About six months."

"You first met her last January?"

"Yes."

"Paul first met Julie last January."

"So?"

"You didn't tell the police that Susan was with you when you followed Paul, did you?"

"No."

"Did Susan ask you not to tell anyone she was with you?"

"She asked me to keep her out of this."

"Why?"

"Perhaps because she was afraid of Paul."

"I think Susan's involved in this."

"How?"

"You said it was her idea to follow Paul, didn't you?"

"Yes."

"She tricked you into following Paul that day. That's why she asked you to keep her out of this."

Had Susan really helped set Paul up? Had Susan been playing her all along?

"Maybe it was Sharon who told them?" Emma said.

A shiver went up her spine. As they followed the man pretending to be Paul that day, Susan had known that he was going to kidnap and murder a woman. She had known that and she had been absolutely calm.

"I think Susan made Sharon up," Wallach said. "Do you know where Susan lives?"

"No."

Susan had never invited Emma to her place.

She didn't want me to know where she lived.

"Will you give me her phone number now?"

"Yes."

After Emma told Wallach Susan's number, he said, "Can you meet her for coffee in the next few days?"

"What for?"

"I'm going to follow her back to her place."

"When do you want me to meet her?"

"Whenever she can. Do you have her picture?"

"No."

"How old is she?"

"Thirty, thirty-five."

"What's her last name?"

"Miller."

Was Susan Miller a fake name?

"How did you meet her?"

"We met while I was jogging."

"You probably don't remember her license plate number."

"No, I don't remember it."

Her call to Susan went straight to voice mail, and Emma sent her a message saying: "Hi. You wanna hang out tonight or tomorrow night?"

Susan replied an hour later: "I can't. I'm still in California. Sorry!"

Emma texted to her: "When are you coming back?"

Susan responded: "In a few weeks."

Emma called Wallach and told him that Susan couldn't meet her because she was in California.

"She's probably lying," Wallach said. "Did she tell you when she was coming back?"

"She said she's coming back in a few weeks."

2

Hopper pulled out a piece of paper with Susan's phone number on it and put it in front of Mathis. "Can you check if any members of the Wolf Brigade contacted this number?"

"Whose number is this?" Mathis asked.

They were sitting in Randy's Barbeque, a small restaurant down the street from Dallas Police Headquarters.

"Another person hired to harm Paul Marston. She calls herself Susan Miller. Probably a fake name."

"Is it a burner phone?"

"Yes. Could you get its geolocation records for the last three months?"

"Maybe."

"It would be great if you could also get geolocation records for the other two numbers."

"You're trying to track them down?"

"Yes."

"I have an idea. When this Julie used her burner phone, she probably had her regular phone with her. Check if there was a phone that was connected to the same cell towers as her burner phone whenever it was connected to the network."

"Great idea. Could you get the cell tower records? I'll owe you one."

Mathis took a sip of Diet Coke. "I'll try."

3

Wallach stopped by Emma's house at six o'clock and showed her photos of female members of the Wolf Brigade. None of them looked like Susan.

"Susan's using a burner phone, like Julie and Zheng," Wallach told Emma. "What do you think about that?"

"I think you're right. She's involved in this. Did you call or text her?"

"No. We're trying to get her phone's location."

"I feel like a fool, you know. Susan played me like a fiddle."

Chapter 32

1

After leaving the Dallas FBI field office, Robert went to the Bank of Texas corporate headquarters in Fort Worth and met with Michael Armstrong, the Vice President for the Dallas Region.

"I need an emergency loan," he told the vice president. "Three hundred thousand. I'll put up my house as collateral."

"How much equity do you have in it?"

"Over three hundred thousand."

Armstrong was probably figuring out the loan's monthly payments for different lengths of repayment (as an experienced banker, he could do such calculations in his head in seconds). Robert hoped the vice president would come to the conclusion that he would have no trouble paying off the loan in twenty years.

"What do you need the money for?"

"For ransom. My wife's been kidnapped."

Armstrong's expression didn't change, which Robert took to mean that the police had told his bosses about Tammy's kidnapping.

"Let me talk to Mr. Davies," Armstrong said.

Brad Davies was the CEO of the bank.

"I'll give the money back in a week. The kidnappers are going to be arrested before they get their hands on it."

"I have to talk to Mr. Davies."

"The deadline's in two days."

"We'll make a decision before it. I'm sorry about what happened to your wife, Bob. If you want, you can take a few days off."

"No. Thank you."

On his way back to the office, Robert called his son and asked how much money he had in his bank account.

"About ten grand," Jim said. "Why?"

"I need a surgery. It's very expensive and my health insurance doesn't cover it. How much are your stocks worth?"

"Maybe five grand. How much do you need?"

"Can you wire me nine grand?"

"Sure."

"Today."

"Okay. What kind of surgery are you having?"

"They're removing a portion of my liver. It's not cancer. I'll be fine."

Did he need the entire five hundred thousand dollars? Were the kidnappers going to count the money right after picking it up?

He had two hundred and two grand now. It took one hundred and one packs of twenty-dollar bills to make two hundred and two grand. One hundred and one packs looked like a lot of money. The kidnappers wouldn't be able to tell there was only two hundred and two thousand dollars in the ransom bag when they looked inside it. The cops might trail them for a while after they picked up the ransom. What were the chances that the kidnappers would be captured before they could count the money? Robert thought they were fairly good.

But he couldn't take chances with Tammy's life. He had to do everything he could to raise the rest of the money.

Two hours later, Jim told Robert that he had wired him the money.

2

"Dammit," Robert said under his breath after listening to his messages in his office on Wednesday morning: none of them concerned his loan request.

He fought the urge to ask Armstrong if Davis had signed off on the loan, but finally gave in at eleven o'clock.

"Brad hasn't made a decision yet," Armstrong told him. "I'll call you as soon as I hear from him."

Robert called Pendergrass and asked him if he had talked to his boss about the ransom money.

"He said he'd think about it," Pendergrass said. "We don't usually do that, you know."

When Robert answered his desk phone at half past one, he hoped it was Armstrong calling to tell him that the bank would loan him the money.

"Do you have the money?" the caller asked.

It was Tammy's kidnappers.

"Yes."

"Five hundred grand?"

"I have two hundred thousand dollars right now."

"We want five hundred, Robert."

"I need more time."

"I'm sure there's three hundred grand in the vault."

"The vault has a dual-control combination lock. It takes two people to open it—me and the assistant manager."

"Borrow from your friends. You must have a lot of rich friends."

"I need more time."

"I'll give you two more days. Borrow the money from your friends, Robert."

"Can I talk to Tamara?"

"Yes. But not today."

"I want to talk to her before I give you the money. I want to make sure she's alive."

"Don't worry, Robert. You'll talk to her."

The kidnapper hung up.

They had given him two more days and they hadn't promised to chop off Tammy's ear or finger to punish him for failing to meet the deadline. It meant that the kidnappers might have some humanity in them.

Robert called Pendergrass and told him that the kidnappers had called his office phone.

"They gave me two more days to get the money."

Were the police tapping his desk phone?

"Did they let you talk to Tamara?"

"No."

Then Robert called Ferland. He told the detective about the kidnappers' call and asked if the police were tapping his desk phone.

"No, we're not tapping it," Ferland replied. "What number did they call from?"

"I don't know."

"What's your office phone number?"

Robert told Ferland his branch's number.

Ferland called Robert on the cellphone two hours later and said that he had bad news.

"Tamara's dead. Her body was found a few hours ago. I'm very sorry."

Robert turned pale and felt his heart seize up.

The kidnappers had killed Tammy. Why?

How long had she been dead?

"Where?" Robert asked hoarsely.

"In a wooded area on Persimmon Road in southern Dallas."

Robert blinked away the tears. "How was she killed?"

"Stabbed in the chest and stomach."

"Are you sure it's Tamara?"

"We found Tamara's driver's license on the body. But we need you to identify her, of course."

"Do you know when she was killed?"

"About forty-eight hours ago."

The kidnappers had killed Tammy shortly after they took her. They probably hadn't let him talk to her when they first called him because she had already been dead.

"When do you want me to identify her?"

"Can you do it now?"

"Yes."

Chapter 33

1

The door opened, and an attendant wearing green scrubs wheeled in a gurney with a body on it. The corpse was completely covered with a white sheet. Robert drew a deep breath and clenched his teeth as he stepped up to the gurney.

Ferland nodded, and the attendant lifted the sheet.

It was Tammy.

"Oh my God," Robert muttered, staring at his dead wife's gray face, forcing himself not to imagine what her body looked like now.

"Is it Tamara?" the detective asked.

Robert thought of the kiss Tammy had given him in the foyer before he left for work last Monday, seven hours before she was kidnapped. She had kissed him and said that she loved him. He had replied that he loved her, too.

"Yes." Robert's eyes filled with tears and he wiped them away.

Ferland said to the attendant, "Take it away."

The attendant put the sheet back and pushed the gurney out of the room.

"Let's go," Ferland said.

"They killed her shortly after they kidnapped her," Robert said as they walked down the hallway.

Ferland nodded. "It seems so."

"Why did they kill her? They knew I'd need proof of life."

"I don't know. What do you think?"

"Maybe they killed her to prevent her from escaping."

The kidnappers couldn't have stabbed Tammy in the chest and stomach by accident, could they?

"They called your office phone from a burner cell. Not the one they called you from the first time."

"What are you going to do now?"

"We won't tell the media that your wife's body was found. I want the kidnappers to think you still believe Tamara's alive. The next time they call you, tell them that you have the money."

Hopefully the kidnappers hadn't seen the police pick up Tammy's body.

They stepped out of the building into the bright sunshine. Ferland put on his sunglasses and continued, "We'll capture them when they pick up the ransom. Don't tell anyone, including your son, that Tamara's dead. "

"I could text the kidnappers that I have the money."

"Okay. Do that."

When Robert got home, he sent the kidnappers a message saying: "I have the money. Please call me."

He changed his clothes, then picked up a framed photograph of him and Tammy from the dresser and stared at it for some time before bursting into tears.

Twenty minutes later Armstrong called Robert and told him that Brad Davies had approved his loan request.

"Thank you, Mike, but I found the money," Robert replied. "The FBI will give it to me."

2

Robert was sitting on the couch in the living room drinking vodka that evening when the doorbell rang. He staggered to the front door, opened it, and saw Ferland and Jovanovic.

"Good evening, Mr. Lochner," Jovanovic said. He was carrying a black messenger bag.

"Good evening," Robert replied. "I texted the kidnappers. They haven't answered yet."

He felt drunk, but the pain was still there, brutal, unbearable. He intended to drink until he passed out.

"Do you mind if we have a look around the house?" Ferland asked.

"Sure."

Robert thought of offering the detectives vodka, but he wasn't drunk enough to actually do it.

"I'm sorry about your wife," Jovanovic said when he came in.

"Thank you."

Robert followed the detectives into the kitchen. Jovanovic put on latex gloves, then took a trigger-spray bottle from his bag and began to spritz the floor with its contents. Robert peered at the bottle's label and saw that it read LUMINOL.

The police used luminol to detect traces of blood, didn't they? As far as he knew, blood made luminol glow.

Why were they looking for traces of blood in his kitchen?

"Turn off the lights," Jovanovic told Ferland, and he did.

The darkness revealed no glowing spots on the floor. Ferland switched on the lights. Jovanovic sprayed the luminol for another fifteen seconds and Ferland turned off the lights again. Between the stove and the kitchen island there was a three-by-three-foot fluorescent stain that looked like a postmodernist painting.

Was it Tammy's blood?

"What are you looking for?" Robert asked Ferland when the detective flicked on the lights.

"I'll explain in a minute."

Why weren't the kidnappers calling? It had been over four hours since he had texted them. Did they know that Tammy's body had been found?

Jovanovic picked up his bag and went outside; Robert and Ferland moved into the living room.

"Do you mind if our crime scene investigators do some tests in your house?" Ferland asked.

"What tests?"

"You saw that glowing stain, didn't you? There appear to be traces of blood on your kitchen floor, Robert, and I believe it may be your wife's blood. Perhaps Tamara was knifed during the abduction."

"Oh."

Maybe the kidnappers had killed her in the house.

"Did you see any blood anywhere in the house when you came home on the day of the kidnapping?"

"Blood? No."

"Did you find any bloody towels or anything like that in the house after the kidnapping?"

"No."

"So, can our crime scene investigators examine your kitchen and bathrooms?"

"Sure."

Ferland walked to the front door, opened it, and let in Jovanovic and two men carrying briefcases (their name tags said Rendon and Cooley).

Jovanovic sent Rendon to the bathroom and led Cooley into the kitchen.

"Maybe the kidnappers killed Tamara in the kitchen," Robert told Ferland.

"It's certainly possible. Do you mind if we search your car?"

Why did they want to search his car? Did they think the kidnappers had been inside it?

"Okay," Robert said.

"When did you text the kidnappers?"

"Four hours ago. Are you going to provide the ransom money?"

"Yes."

Jovanovic walked up to Ferland and whispered something in his ear.

"The tests showed that there really are traces of human blood on your kitchen floor," Ferland told Robert. "We'll run a DNA test to see if it's Tamara's."

"It has to be hers," Robert said.

"Can you give your car keys to Detective Jovanovic?" Ferland asked.

"Yes."

Robert went to the master bedroom, grabbed his keys from the dresser, and returned to the living room.

"The first floor bathroom is clean," Rendon told the detectives as Robert handed his car key fob to Jovanovic. "I'm going upstairs."

Jovanovic and Cooley left the house. Fifteen minutes later, Jovanovic came back and told Robert, "We need to take your car to the lab."

"Why?"

"We found some evidence in it."

"What kind of evidence?"

"Fingerprints that might belong to your wife's killers. Do you mind if we take your car to the lab?"

"Sure."

Robert was beginning to feel that something wasn't right, that the detectives were lying to him, that they weren't on his side.

Why would the kidnappers' fingerprints be in his car?

Rendon found no traces of blood in the bathrooms on the second floor. The detectives and crime scene investigators left after a police flatbed truck picked up Robert's Lexus.

Robert stood in the kitchen for a minute picturing the kidnappers stabbing Tammy, her blood spilling on the floor, then poured himself another glass of vodka and took a swig. He finished the whole bottle before passing out.

Chapter 34

1

His head was throbbing when Robert woke the next morning. He checked his phone and saw there were no missed calls and no new text messages.

Why weren't the kidnappers calling? Were they going to wait until Saturday?

Maybe they had gotten rid of the phone they had used to make the first call?

Robert called the assistant manager of his branch and told him that he was sick and couldn't come to work today. Then he sent the kidnappers another text saying that he had the money and asking them to call him. He realized that it wouldn't make them respond sooner, but he couldn't just wait and do nothing.

Robert grabbed a bottle of vodka from the pantry, and as he twisted off the cap, it occurred to him that if the kidnappers heard his slurred voice, they might figure out that he had learned Tammy was dead. He needed to stay sober until Tammy's killers were caught.

He took two aspirin, washed his face, and made coffee. Although he hadn't eaten since last night, he wasn't hungry. As he drank coffee, Robert wondered what Detectives Ferland and Jovanovic were up to. Why had they searched his car? It had been in the bank's parking lot when Tammy was kidnapped and when she was murdered.

Did the detectives suspect he might have had something to do with Tammy's kidnapping and murder?

Did they suspect he had killed her?

It didn't matter what Ferland and Jovanovic thought. Sooner or later the kidnappers would call and arrange an exchange, and the cops would arrest them when they picked up the money.

At seven o'clock the doorbell rang. It was Ferland and Jovanovic.

"The kidnappers haven't called yet," Robert told them.

"How are you holding up?" Ferland asked.

"Not good."

"A DNA test showed that the blood found in your kitchen belonged to your wife," Ferland said.

"Tamara might have been killed in the kitchen," Jovanovic said.

"Yes."

"We found traces of your wife's blood on one of your kitchen knives. It might have been used to kill her."

Robert nodded. "Did you find any fingerprints on the handle?"

"No. There were no fingerprints on the knife," Ferland said.

"It's strange that the kidnappers killed Tamara so early, isn't it?" Jovanovic said. "Usually kidnappers keep their hostages alive at least until the ransom call."

"I wonder why they aren't calling," Ferland said.

"Maybe they threw the first burner phone away," Robert said.

"Did you drive your car to work on the day of the kidnapping?"

"Yes."

"Did you lend it to anyone that day?"

"No."

Where was Ferland going with that?

"Robert, we found Tamara's blood in the trunk of your car."

Robert frowned. "How did it get there?"

"You don't know how it got there?"

"No."

How had Tamara's blood gotten in the trunk of his car?

"Are you sure Tamara was kidnapped?" Jovanovic asked, his eyes fixed on Robert's.

"What? Yes, I'm sure."

Robert broke into a sweat.

They did suspect he had murdered Tammy. They thought he had made up the kidnapping story.

"Did your wife have life insurance?" Ferland asked.

"Yes."

"Are you the beneficiary?"

"Yes."

"How much was she insured for?"

"Eight hundred thousand."

Did the police think he had killed Tamara for the insurance money?

He needed a lawyer. And he needed to stop talking to the detectives right now.

"That's a lot of money," Jovanovic said.

"What does that have to do with my wife's kidnapping?"

Ferland took a folded document from his inside pocket and put it on the table. "We have a warrant to search your house, Mr. Lochner." He got up.

"Searching my house isn't going to help you find Tamara's killers."

Ferland pulled out a pair of handcuffs. "Robert Lochner, you're under arrest for the murder of your wife, Tamara Lochner."

"I didn't kill my wife!"

"Stand up and put your hands behind your back."

Robert rose to his feet. "Please don't do it. The kidnappers are going to call soon. We have to catch them."

"Your wife wasn't kidnapped, Robert." Ferland cuffed Robert's hands behind his back. "You murdered her."

"Can you give my phone to my friend? The kidnappers might call tonight."

"If they call, I'll talk to them."

"Tell them you're my friend."

Chapter 35

1

Robert was taken to the Dallas County jail, and it was half past nine when the booking process was completed and he was allowed to make a phone call. He dialed Seth Sulkin's cell number and prayed that his friend would answer. Sulkin picked up on the third ring.

"Seth, I need your help," Robert said.

"What happened?"

"I'm in jail. The cops think I killed Tamara."

"What?"

"Do you know any good lawyers?"

"Yes. When did they arrest you?"

"Two hours ago. Call the best lawyer you know and tell him I need his help."

"Sure."

Robert barely slept that night. He wondered if the kidnappers had called and if Ferland had talked to them. They would definitely call on Saturday because Saturday was the deadline (unless they found out that he knew Tammy was dead).

Would Ferland keep his promise to talk to the kidnappers? Would they believe him?

They wanted the ransom money, so they would probably be inclined to believe Ferland.

How had Tammy's blood gotten in his trunk? It must have been planted there by the kidnappers; he could think of no other explanation.

At eight o'clock the next morning, a guard told Robert that his lawyer was there to see him, and escorted him to the attorney conference room. The lawyer's name was John Laporte. He was in his forties, trim, with an aquiline nose and gray eyes.

"Why do the cops think you murdered your wife?" Laporte asked Robert.

Robert told him about the kidnapping, the traces of blood found in his kitchen and the trunk of his car, and Tamara's life insurance policy.

"Did the police record the kidnappers' second call?" Laporte asked.

"No. They weren't tapping my office phone and the kidnappers used another burner phone to make the call."

"How do you think Tamara's blood got in your trunk?"

"I believe the kidnappers planted it. They set me up."

"Why would they do that?"

"So the cops won't look for them."

"Where's your cellphone now?"

"I think Detective Ferland has it. Can you get it back? The kidnappers will call tomorrow: tomorrow is the deadline."

"I'll try. Don't talk to the cops without me." Laporte glanced at his watch. "Your arraignment is in an hour. We'll talk more later."

"Do you think they'll release me on bail?"

"They probably will. You have no criminal record, do you?"

"No."

2

Despite Laporte's persuasive (at least to Robert) arguments, the judge denied Robert bail. Laporte called Ferland and asked him to give Robert's phone back. The detective said that he couldn't return the phone because it was evidence.

"If the kidnappers call, I'll talk to them," Ferland said.

Laporte told Robert that the news of his arrest might hit the Internet today.

"If the kidnappers find out you were arrested for Tamara's murder, they won't call," he said. "I requested a gag order. Hopefully, it's granted."

At four o'clock, Robert called his son and told him about the kidnapping, Tamara's death, and his arrest. Jim started crying.

"Don't tell anyone about this," Robert said.

"I'll be in Dallas tomorrow. What jail are you in?"

"Dallas County jail, the North Tower Detention Facility."

Three hours later a guard took Robert to an interview room, where Detective Ferland was waiting for him.

"Let me call my lawyer," Robert said.

"You don't need him," Ferland replied. "This is not an interrogation. I just want to give you an update."

Had the kidnappers called?

"Okay."

"Do you have a pair of black sweatpants?"

"Yes."

"During the search, we found a pair of black sweatpants in the master bedroom closet. We examined them and discovered a blood stain. The blood belonged to your wife."

"I didn't kill Tamara. The blood was planted by the kidnappers. They set me up."

"They set you up?"

"Don't you find it suspicious that there's so much evidence against me? If I were the killer, I would have gotten rid of the sweatpants and the knife. I'm a smart guy, you know."

"Even smart people make mistakes. By the way, juries love it when there's a lot of evidence. The more evidence the better."

Robert had served on a jury several years ago and he knew that Ferland was right: jurors loved physical evidence.

"If I were the killer, I would have buried Tammy's body."

"You didn't bury Tamara because if her body wasn't found, you wouldn't have gotten the insurance money. You left Tamara's driver's license on her body to make it easy to identify her."

"Do you have my phone with you?"

"Yes."

"Can I see it?"

Would Ferland believe that Tammy's abduction was real if the kidnappers called? He might decide that Robert had asked someone to pretend to be the kidnappers.

"Sure." Ferland reached into his pocket and brought out Robert's cellphone.

"Is it on?"

"No." Ferland pressed the power button, and the phone came on.

"How are you going to answer the kidnappers' call if the phone's off?" Robert asked.

"No one's going to call." Ferland opened the call history on Robert's phone and showed it to him. "They haven't called yet. See? No unknown numbers."

"They'll call tomorrow. Tomorrow's the deadline. Please keep the phone on."

"Okay. But we both know no one's going to call. No one kidnapped your wife, Robert."

"My son's coming to Dallas tomorrow. Can you give my phone to him?"

"No. It's evidence." Ferland pocketed the phone. "It was an accident, wasn't it, Robert? You didn't mean to kill Tamara, right?"

"I didn't kill my wife."

"You'll feel a lot better if you confess. Tell the truth, Robert, get this burden off your chest."

"Can I go back to my cell?"

"Sure."

Chapter 36

1

Did Tammy's killers intend to frame me for her murder from the very beginning or was setting me up an afterthought, Robert wondered when he returned to his cell.

Ransom kidnappers didn't frame their hostages' spouses for murder: if the spouse was arrested, who would pay the ransom? Ransom kidnappers wouldn't have planted Tammy's blood in his trunk and on his sweatpants. That meant that Tammy's killers weren't ransom kidnappers.

They had probably killed Tammy in the kitchen. They must have stabbed her to death with one of the kitchen knives. They had let some blood spill out on the floor so its traces would later be found by the police. They had probably driven Tammy's or their car into the garage and put Tammy's body in the trunk.

When had they planted Tammy's blood in his trunk?

They might have done it while he was at work. He should ask Ferland to check the bank parking lot surveillance footage.

Tammy's killers probably knew there was a security camera in the bank parking lot.

Who had set him up?

Was it someone who hated him? Someone who held a grudge against him?

It could be a disgruntled employee he had fired. Or someone whose loan application was denied by his branch.

Robert knew of at least one ex-employee who he thought hated his guts: Brian Harbour, the assistant manager he had fired a year ago for sexual harassment.

It could be someone who wanted his job (the current assistant manager, for example). Some people would stop at nothing to advance their careers.

Maybe killing Tammy was the primary objective, and the perpetrators had framed him to keep the police from looking for them? It was perfectly possible that Tammy had had an enemy who would want to kill her. People kill for the most trivial reasons. It could have been a student Tammy had given a bad grade to.

They would look into Harbour first. Robert called Laporte and asked him to come see him tomorrow.

2

As he walked to the attorney conference room, Robert found himself hoping that Tammy had been kidnapped for ransom and that her abductors would call today. The kidnappers could be arrested today, and then his nightmare would be over.

He asked Laporte if the judge had granted the gag order, and the lawyer shook his head.

"The good news is, this morning I searched online for news about you and Tamara and found nothing," Laporte said.

"I'm beginning to think they killed Tamara to set me up for her murder. It's possible, isn't it?"

"Sure."

"I need you to look into one of my former employees. His name's Brian Harbour. He was the assistant manager at my branch. I fired him a year ago. I think he might be behind this."

"What did you fire him for?"

"Sexual harassment. Find out if he's doing well financially. Find out if he has an alibi."

"Okay. Can you spell his last name for me?"

"H-A-R-B-O-U-R."

"How old is he?"

"He's in his late thirties."

"Can you think of anyone else who could be behind this?"

"It could be someone whose loan application we rejected."

"Did any of the people whose loan applications you rejected threaten you?"

"Not that I know of."

"I'll ask the bank."

At five in the afternoon, Robert was told he had a visitor. When he reached his seat in the visitation room, he saw his son on the other side of the glass partition. Robert sat down, lifted the receiver, and put it to his ear.

"How are you, Dad?" Jim asked.

"I'm okay."

"Why do the police think you killed Mom?"

"The kidnappers killed her in our kitchen. The police found traces of her blood on the floor. They don't believe she was kidnapped. They think I murdered her."

"Where's Mom's body?"

"Probably in the county morgue."

"Do you have a lawyer?"

"Yes."

"Is he good?"

"Yes. Go to my house and stay there until tomorrow morning. The kidnappers might call my landline today. If they call, ask them where to drop off the ransom and then call Detective Beau Ferland at the Richardson Police Department. The police will provide the ransom money."

"Okay. What's your lawyer's name?"

"John Laporte."

Chapter 37

1

Susan's phone geolocation records showed that she had lied every time she said she was in California, just as Emma had suspected. None of the cell towers that Susan's burner phone had connected to in April, May, and June was outside the Dallas area. Unfortunately, the geolocation records hadn't provided enough information to figure out where Susan lived or worked.

On Saturday, Emma visited Paul.

"I'm going to tell Korbin that it wasn't you who kidnapped Alison Bowles," she told him.

"I don't think it's going to work," Paul replied.

"There's no harm in trying. Did you tell the police that Julie provided Alison's killer with your semen?"

"No. They'd laugh at me if I told them that."

"Did Jonah tell you about Susan?"

"Yes. She tricked you into following me."

"Yes, she did. Who else besides Matt Sawyers might have set you up?"

"I think about this every day, but so far I haven't been able to come up with another suspect." Paul sighed. "I've spent so much money on lawyers. I'll ask my parents to help you pay the mortgage."

"No. Let them use that money to pay your lawyers. I'll get a second job if I have to. Or sell the house."

2

While Emma was in the visitation room of the county jail, Hopper arrived at Luke Mathis's house in northwest Dallas to work on the cell tower records: the detective had decided not to give the records to him.

Hopper found that Julie's burner cell had been off since May 4. Between December and May the phone had connected to twenty-three cell towers, all of which were in the Dallas area. Hopper went through thousands of phone numbers and discovered no phones that had been connected to the same cell towers as Julie's burner cell whenever it was connected to the network. There were phones that had been connected to the same cell tower at the same time as Julie's cell in different locations, but the number of locations didn't exceed three for any of them, except for Paul Marston's phone.

Hopper reported his findings to Wallach, and the lawyer instructed him to check out the owners of the phones that had been connected to the same cell tower at the same time as Julie's cell in three locations (there were four of them). Hopper found out that the phone numbers belonged to individuals, two of whom were females. Mathis provided him with the women's photos, and he discovered that one of them was black and the other white. The white woman was twenty-eight years old and her name was Sandra Carrington. When Wallach showed Paul Sandra Carrington's picture on Sunday, he said that she wasn't Julie.

3

Robert called Jim on Sunday morning, and his son told him that the kidnappers hadn't called.

"Did I receive any packages?" Robert asked.

In the movies, kidnappers sometimes sent burner phones to those who they wanted to communicate with.

"No," Jim replied.

"Did you call the morgue?"

"It's closed on Saturdays and Sundays."

"Did you see any news stories about my arrest online?"

"Yes."

Now that the news of his arrest had hit the Internet, there was no point in delaying Tammy's funeral.

Chapter 38

1

Ferland came to see Robert again on Monday. The detective showed him the call log on his phone (there were no unknown numbers in it) and said, "The kidnappers didn't call."

"They must have found out I was arrested for Tammy's murder."

"We found your wife's car. It was parked on a residential street in Garland, about five miles from your house."

"Did you find any blood in it?"

"No."

"Did you check the trunk?"

"Yes. No blood."

"The kidnappers might have planted Tammy's blood in my trunk while I was at work on the day of the kidnapping. You need to check the bank parking lot security footage."

"No one planted Tamara's blood in your trunk. You killed her."

"I didn't kill Tammy! I was framed. I think they murdered Tammy to set me up."

"Why would anyone frame you, Robert?"

"Out of spite. It could be someone whose loan application we rejected. Some people get really upset when a bank denies them a loan."

"Well, feel free to hire a private investigator to look into this, Robert."

"A year ago, I fired the assistant manager for sexual harassment. His name's Brian Harbour. He might have set me up to get back at me. Ask him where he was on the day Tamara was murdered, check his text messages, his emails."

"We're not going to do that. You know why? Because you killed Tamara." Ferland leaned forward. "I wonder who your accomplice is."

"Why do you think I had an accomplice?"

"Someone called you from those burner phones and we know it wasn't you. Did your accomplice help you dump Tamara's body? Is it a woman? Were you sleeping with her?"

"I never cheated on my wife. And I didn't kill her."

Robert called his son at two in the afternoon and asked if he had phoned the county morgue.

"Yes," Jim said. "Mom's body's there. The funeral home will pick it up tomorrow morning."

"When do you plan to have the funeral?"

"Thursday. They're not going to let you come, are they?"

"I'll ask."

"I talked to Detective Ferland today. He said they found Mom's blood in your trunk. He said you killed her for insurance money."

"The blood was planted."

"Who planted it?"

"The killer. He wanted to frame me for Tammy's murder."

"Why would anyone want to frame you, Dad?"

"I was framed, Jimmy. I don't know who or why, but I'll figure it out."

"Mom's life was insured for eight hundred thousand dollars. You killed her, didn't you?"

Robert felt his chest tighten.

My son thinks I murdered his mother, the most important person in his life. What could be worse than that?

"I didn't kill Tammy. I swear."

"Were you cheating on her?"

"No. I loved Tammy more than anything. You know that, Jimmy."

"Goodbye, Dad." Jim hung up.

Robert called Laporte and told him that he wanted to go to Tamara's funeral. The lawyer said that he would file a request for temporary release and that there was a fair chance it would be granted.

2

Emma told the officer at the front desk of Dallas Police Headquarters that she wanted to talk to Detective Korbin, and five minutes later Korbin came to the lobby.

"How are you doing, Emma?" he said.

"I'm fine."

"What can I do for you?"

"I think Paul's innocent. I think he was framed."

"I don't understand."

"I'll testify that the man I saw kidnap Alison Bowles wasn't Paul."

Korbin frowned. "Why do you think Paul's innocent?"

"His mistress moved out of her house shortly after his arrest and she wiped off all her fingerprints before she left. She doesn't want to be found because she helped frame Paul: she obtained the semen you found on Alison Bowles."

"Who told you that Paul's mistress moved out of her house and wiped off all her fingerprints?"

"Paul's private investigator. You need to find Paul's mistress and interrogate her. She knows who murdered Alison Bowles."

"Emma, this sounds absurd."

"You also need to find the woman who tricked me into following Paul. I'll give you her phone number."

"Someone tricked you into following Paul?"

"Yes. But the man I followed, the man I saw kidnap Alison Bowles wasn't my husband. He pretended to be Paul. They wanted me to think Paul kidnapped Alison."

"Emma, Paul is a cold-blooded murderer. He wasn't framed. He raped and killed Alison Bowles, and we have enough evidence to prove that."

"The evidence was planted. Please find Paul's mistress. She knows who the real killer is."

"How do you know Paul's PI is telling you the truth?"

Emma pulled out a piece of paper with Susan's number on it and held it out to Korbin. "Could you find out who this number is registered to?"

Korbin took the piece of paper. "Whose number is it?"

"It belongs to the woman who tricked me into following Paul. Paul's PI told me it was a disposable phone. This woman calls herself Susan Miller, but I don't think it's her real name. I thought she was my friend. She was with me when I tailed Paul that day. It was actually her idea to tail him."

"They're lying to you, Emma. No one framed your husband."

Korbin probably didn't care that she had turned into a defense witness: the jury wouldn't believe her because she was Paul's wife.

"How would you feel if years from now it turned out that Paul was innocent?" Emma said. "You'd never forgive yourself for doing nothing to catch the real killer."

"Paul is the real killer. Have a nice day, Emma," Korbin said, and walked away.

Chapter 39

1

According to online public records databases, there was only one Brian Harbour in the Dallas area who was in his late thirties. Hugh Ruskin, the private investigator hired by John Laporte to look into Harbour, called the Human Resources Department of the Bank of Texas and asked for Harbour's address and phone number. They said they couldn't give him that information.

Ruskin's contact at the DMV searched the DMV database and found only one Brian Harbour in the Dallas area who was in his late thirties. She sent Ruskin the guy's address and photo.

Ruskin arrived at Harbour's apartment in Carrollton at seven-thirty p.m. The place wasn't upscale but not a dump, either. No one answered the door, and Ruskin returned to his car. He waited half an hour, then went back to Harbour's apartment and rang the bell. Again there was no answer.

The lights were on in Harbour's living room when Ruskin came back to his apartment building at half past eight. Harbour opened the door without asking who it was. He was fit, with deep-set eyes, dark hair combed straight back, and a goatee.

"Are you Brian Harbour?" Ruskin asked.

"Yes."

"Did you work at the North Dallas branch of the Bank of Texas until a year ago?"

Harbour nodded. "Yes. Who are you?"

"My name's Hugh Ruskin. I'm a private investigator."

"How can I help you?"

"Do you remember where you were on the morning of June eighth?"

"What day of the week was it?"

"Monday."

"I was at work."

"What do you do for a living, if you don't mind my asking?"

"I sell furniture. Are you looking for a new couch?"

"As a matter of fact, I am. What's your store's address?"

"It's in Irving, at MacArthur Boulevard and Airport Freeway. Buena Vista Furniture. Ask for me, okay?"

"Sure."

The furniture store was probably paying Harbour half of what of he had made at the Bank of Texas. Harbour couldn't be happy with his current situation.

Harbour asked, "What are you investigating?"

"My case involves Robert Lochner. Do you remember him?"

"Are you talking about my former boss at the bank?"

Ruskin nodded. "Yes."

"Yeah, I remember him. What did he do?"

"That's what I'm trying to figure out."

"Did he embezzle from the bank?"

"I don't know."

"Was he fired?"

"Yes."

"Poor guy," Harbour said without any sincerity. "I'm surprised he lasted that long in that job. He's not a smart guy, you know." He smiled. "Have you ever served on a jury?"

"No."

"Robert has. You know what they say about people who serve on juries?"

"What?"

"They were too dumb to get out of jury duty." Harbour grinned.

"I suppose you don't know what kind of trouble Robert's in."

"What is it?"

"He's been accused of killing of his wife."

"Wow." Harbor looked surprised. "He killed his wife? Jesus. Why?"

"I don't know."

"Is he in jail?"

"Yes. He says he didn't do it. Do you think he's capable of murder?"

Harbour shrugged. "Was she cheating on him?"

"I don't know."

"Do they have proof that he killed her?"

"There's some evidence against him, but the question is, will it be enough to convict him?"

"Well, if he did it, I hope he goes to prison."

"Are you still mad at Robert?"

"I've never been mad at him."

"Even when he fired you?"

"I wasn't mad at Robert when he fired me. Being angry is bad for your health. He fired me because he saw me as a competitor."

"You're probably glad that he's going to prison."

"Would you be glad if you were in my shoes?" Harbour smiled.

Harbour obviously hated the idea of serving on a jury, but he would probably pay money to be a juror at Robert Lochner's trial.

"Did you ever meet Robert's wife?"

"No. Who do you work for?"

"The bank. Do you know if Robert cheated on his wife?"

"No. Was his wife rich?"

"No."

"How long has he been in jail?"

"Four days."

"Did his wife have life insurance? Maybe he killed her for insurance money."

"She did have life insurance. Thank you for your time, Brian. Can I have your phone number in case I need to get in touch with you?"

"Okay." Harbour told Ruskin his phone number, and the private investigator headed back to his car.

2

On Tuesday, Ruskin and his partner Albert Cruz went to the furniture store where Brian Harbour worked. Buena Vista Furniture was fairly large and sat next to a Mexican restaurant. A sign in the window announced discounts of up to fifty percent. Ruskin stayed in the car, and Cruz went into the store. A sales clerk named Steve asked the private investigator if he could help him, and Cruz said that he wanted to talk to the manager. He spotted Harbour with a customer near a leather sofa thirty feet away. Steve left and came back a minute later with the manager, who introduced himself as Henry.

"I'm Albert Cruz," Cruz told Henry. "I'm a private investigator. I have a question about one of your employees, Brian Harbour."

"What do you want to know?"

"Was he at work on June eighth?"

"Why do you want to know that?"

"I'm just trying to establish Mr. Harbour's whereabouts on June eighth. It has nothing to do with your store."

Henry stared at Cruz for a long moment and then said, "Follow me."

They went to the manager's office in the back of the store, where Henry sat at his desk and started clicking his computer mouse.

"On June eighth Brian called in sick," Henry finally said. "What did he do?"

Had Harbour lied to Ruskin, or had he forgotten that he had called in sick on June 8?

"I believe he might be a witness in a case I'm investigating. Thank you for your help, Henry."

When he and Cruz got to the office, Ruskin called Laporte and gave him an update on Brian Harbour.

"He's making much less than he did at the bank," Ruskin said. "I'm sure he still hates Lochner."

On Wednesday, Laporte visited Robert in jail and told him what his private investigators had found out about Harbour.

"So he wasn't at work that day?" Robert said.

Laporte nodded.

"And he lied to your PI. I think he did it. We need to tell Ferland about him."

"I'll talk to Ferland today."

"What about my request for temporary release? Will they let me go to Tammy's funeral?"

"No. I'm sorry, Robert."

Although Robert had expected his request for temporary release to be denied, he felt a pang of disappointment.

"Did you ask the bank about the threats from those whose loan applications we rejected?" he asked.

"Yes. They haven't responded yet."

3

Ferland came out of the Richardson Police Department building as Laporte approached it.

"Good afternoon, Detective," the lawyer said to Ferland. "Do you have a few moments?"

"Yes." Ferland stopped.

Laporte gave the detective Brian Harbour's photograph and a sheet of paper with his name, address, and phone number, and said, "This is Brian Harbour. He used to work at Mr. Lochner's branch. My client fired him for sexual harassment a year ago. We believe he framed Mr. Lochner for his wife's murder to get even with him."

Ferland put the photograph and the sheet of paper in his pocket. "Thanks for the information. Have a nice day," he said, and started walking.

"He called in sick on the day of Tamara Lochner's murder," Laporte said, following the detective. "You need to look into him."

"Have a nice day."

Chapter 40

1

Emma called Detective Korbin on Wednesday and asked if he had found out who Susan's number was registered to.

"It's a disposable phone, but it doesn't mean this Susan woman framed your husband," Korbin said.

"You need to find her. She knows who killed Alison Bowles."

When she came home from work, Emma sent Susan a message saying: "Hi, Susie. Where in California are you? Ollie and I may go there soon. Let's hang out. I miss you."

This probably wouldn't work, but she had to try.

As she scrolled through the TV guide, Emma saw that Sicario was on one of the channels. It was one of Paul's favorite movies, in part because Benicio Del Toro's character, Alejandro, was a former prosecutor.

Emma tuned the TV to a cooking competition show and put the remote on the coffee table.

Suddenly an idea struck her. In Sicario, Alejandro took on a drug cartel when he was a prosecutor, and the cartel punished him by murdering his wife and daughter. Maybe the people who had framed Paul were after him because of something he had done when he worked in the district attorney's office? Paul had put a lot of people behind bars, and Emma was willing to bet that many of them would have loved to get even with him.

It was probably someone who had been released from prison last fall or December.

It must be someone convicted of a violent crime.

Was Alison Bowles's kidnapper the person put in jail by Paul, or was he just a helper?

Why had Susan and Julie, or whatever their real names were, helped set Paul up? Were they relatives of the guy Paul had put in jail? Was one of them the man's girlfriend?

2

Emma put the phone to her ear as Paul sat down in front of her. He picked up the receiver on his side of the glass and said, "Hi, honey. I'm so glad to see you."

"I miss you, honey," Emma said.

"I miss you, too."

"Did Jonah find any evidence that you were framed by Sawyers?"

"No."

"Maybe you were framed by someone you put in prison when you were a prosecutor? Have you considered this possibility?"

"No." Paul furrowed his brow. "I think you may be right."

"It's probably someone who got out of prison last fall or December, someone convicted of a violent crime."

Paul nodded.

"If it was the guy you put in prison who kidnapped Alison, then we can narrow the search to white men about your height."

Paul smiled faintly. "I'm so lucky to have you in my life."

"Susan and Julie may be this guy's relatives."

When Emma left the county jail, she called Jonah Wallach and told him that Paul might have been framed by someone he had put in prison.

"It might be someone who thought that he was wrongfully convicted or that his sentence was too harsh," Wallach said.

Susan texted Emma back later that evening saying: "Sorry for the late reply. I'm very busy. I'm in Fresno right now. Let's hang out when I come back to Dallas. How are you doing? I hope everything's fine."

Emma replied: "I'm fine. Come back soon."

The next day Wallach visited Paul, and he asked his lawyer to get a list of people he had put in jail for violent crimes who had been released from June through December of last year.

Chapter 41

1

Robert called Jim on Friday morning, but his son didn't answer. Five hours later he sat across from Jim in the jail visitation room.

"Thanks for coming, Jimmy." Robert's throat tightened.

"They didn't let you go to the funeral?"

"No. Where did you bury Tammy?"

"The Forest Lawn Cemetery."

"I didn't kill Tammy, Jimmy. I was framed. I didn't kill her."

Jim looked at him for a long time and then said, "When we talked last Saturday, you didn't tell me they found Mom's blood in your trunk. Why?"

Robert swallowed. "Because I didn't want you to think I might have killed Tammy."

"I talked to Seth Sulkin at the funeral. He's sure you didn't kill Mom. He said you looked terrified when you came to his house on the day of the kidnapping. He's sure you weren't faking it."

"I didn't kill her, Jimmy. I'm innocent."

"So you're saying they killed Mom to frame you?"

"Yes."

"And you still have no idea who might have done it?"

Robert couldn't tell if his son believed he was innocent.

"I think it might be a man named Brian Harbour. He was the assistant manager at my branch. I fired him for sexual harassment last year. I think he framed me to get back at me for firing him. My lawyer's private detective found out that Harbour called in sick on the day of Tammy's murder."

"Did you tell the police about him?"

"Yes."

"Are they going to investigate him?"

"I don't know. But I wouldn't bet on it."

"Do you think you can prove that you were framed?"

"I don't know. I guess we'll have to find the real killers."

"I hope you find them, Dad."

Robert's heart sank a little when his son said "you" and not "we." Did Jim not want to help him prove his innocence?

"We'll find them, and they'll pay for what they did to Tammy," Robert said.

"Is there anything I can do to help?"

"Right now, all I need you to do is believe me."

"I believe you, Dad."

Robert smiled. "Thank you, Jimmy."

"I'm leaving Dallas in two days. I'll come back in August."

"Okay."

"Call me at least once a week."

"Okay."

Robert called Laporte later that day, and the lawyer told him that the Bank of Texas hadn't received any threats from people whose loan applications were rejected.

Chapter 42

1

As a prosecutor, Paul had handled on average about thirty-five violent crime cases a year, and he figured that the list he had asked Wallach to obtain would contain about twenty names. He decided that they would first focus on Caucasian men who went to trial (he expected there would be only a couple of people fitting these criteria).

On Sunday, Paul had a visitor. He was in his thirties, lean, with long brown hair and a short beard and mustache, wearing a blue shirt and horn-rimmed glasses. Paul didn't recognize him. He wondered if the guy was a journalist or Alison Bowles's relative.

"Good morning, Paul," the visitor said.

"Good morning."

"My name's John Colter. I'm a volunteer for the Innocence Initiative of Texas."

"What can I do for you, John?"

"You represented one of our clients a year ago. His name's Travis Mosby."

Paul nodded. "I remember him."

Mosby had spent nine years in prison for a murder he hadn't committed before they got him released.

"I read about you in the news, and I wondered if you really did it."

"I didn't kill that woman. I was set up."

"You don't look like a killer, Paul. I think you're a kind man. You represented Travis Mosby for free, and you did a great job."

"It was a team effort."

"I don't think it would have succeeded without you."

"Thank you."

"You said you were set up. Do you know who did it?"

Paul shook his head. "No."

"Do you think you can prove you were set up?"

"I don't know."

"Is the prosecution's case strong?"

"Yes."

"I can't even imagine what it's like to be in prison for a crime you didn't commit. I'd probably go insane."

"To be honest, I'm pretty close to going insane." Paul managed a weak smile.

"Is there anything the Innocence Initiative can do to help you?"

"You could help me find the people who framed me."

"Do you have any idea who might have set you up?"

"It could be a former client of mine or someone I put in jail."

"Someone you put in jail?"

"I used to be a prosecutor."

"Did you see Cape Fear?"

"Yes."

"The guy played by De Niro wanted to punish his former lawyer because he thought he did a bad job defending him. I don't remember who played the lawyer."

"Nick Nolte played the lawyer."

"It's a good movie."

"A classic."

"How long were you a prosecutor?"

"Eleven years."

"You must have put a lot of people in jail."

"Hundreds."

"Do you want me to ask the Innocence Initiative to help you?"

"I don't want them to spend their resources on me. I have a good lawyer."

"Okay. I'll follow your case. Your trial starts in October?"

"Yes."

"I wish you luck."

"Thank you."

Paul thought of telling John that he was considering a plea deal (he'd been considering it for a month, actually) and decided not to: he believed it would upset the guy.

Chapter 43

1

Dennis Almanza spent a minute scrolling through his Facebook timeline, checking out the pictures posted by his friends in the last two days (his favorite was a photo of a Chihuahua wearing a sombrero), then clicked on the post box and typed: "Today I mailed my DNA sample to My Family Tree. Can't wait for the results!"

He reread his post and clicked Share.

My Family Tree was a genealogy company that helped people discover their ancestry by means of DNA testing. Their website said that he would receive his results online in four weeks. Dennis's grandparents had immigrated to the United States from Spain, so he might turn out to be a descendant of a Spanish king. That would be nice, wouldn't it?

Dennis had read on the Internet that one in two hundred men, about sixteen million individuals alive today, were direct descendants of Genghis Khan. Impressive, right? According to some estimates, Genghis Khan had impregnated over a thousand different women.

Three weeks ago, while they were watching Sherlock in his studio apartment in Central Los Angeles, Lisa, his girlfriend, had told him that actor Benedict Cumberbatch (who played Sherlock Holmes in Sherlock) was related to Richard III. She found this fact amazing and Dennis didn't. Cumberbatch was a global movie star and probably didn't care that he was a descendant of Richard III.

Lisa had sent her DNA sample to My Family Tree last February and learned that none of her ancestors was royalty or famous.

"You should send them your DNA sample," she had said to Dennis. "Maybe you have royal blood."

Eight days ago, Lisa had told Dennis that Brad Pitt and Angelina Jolie, her favorite famous former couple, had royal ancestry, like Cumberbatch: Pitt was related to King Henry II of England and Jolie to King Philip II of France. Dennis had said that he had decided to send his DNA sample to My Family Tree, then had gone to the company's website and ordered a DNA kit. The kit had arrived today.

Collecting a DNA sample was easy: he needed to put about a quarter of a teaspoon of his saliva in a plastic tube. He had placed the sample in a prepaid mailing box that came with the kit and then dropped the package off at the post office.

Lisa came to Dennis's apartment at eight that night, and he told her that he had received the DNA kit and mailed his DNA sample.

"What if it turns out you have royal blood?" Lisa said. "Are you going to get snobby?"

"Of course." Dennis grinned. "I'll demand that commoners bow to me."

"You could be related to Picasso. It would be so cool if you were his relative, wouldn't it?"

"Yeah."

They made love and then watched TV until they fell asleep.

Chapter 44

1

On Monday, June 30, Jonah Wallach received a list of people Paul Marston had put in jail for violent crimes who had been released from June through December of last year. There was only one Caucasian man on the list who went to trial—Sean Kowalik.

Kowalik had been sentenced to eleven years for aggravated assault and served ten before being paroled in June of last year. Paul had been the lead prosecutor at his trial. Kowalik was forty-two years old and six feet tall, one inch shorter than Paul Marston. At the time of his arrest eleven years ago he had weighed one hundred and sixty-nine pounds, six pounds less than Marston. How much did Kowalik weigh now? Was he fat?

Hopper got Kowalik's address from his friend at the Texas Department of Criminal Justice. Kowalik lived in an apartment complex in the Dallas suburb of Garland. He had a six-year-old black Dodge Charger registered to him.

Hopper checked Julie's and Susan's phones' geolocation records and found that they had never connected to any cell towers near Kowalik's place. He spent two hours searching public records for Kowalik's relatives and discovered that he had a sister. Her name was Linda Brown and she was thirty-five years old. Kowalik had been married once, to a woman named Patricia Shields. The marriage had lasted two years and ended in divorce three years before he went to prison. Kowalik had no children. It was unlikely that his ex-wife would have helped him frame Paul Marston, but Hopper got her picture anyway.

When Kowalik was released, a GPS ankle monitor had been placed on him, but it had been removed on April 6 of this year, thirteen days before Alison Bowles was murdered.

Hopper figured that if Kowalik had framed Marston, Susan, Julie, or Edward Zheng might visit him, so he decided to put his apartment under video surveillance for a few days. Early the next morning, he went to Kowalik's place, found his Dodge Charger in the parking lot, and put a GPS tracker on it. An hour later, Hopper photographed Kowalik as he walked to his car.

The guy was about Paul Marston's build and could be mistaken for him.

When Kowalik drove away, Hopper drilled a small hole at eye level in the wall beside the apartment door across from Kowalik's and installed a thermometer-shaped spy camera. The camera had a motion detector, a memory card that could hold up to ten hours of video, and a battery life of twenty days in standby mode. He would retrieve the memory card and replace it with a blank one in two days.

2

"There's only one white guy who went to trial," Wallach said as Paul scanned the list. "Sean Kowalik."

He pulled out Kowalik's photograph and put it on the table.

"Do you remember him?" Wallach asked.

Paul picked up the photo. "Vaguely."

"He went to prison eleven years ago and was released in June of last year. He's forty-two and about your height."

"When did you take this picture?"

"Yesterday."

"Do you have his address?"

"Yes."

"Is he married?"

"No."

"Does he have any sisters or daughters?"

"He has a sister. Linda Brown. Thirty-five years old."

"Do you have her picture?"

"Not yet."

Paul put Kowalik's photograph down and looked at the list. "Aggravated assault."

"He spent ten years in prison. I bet he hates your guts." Wallach took out Kowalik's ex-wife's picture and placed it on the table. "This is his ex-wife. Do you recognize her?"

"No. Has his ankle monitor been removed?"

"Yes. Last April, two weeks before Alison Bowles's murder."

"Can you put his place under surveillance? Julie might visit him."

"We already did."

"We need to get his phone records and check his most frequently called numbers."

Wallach nodded. The person who had framed Paul must have called and texted Julie and Susan regularly.

"What else do you think we could do?" Paul asked.

"Hopper and I are working on it. We need to be careful so Kowalik won't find out we're looking into him."

"Right."

3

At six o'clock Wallach texted Kowalik's picture to Emma, then called her and asked if she had ever seen him.

"No," Emma replied. "Who is he?"

"One of the people Paul put in jail. His name's Sean Kowalik. He got out in June of last year. He's about Paul's height and build. He might be the man you saw kidnap Alison Bowles."

"What was he in prison for?"

"Aggravated assault. He served ten years."

"Is he married? Does he have any sisters or daughters or female cousins?"

"He's not married. He has a sister and she's about Susan's age. I'll send you her picture as soon as I have it."

"Where does he live?"

"Garland. We put his place under surveillance. Don't look for his address, Emma. I don't want him to see you."

"Okay."

Wallach texted Kowalik's ex-wife's picture to Emma and said, "I just sent you his ex-wife's photo. Does she look like Susan?"

"No."

Chapter 45

1

Kowalik's sister lived in Albuquerque, New Mexico. It took Hopper two days to verify that the thirty-five-year-old Linda Brown in Albuquerque was the one he was looking for. His contact at the New Mexico Motor Vehicle Division sent him Kowalik's sister's photo, which was fourteen years old. Trying to find a more recent picture of Kowalik's sister, Hopper searched for her on Facebook, but none of the Linda Browns on the website looked like her.

"Do you want me to go to Albuquerque and take her picture?" Hopper asked Wallach.

"Let me show this photo to Emma first," the lawyer said.

After texting Linda Brown's picture to Emma, Wallach called her and asked if the woman looked like Susan.

"No," Emma replied. "It's not Susan. Is she Sean Kowalik's sister?"

"Yes. Are you sure it's not Susan? This photo is fourteen years old."

"Do you have her address? Can you go to her place and take her picture?"

"Yes. Does Susan still answer your texts?"

"Yes. Two weeks ago I told her that Ollie and I might go to California soon and suggested that we meet. She said we'd meet when she came back to Dallas."

"These bastards are cautious. She probably intends to never see you again."

"Was Kowalik released on parole?"

"Yes."

"People released on parole have to wear an ankle monitor, don't they?"

"Kowalik's ankle monitor was removed on April sixth because his sentence ended."

Alison Bowles had been murdered on April 19. It was too risky to kidnap and kill someone while wearing an ankle monitor, so Kowalik had waited until it had been removed.

2

These bastards are cautious.

They weren't always cautious, though. Alison's kidnapper had put her in the trunk, which was risky.

They must have really wanted me to see Paul abduct a woman.

Suddenly Emma remembered something Connie Bowles had said. Connie had wondered why Alison hadn't come to her house at one o'clock and hadn't answered her calls and texts before the abduction.

Maybe Alison had been kidnapped before one o'clock? Maybe the woman who had climbed into the trunk was an accomplice of the people who had framed Paul?

Staging the kidnapping would have been a safe thing to do.

Emma called Wallach and told him her theory. The lawyer said that she might be right.

3

Hopper went to Kowalik's apartment that afternoon, retrieved the memory card from his hidden camera, and replaced it with a blank one. He watched the surveillance footage at the office and saw that Kowalik had had no female visitors. None of the three men who had come to Kowalik's place looked like Edward Zheng. The guy appeared to live alone.

On Friday, Hopper flew to Albuquerque and photographed Linda Brown when she arrived home at six p.m. He emailed her pictures to Wallach, who then texted them to Emma. When Wallach called her, Emma said that Kowalik's sister didn't look like Susan.

Hopper drove to the airport and caught a plane back to Dallas. While the private investigator was in Albuquerque, Luke Mathis had sent him Kowalik's cellphone records for the last seven months; Hopper examined them when he got home. He made a list of Kowalik's ten most frequently called and texted numbers and asked his friend Mark Bessant, who worked in the Dallas PD's Criminal Investigations Division, to find out who

they belonged to. Bessant said he would give Hopper the
information next Monday.

Chapter 46

1

Early Saturday morning, Hopper retrieved the memory card from his hidden camera and viewed the surveillance footage at home. (It was the Fourth of July, but he didn't mind working on holidays.) A woman in her thirties with long dark hair had spent two hours at Kowalik's apartment on Thursday night. On Friday night, Kowalik had had another female visitor, who had stayed at his place for four hours. She was also in her thirties and had short dark hair.

Hopper emailed Wallach pictures of the women and then texted them to Emma (he was impatient to find out if either of the women was Susan).

2

Her phone rang while Emma was washing dishes in the kitchen. An unknown number.

"Good morning," a man said. "Is this Emma Marston?"

"Yes."

"I'm sorry to bother you on a holiday. My name's Victor Hopper. I'm a private investigator. I'm helping Jonah Wallach with your husband's case."

"Jonah told me about you. Thank you for everything you've done for Paul."

"You don't have to thank me, Emma. I just texted you two pictures. These women visited Sean Kowalik at his apartment. Does either of them look like Susan?"

Emma opened Hopper's message and tapped the first photo. The image appeared to be a screenshot from a video. The woman in the picture stood in the doorway of an apartment or house (Emma figured it was Kowalik's place). The camera was positioned outside the door. The woman was young, with long dark hair. She didn't look like Susan.

The second image was also a screenshot and depicted a young woman standing in the same doorway as the woman in the previous picture. Her hair was dark and short. She wasn't Susan, either.

"Neither of them looks like Susan." Emma sighed. "Is this Kowalik's place?"

"Yes."

"I think Kowalik framed Paul."

"Why do you think so?"

"Alison Bowles was murdered shortly after his ankle monitor was removed."

"If he framed Paul, I hope we can prove it."

"I wish we could grab him and force him to confess."

"Unfortunately, this confession wouldn't be admissible in court. I think our best bet is to try to get Susan or Julie to rat him out."

3

At two o'clock, Emma and Ollie arrived at her parents' house. The place was full of delicious aromas, and Emma's mouth watered as soon as she entered.

Rosie locked the front door and said to Emma, "Happy Independence Day, honey."

Emma's mother was wearing her favorite Michael Kors floral jumpsuit.

"Happy Independence Day, Mom," Emma replied.

Rosie kissed her on the cheek and then hugged Ollie. "Are you hungry, sweetie?" she asked the boy.

"No. Did you make a cake?"

"Yes. I made a German chocolate cake."

"Cool!" Ollie smiled.

They went into the living room, where Emma's father was watching TV.

"Hello." Phil smiled at Emma and Ollie.

"Hi, Dad."

"Hi, Grandpa." Ollie hugged Phil and then sat down on the sofa.

"Do you need any help in the kitchen?" Emma asked Rosie.

"Yes."

When they walked into the kitchen, Rosie said in a low voice, "How is Paul doing?"

Emma had been able to convince her parents that Paul had been framed, and his status as their beloved son-in-law had been restored.

"He's okay."

"You still don't know who set him up?"

"No."

Rosie sighed, put a hand on Emma's shoulder, and squeezed it.

"So what do you need me to do?" Emma asked.

Rosie pointed at a stack of dinner plates on the counter and said, "Put them on the table in the dining room."

"Okay."

Why hadn't Kowalik punished the judge who presided over his trial? Emma wondered as she arranged the plates. It was the judge who had given him a long sentence.

Why hadn't he punished the jurors? It was them who had convicted him.

Maybe he's already taken his revenge on the judge? And maybe he's already started getting even with the jurors.

They should find out if the judge was alive and if he was a suspect in a crime. If he was fine, they would warn him about Kowalik.

Maybe the judge will help Paul prove his innocence.

When she finished arranging the plates, Emma went outside and called Hopper.

"Do you have a minute?" she asked him.

"Yes."

"I think Kowalik might have killed the judge who presided over his trial, or set him up for murder. You need to find him. If he's alive, you should warn him about Kowalik."

"Let me find his name. I think I have it."

"Kowalik may take revenge on the jurors, too. Can you check on them?"

"We'll try."

Half a minute later Hopper said that the name of the judge who presided over Kowalik's trial was Maurice Woodworth.

"We'll check on the second-chair prosecutor, too," Hopper said.

"Do you have his name?"

"No."

After she hung up, Emma googled Judge Maurice Woodworth and found that he was alive and still worked as a judge in Dallas County. She sent Hopper a message saying: "Maurice Woodworth is alive. Please warn him. Ask him to help Paul."

Chapter 47

1

Hopper called Wallach at seven o'clock and told him about Emma's concern that Kowalik might take revenge on the judge and jurors. The lawyer said that he would talk to Maurice Woodworth tomorrow. Hooper texted him the judge's address and phone number.

Wallach went to Woodworth's house the next morning without calling in advance. Luckily, the judge was home and agreed to speak with him.

Maurice Woodworth was in his late fifties, stocky, bald, with a fringe of gray hair. He had a reputation as a tough, no-nonsense judge. Wallach had tried two cases before Woodworth, most recently a year ago.

"Do you remember Sean Kowalik?" Wallach asked the judge. "You presided over his trial eleven years ago."

Woodworth shook his head. "No. I don't remember him."

"He was convicted of aggravated assault and sentenced to eleven years. He got out last year. I believe he might try to kill or harm you out of revenge."

"Why do you think so?"

"I don't want to reveal my sources. Kowalik might try to frame you for murder. Have you been accused of any serious crimes recently?"

"No."

Wallach pulled out Sean Kowalik's and Linda Brown's pictures and gave them to Woodworth. "Do you recognize them?"

"No. Who are they?"

"Sean Kowalik and his sister. Be careful if you see them."

"Did you tell the police about this?"

"No. I can't prove that Kowalik is after you."

"How is Kowalik's sister involved in this?"

"I believe Kowalik might get her to help him."

"Can I keep the pictures?"

"Yes. Please take this seriously, Judge. Better safe than sorry."

Woodworth nodded. "Right." He put the photos on the coffee table. "Did you represent Kowalik at the trial?"

"No."

"You tried a case before me last year, didn't you?"

"Yes."

"You did a fine job, as I remember."

"Thank you, Judge."

"Is Kowalik on parole?"

"His parole ended last April. If you decide to get the police involved, please make sure he doesn't find out he's being investigated."

"Okay. Do you have anything else to tell me?"

"No."

"Thank you for the warning, Jonah."

They got up.

"If you see Kowalik, please let me know," Wallach said.

"Okay."

"Do you carry a gun?"

"No. I guess I should start carrying one."

The second-chair prosecutor in Kowalik's case was Stacy Anders. On Tuesday, the Dallas County District Attorney's Office told Wallach that she had quit five years ago. Wallach searched the website of the State Bar of Texas for Stacy Anders and found one lawyer by that name, who worked for a law firm in Fort Worth. He called her and she told him that she used to work in the Dallas County DA's Office and that she knew Paul Marston. Wallach warned Anders about Kowalik and then asked if she had been accused of any serious crimes recently.

"No," she replied.

"Please watch your back, Stacy. I'll send you pictures of Kowalik and his sister."

After Anders gave him her email address, Wallach said, "I've already warned Paul and the judge."

Wallach didn't tell Anders that he was Paul's lawyer and that Paul might have been framed by Kowalik.

He wrote a request for the names of the jurors in Kowalik's trial and filed it at the Dallas County Clerk of the Court's Office before heading to the county jail to see Paul.

2

"Any good news?" Paul asked.

He expected Wallach to say that he had no good news for him. He believed it was the right attitude: if you expect the worst, you won't be disappointed. Paul was usually a glass-half-full kind of guy, but only a delusional idiot could be an optimist in his situation.

Paul's pessimism didn't prevent him from wanting to do everything he could to prove that he had been set up. He knew he needed to follow the example of that frog who fell into a pail of milk and kept swimming until the milk turned into butter; however, he didn't think his story would have a happy ending.

When he talked to Emma, Paul put on an optimistic façade so as not to dishearten her; she still didn't know he was considering a plea bargain.

"No." Wallach pulled out two photographs and handed them to Paul. "These women visited Kowalik last week. Do you recognize either of them?"

"No. Did you check Kowalik's phone records?"

"Yes. We checked his ten most frequently called and texted numbers. Four of them belong to women: his mother, his sister, and these two gals. As for men, none of them looks like Edward Zheng."

"Can you check everyone Kowalik called or texted in March and April?"

"Okay." Wallach put the photographs back in his pocket. "Emma believes that Kowalik might get revenge on the judge who presided over his trial and the jurors."

Paul nodded. "Yeah. Why didn't I think of that? Did you check on them?"

"The judge is fine, and he's not a suspect in any crime. We haven't checked on the jurors yet."

If they try to frame Judge Woodworth, we may get an opportunity to track down Susan and Julie, Paul thought. We might be able to catch them in the act.

"If they try to frame the judge, they might use the same methods they used with me," Paul said. "You need to ask the judge if he made any new friends in the last six months."

"Okay."

"Tell him what happened to me. Tell him about Susan and Julie."

"Okay."

"Did you check on my second chair?"

"She's fine."

"Stacy Anders was my second chair in the Kowalik case, wasn't she?"

"Yes." Wallach took out another photograph and gave it to Paul. "This is Kowalik's sister. Do you recognize her?"

"No."

3

Wallach called Woodworth at home at seven that evening. The judge knew that Paul Marston used to be an assistant district attorney, and he had heard of his case. Wallach explained how Paul had been framed and then told Woodworth that Kowalik might set him up using the same methods he had used with Paul.

"So Marston claims he's innocent?" Woodworth asked.

"Yes. And I believe him."

"He took a plea deal, didn't he?"

"Yes. It was an Alford plea. I'm not trying to convince you that Paul's innocent, Judge. I just want you to be forewarned."

Chapter 48

1

On Wednesday, July 8, Detective Ferland told Robert that he had reviewed the footage from the bank parking lot security cameras and seen no one get into Robert's car or open its trunk.

"That means Tamara's blood was planted while my car was in my driveway," Robert said.

"No one planted Tamara's blood, Robert."

"Are you looking into Brian Harbour?"

"No. There's no evidence that he killed your wife."

"He hates me. He had a motive to set me up."

"Is Brian Harbour the only person you've ever fired?"

"No."

"Should we look into all the other people you've fired?"

Two days later, Robert had a visitor. On the way to the visitation room, he wondered if it was Seth Sulkin. It couldn't be his son, because Jim was going to come to Dallas in August.

Brian Harbour was waiting for him on the other side of the partition. Robert stopped in his tracks for a moment when he saw him.

Did he come to gloat? Robert wondered.

Conversations between inmates and visitors might be recorded here. He needed to get Harbour to incriminate himself.

Robert sat down and picked up the phone.

"Hello, Robert," Harbour said.

"Hello, Brian."

"Long time no see."

"Yeah. How are you doing?"

"I'm sorry about your wife."

"Thank you."

"They say you killed her."

"I didn't kill her."

"A private detective came to me about three weeks ago. He told me about your situation. He said they had evidence against you."

"It was planted."

"He asked me where I was on the morning of June eighth. When he left, I looked you up on the Internet and found out that your wife was murdered on June eighth. Why did he ask me where I was on the day of your wife's murder?"

"I don't know."

"I think you do. He works for you, doesn't he?"

"Why are you here, Brian?"

"Did you tell the police I killed your wife?"

"Did you kill her?"

"Of course not. Why would I kill her?"

"To set me up for her murder."

"What?" Harbour raised his eyebrows. "You think I killed your wife to set you up for her murder?"

"It's possible."

"I can't say I don't enjoy your misfortune, but I had nothing to do with it."

"You hate me, don't you, Brian?"

"You really think someone killed your wife to set you up for her murder?"

"Someone killed her and then planted her blood in my trunk."

"Wow. If you didn't do it, then you really were set up."

Was Harbour telling the truth?

He sounded sincere, but Robert had trouble trusting him. Maybe Harbour was just a good liar.

"I *was* set up," Robert said.

"It wasn't me, okay? I didn't kill your wife. Don't waste your time on me, Robert."

"You told the PI you were at work on the morning of June eighth. You lied. You called in sick that day."

Harbour smiled. "So that private detective does work for you?"

"Yes."

"I forgot I called in sick. My memory isn't perfect, okay?"

"Who do you think framed me?"

"It must be someone whose life you ruined."

"I ruined your life."

"You didn't ruin my life. I'm doing okay and I'm as healthy as a horse."

And you're not in jail, Robert thought.

"In that case, I've never ruined anyone's life," Robert said.

"Did you ever run over and kill or maim anyone?"

Robert shook his head. "No."

"Did your wife ever run over and kill or maim anyone?"

"No."

"You never accidentally killed or crippled anyone?"

"No."

"What did your wife do for a living?"

"She was a high school teacher."

"Did she cheat on you?"

"No. I think it might be someone whose loan application we rejected."

Harbour nodded. "That's possible. The bad news is that there are too many potential suspects."

"Yeah."

"When is the trial?"

"In December."

"What does your lawyer say about your chances?"

"They aren't great. Does that make you happy?"

"No. I'm very sorry this happened to you, Robert. I think you're innocent."

Chapter 49

1

Victor Hopper had said that their best bet was to try to get Susan or Julie to rat out Alison Bowles's killer. They could ask the Wolf Brigade gang to help them with that. Gangsters were good at intimidating people. Emma was willing to talk to Rod Sawyers herself and even assist his men in strong-arming Susan and Julie if she had to.

On Monday, July 13, Emma asked Hopper if any other women had visited Kowalik's apartment.

"No," Hopper said.

"Have you warned the jurors?"

"We got their names last Friday. So far we've warned four of them."

On Wednesday, Emma visited Paul, and he told her that the prosecutors had offered him a plea bargain and that he was thinking of taking it.

Emma's heart sank.

"Don't take it," she said. "We're going to find whoever framed you. I think it's Sean Kowalik."

"Even if we find the people who framed me, how are we going to get them to confess? Alison Bowles's killer will never confess to her murder. Susan and Julie won't cooperate with the police because we have no evidence that they set me up."

Emma wanted to tell him that Susan and Julie would cooperate with the cops if Rod Sawyers's men or some other goons put pressure on them, but she couldn't do that because their conversation was monitored.

"What are the prosecutors offering?" she asked.

"Life sentence. I'll be eligible for parole in thirty years."

Thirty years. Paul would be seventy-two years old when he became eligible for parole.

If he went to trial and lost, he would face a death sentence.

"Do you think it's the best deal you can get?" Emma asked.

"Yes."

"What are the chances that you won't be sentenced to death if you lose at trial?"

"Zero. I'm going to ask for an Alford plea."

When a defendant entered an Alford plea, he maintained his innocence but admitted that the evidence presented by the prosecution would likely persuade a judge or jury to find him guilty beyond a reasonable doubt.

"When are you going to take the plea bargain?"

"This week."

"Why not wait until October?" Emma felt tears prick her eyes.

"What's the point? Look, honey, I've thought this through. It's a good plea deal. It's the best deal I can get. I'll live another twenty years after I get out of prison. Maybe thirty. One of my great-grandfathers lived to be a hundred. And I'll probably still look good when I get out." Paul smiled.

Emma swallowed the large lump in her throat. "If we find a way to get Susan and Julie to confess, they'll reverse your conviction, right?"

"Yes. This kind of thing happens all the time."

Emma wiped away her tears. "Then we'll keep looking for the real killer."

Paul nodded. "Can you bring Ollie to see me tomorrow?"

"Sure."

2

When she got home, Emma called Hopper and asked him how they were going to get Susan and Julie to rat out Alison Bowles's killer.

"Honestly, I don't know," Hopper replied. "We have to find them first."

"I could hire some people to lean on them. What do you think about that?"

"Lean on them? You know people who could lean on them?"

"Maybe Rod Sawyers will help us."

"Rod Sawyers? That's an interesting idea, Emma. Let's talk about it when we find Susan and Julie."

"Ask Jonah what he thinks about that."

"He'll say it's a bad idea."

Chapter 50

1

When Dennis opened his account on the My Family Tree website on Friday, July 17, he saw that his DNA test results had been posted. He checked the profiles of the people whose DNA matched his, examined their family trees, and was disappointed to find he wasn't related to royalty or any famous people.

However, it was still possible that he had royal blood, since none of the family trees went more than six generations back.

Lisa came to his apartment that night, and Dennis informed her that he had found no royals or famous people among his DNA matches or in their family trees. Lisa laughed and said, "I still love you, baby."

He loved Lisa with all his heart and he thanked God for leading him to her. She was smart, beautiful, caring, and good in bed. Dennis knew her love for him was real, since he wasn't rich and didn't have much to offer.

On Tuesday, July 28, at six p.m., while Dennis was making a ham sandwich, his doorbell rang. When he opened the door, he saw two tall, solidly built men in dark suits. One of them held up a police badge and said, "Dennis Almanza?"

"Yes."

"I'm Detective Richard Viera with the Los Angeles Police Department. And this is my partner, Detective Sam Bellis."

Dennis's pulse quickened. "How can I help you?"

"We have a few questions for you. Can we come in?"

"Sure."

Was someone he knew a suspect in a crime?

Was he a suspect?

The detectives entered the apartment.

Viera asked, "Where you were on July twenty-fifth between nine and eleven p.m.?"

Dennis felt a sinking in the pit of his stomach.

What's this about?

"Was it Saturday?" he asked.

"Yes."

"I was home."

"Can anyone confirm that?"

Lisa had been at his place last Saturday night. She had left around ten in the morning.

"Yes. Lisa, my girlfriend. She was with me that night."

Viera reached into his suit pocket, pulled out a photograph of a young attractive woman with long dark hair, and held it up. "Do you know this woman?"

"No."

"Have you ever met her?"

"No."

"Her name was Stephanie Jarvis. She was murdered on July twenty-fifth. Your DNA was found on her body and underwear."

Dennis broke into a cold sweat. How had his DNA gotten on the body of a murder victim? Was it semen? How the hell did they know it was his DNA?

He had no idea who Stephanie Jarvis was.

"I have nothing to do with this," Dennis said. "I never met Stephanie Jarvis. I was home with Lisa that night. Call her. She'll confirm."

"Sure." Viera stood up and took out a pair of handcuffs. "Dennis Almanza, you're under arrest for the murder of Stephanie Jarvis."

Dennis's heart was hammering. "I didn't kill this woman! I never met her!"

2

Dennis looked at the crime scene photos of Stephanie Jarvis for a few seconds and then raised his eyes to Detective Viera's face.

Stephanie appeared to have been stabbed: her shirt was covered with blood.

"How was she murdered," he asked.

They were in an interview room at Los Angeles Police Headquarters. Viera and Bellis sat across the table from him with solemn expressions on their faces.

After he was booked, Dennis had called Lisa, but she hadn't answered. Then he had phoned Kevin Worley, his best friend in Los Angeles, and told him that he had been arrested and that he needed a lawyer.

"She was stabbed in the chest and stomach," Viera replied. "Did you forget what you did to her?"

"I didn't kill her."

When Lisa confirmed his alibi, would the police believe her?

An alibi corroborated by a girlfriend was worthless. There was no way he could prove he had been home on the night of the murder.

I'm definitely going to jail.

Gooseflesh broke out all over Dennis's body.

"And you didn't know her?" Bellis said.

"No. Where did you find her body?"

"In an alley in Cypress Park. You forgot?"

Cypress Park was a neighborhood in northeast Los Angeles.

"You said you found my DNA on her body. What kind of DNA was it?"

"Semen. You raped Stephanie before killing her."

"Where did you find it?"

"In the groin area. You must have spilled some of your semen when you took off the condom."

"How do you know it's my semen?"

Viera said, "We found your DNA profile in the database of a company called My Family Tree. You sent them your DNA sample a month ago."

"They let you search their database?"

"Yes. DNA testing companies have helped catch a lot of killers and rapists."

"I didn't kill that woman."

"But you had sex with her that night, didn't you?"

"No. I never met her."

He could tell them that he'd had sex with Stephanie a few hours before she was murdered and his semen had gotten on her during that encounter.

That wouldn't help him. It was a stupid idea.

"You're in big trouble, Dennis," Bellis said. "Your semen was found on the victim's body and you have no alibi."

"I have an alibi."

He had never met Stephanie Jarvis, which meant that the semen found on her body wasn't his. The people who had run the DNA test must have made a mistake. What other explanation could there be?

Maybe My Family Tree recorded the killer's DNA profile under my name by mistake?

Could his semen have been planted on Stephanie's body? Where would they have gotten it? He had never donated his sperm.

Maybe they had taken one of his used condoms from his garbage?

"Tell us what happened, Dennis," Viera said in a soft voice.

"I didn't kill Stephanie Jarvis. I'm not saying anything else until my lawyer gets here."

3

After the interview, Dennis was transferred to the Men's Central Jail in downtown Los Angeles. The lawyer Kevin Worley had found for him came the next morning. His name was Jeremy Hausler and he specialized in criminal defense. He was in his late thirties, lean, with short dark hair and gray eyes.

Dennis was glad he could afford a lawyer: his parents had promised to help him pay his legal bills.

"What did you tell the police?" Hausler asked Dennis.

"I told them that I didn't kill Stephanie Jarvis, that I was at home with my girlfriend on the night of the murder."

"From now on, don't talk to the police without me."

"Okay."

"Did you know Stephanie Jarvis?"

"No. I never met her."

"How did your semen get on her body?"

"I don't know. It might have been planted. Or maybe it's not my semen. Can you do an independent DNA test on it? I think the crime lab might have made a mistake."

"Sure."

"You need to call my girlfriend. Her name's Lisa. I was home with her on the night of the murder. She came around six and left around ten in the morning."

"Okay. What's her number?"

Dennis told Hausler Lisa's phone number.

"Can anyone else confirm you were at home that night?" the lawyer asked.

"No. What are my chances? Please be honest."

"It's a tough case, Dennis. Your semen was found on the victim's body. That's an extremely powerful piece of evidence."

Dennis was arraigned an hour later. He was charged with murder with a special circumstance allegation of murder during a rape. He was denied bail because of the special circumstance. The special circumstance made Dennis eligible for the death penalty; although there was a moratorium on executions in California right now, prosecutors were allowed to seek capital punishment.

Chapter 51

1

The prosecutors offered Robert a thirty-year plea bargain, and according to Laporte, it was the best deal he could get. He would be eligible for parole after serving fifteen years. If he was found guilty at trial, he would face life in prison.

The idea of pleading guilty to a murder he hadn't committed—the murder of the love of his life—sickened Robert, but he was pretty sure that he would lose at trial, and he didn't want to risk getting a life sentence.

The search for the real killers had stalled: Robert doubted Brian Harbour was the murderer, and he had so far been unable to think of anyone else who could be a plausible suspect.

Harbour visited Robert again on Thursday, July 30.

"Did you figure out who set you up?" he asked.

"No."

"I've been thinking about this since we last talked. I want to help you, you know. I think I might have figured out who framed you."

"Who is it?"

"There's at least one person whose life you ruined. Apparently you forgot him."

"Who is it?" Robert asked impatiently.

"You were on a jury a few years ago, weren't you?

Robert nodded. "Yes."

"You found the guy guilty, didn't you?"

"Yes."

"What was he on trial for?"

"He killed someone."

"What sentence did he get?"

"Thirty-five years."

"That's a long sentence. If I were him, I'd be really pissed off at you."

Harbour was right. That guy must have hated every member of the jury that heard his case.

What was his name?

His last name was Becker or Decker. Robert forgot the man's first name.

There were twelve people on the jury. Why did he pick me?

Because I was the foreman.

"He must still be in prison," Robert said. "Who did this?"

"Probably his siblings. How old is he now?"

"About sixty."

"It could be his children. They probably think he's innocent. You put this guy in jail for a crime he didn't commit, so they framed you so you'd go to jail for a crime you didn't commit. I think that's what they call poetic justice."

Was Becker/Decker going to take vengeance on the other members of his jury?

He probably was. Would he set them up for murder, too? Would he kill them?

What about the judge who presided over his trial? Would Becker/Decker punish him?

Maybe he has already punished the judge.

"I think he's going to get revenge on the other jurors and the judge," Robert said.

Harbour nodded. "Definitely."

He had to warn the jurors and the judge about Becker/Decker.

"Thank you for figuring this thing out, Brian," Robert said.

"You're welcome. Do you remember the guy's name?"

If Tamara had been murdered by Becker/Decker's relatives or friends, how would he prove that?

"No. I'll ask my lawyer to find it out."

"Do you want me to help you track down his children and siblings?"

"I'll ask my lawyer to do that."

"Okay. Good luck, Robert. I hope everything works out well for you."

"Thank you."

Chapter 52

1

On Friday, July 31, Detective Viera told Dennis that they had examined all his shoes and found traces of Stephanie Jarvis's blood on the bottom of one of his black Nike sneakers.

"Do you know how the blood got there?" Viera asked, a smug look on his face.

It must have been planted.

"No."

His chances of acquittal had been slim before, but now they were nonexistent, weren't they?

"You probably stepped on a drop of Stephanie Jarvis's blood after you killed her."

"I didn't kill her. I have nothing else to say to you, Detective."

"Okay." Viera got up. "By the way, your girlfriend hasn't returned my call yet."

"She's probably busy."

You won't believe her anyway.

"Or maybe she's not willing to commit perjury for you."

Dennis left his cellblock again an hour later, to meet his lawyer. Hausler told him that he had asked the police to provide a sample of the semen found on Stephanie Jarvis's body for an independent DNA test.

"You shouldn't get your hopes up," Hausler said. "The crime lab does make mistakes, but that rarely happens."

"Maybe My Family Tree made a mistake? Maybe they erroneously recorded the killer's DNA profile under my name?"

"They tested the DNA sample collected from you after the arrest. Your DNA matches the semen."

"Did they tell that they found traces of Stephanie Jarvis's blood on one of my shoes?"

"No."

"I think the blood was planted. And my semen was planted, too."

Hausler must have had a lot of clients who said that evidence against them had been planted. How many times had those claims turned out to be true? Probably very rarely, if ever.

"Who do you think planted them?"

The blood might have been planted by the police, but who had planted the semen? He had no enemies whatsoever, and he had no disputes with anyone.

"I don't know."

"How do you think they got your semen?"

"They might have gone through my garbage and found one of my used condoms."

Hausler nodded.

Dennis asked, "Did you call Lisa?"

"Yes. I called her several times, but she never answered or returned my calls."

"You left her a message?"

"Several of them."

"Did you mention that I need her help?"

"I said that I'm your attorney and that it's an urgent matter."

"Tell her that I'm in jail and need her help."

"What's her address? I'll send someone to her place."

"I don't know her address."

"Do you know where she works?"

"No."

"What's her last name?"

"Wilson."

"Maybe she doesn't want to help you? How well do you know her?"

"She's my girlfriend."

Why wasn't Lisa answering? Was she okay? Had something happened to her?

Maybe she had been run over by a car or killed by a robber. Maybe she had slipped and cracked her skull open.

"I'll try to find out her address," Hausler said.

"Maybe she's in the hospital. Can you check the hospitals?"

"Sure."

Dennis wondered if Hausler still believed he was innocent.

Had his lawyer believed him before?

Chapter 53

1

"I think I know who set me up," Robert told Laporte.

"Who is it?" the lawyer asked.

"Seven years ago I served on a jury. I was its foreman. We found the guy guilty and he was sentenced to thirty-five years in prison. His last name is Becker or Decker. I believe his relatives or friends framed me to avenge him."

Laporte wrote down the name. "What was he on trial for?"

"He killed a guy who slept with his wife."

"Did the trial take place in Dallas County?"

"Yes. You need to find out if he has any children or siblings. He's in his sixties now, so his kids, if he has any, are probably adults."

"Was this man involved with organized crime?"

"I don't think so. If he has children or siblings, ask the police to check their emails and text messages."

"Okay."

"Do you think the police will look into him?"

Laporte shrugged. "I don't know. They might."

"I think he's going to get revenge on the other jurors and the judge who presided over his trial, so you need to find them and warn them."

"He probably plans to get even with the prosecutors, too."

Robert nodded. "Yes. Warn them, too. Tell the police that Becker's relatives will try to kill again, so they must be put under surveillance."

"If he has already framed or killed the judge or the prosecutors, it will help you convince the police to look into him, won't it?"

"Yes."

"Have his relatives followed for a week or two."

"Okay."

"If it's technically possible, eavesdrop on them at home for a couple of weeks."

Private detectives weren't allowed to plant bugs in homes, but they could eavesdrop by means of laser microphones that could record sound through windows.

"Okay. They might have left fingerprints in your house or your car."

"Yes. We need to get their fingerprints."

"Do you remember the judge's name?"

"No."

"Do you remember when the trial ended?"

"Late February."

2

When Laporte returned to the office, he wrote a letter to the Dallas County Clerk of the Court requesting the names of the defendant, judge, prosecutors, and jurors in the trial whose jury Robert Lochner had served on seven years ago. He also asked for the addresses where the jurors lived at the time of the trial.

Had Becker set Lochner up for Tamara's murder, or was it another dead end? He was surely a better suspect than a disgruntled loan applicant.

Had Lochner been framed? He struck Laporte as honest, but maybe he was just a good actor.

Laporte searched an online legal case database and found no murder cases where the defendant's name was Becker or Decker, the defendant was found guilty by a jury, and the trial took place in Dallas County seven years ago. Then he searched news articles published seven years ago for "jury foreman Robert Lochner" and got no relevant hits. He figured Lochner had misremembered the defendant's name.

3

Five days later, the Dallas County Clerk of the Court informed Laporte that seven years ago Robert Lochner had served on the jury at the trial of Owen Dekker. Judge Andrew Hollenbeck presided over it. The lead prosecutor was Paul Marston, and Mark Ketteridge was his second chair. The jurors were Dennis Almanza, Celeste Ramos, Robert Lochner, Kevin Huang, Brandon Huber, Olivia Villanueva, Reece Edgehill,

Amalia Calderon, William Stevens, Maria Vasquez, Lawrence Turley, and Benjamin Oglesby.

Laporte knew that Judge Andrew Hollenbeck had retired earlier this year. He had last seen Mark Ketteridge about a month ago, at the courthouse. It had been a long time since he had last seen Paul Marston.

Laporte called Hugh Ruskin and instructed him to find out if Owen Dekker had any children or siblings and where they lived.

"We believe that he framed Robert Lochner," he said. "Robert served on the jury at his trial. Put his children's homes under video surveillance, if possible." Then he asked Ruskin to find the jurors' addresses.

"You think Dekker's planning to frame them, too?" Ruskin asked.

"Yes. Frame them or kill them."

Laporte did an Internet search for "Owen Dekker murder trial" and found out that Dekker had killed a man named Isaac Hemphill, who he believed had slept with his wife, Louise. Dekker had never admitted to the murder.

Laporte found Hollenbeck's home phone number on the Internet, called him, and left a voice mail. Then he phoned the Dallas County District Attorney's Office and was told that Paul Marston had quit four years ago. They didn't know where he worked now. Mark Ketteridge was still alive and still worked in the DA's office, which meant that he hadn't been framed by Dekker yet. Laporte called his office number and left a message.

He figured that Marston had joined a law firm and googled "Paul Marston attorney." What he found shocked him.

Chapter 54

1

"Have you heard from the clerk of the court?" Robert asked Laporte, his heart beating hard. He had been on pins and needles for the last five days, waiting for his lawyer to report what he had found out about Becker/Decker, the judge, the prosecutors, and the jurors.

"Yes." Laporte's eyes lit up.

He has some good news for me, Robert thought.

"Did they give you the jurors' names?"

"Yes. The defendant's name is Owen Dekker." Laporte spelled Dekker's last name.

"Yes." Robert nodded. "Now I remember that it's spelled with two Ks. How old is he?"

"Sixty-two. He's still in prison. The judge's name is Andrew Hollenbeck. I left him a message yesterday. He hasn't called me back yet."

"Maybe he's dead."

"I found no mention of his death on the Internet. If he doesn't call me by six, I'll go to his house. The lead prosecutor was Paul Marston. Guess what happened to him."

"Was he murdered?"

Laporte shook his head. "Last month he went to prison for raping and killing a young woman."

"Did he say he was framed?"

"I don't know. He took a plea deal."

Robert chewed on his lower lip. "This is proof. He was framed, which means I was framed, too." He smiled. "We found him. We found the bastard who set me up."

Laporte nodded.

"Does Dekker have children?" Robert asked.

"He has a son, Tom. He's thirty-nine."

"His son killed Tammy, I'm sure of it. You need to find him."

"We're working on it. He no longer lives at the address the DMV has for him." Laporte opened his briefcase, took out a photograph, and put in on the table. "This is Tom's DMV photo. Do you recognize him?"

"No. Is Owen Dekker married?"

"He was married twice. His first wife, Tom Dekker's mother, died a year ago. His second wife divorced him six years ago."

"Does he have siblings?"

"He has a sister, Caroline. She's fifty-eight."

"She might have helped Tom Dekker kill Tammy."

"I asked Ruskin to find her, too."

"Did they frame or kill any of the other jurors?"

"I don't know yet. The second-chair prosecutor in Dekker's case is alive and hasn't been framed. I talked to him this morning."

"What did he say when you told him about Dekker? Did he take the warning seriously?"

"I think so."

"Please call my son and tell him about Paul Marston. Tell him he was framed by Dekker. Tell him that proves I was framed, too."

"Sure."

Robert could tell Jim about Marston himself, but he thought this information would sound more credible if it came from Laporte.

"What sentence did Paul Marston get?" he asked.

"Life in prison with the possibility of parole."

"Did he know the woman he was accused of killing?"

"No."

"When was he arrested?"

"Last April. He was arrested shortly after the murder."

They waited two months before framing me.

"When are you going to meet him?"

"I'll try to meet him this Saturday."

"What prison is he in?"

"A maximum security prison in Livingston. It's about two hundred miles from Dallas."

"Is he in the same prison as Dekker?"

"No. Dekker's in the Huntsville prison. Huntsville's about forty miles west of Livingston."

"If Marston's married, talk to his wife. Tell her he's innocent."

"Sure."

"When are you going to ask the police to look into Tom Dekker?"

"I want to check if he framed any of the other jurors before I tell the police about him."

2

"Have you talked to Marston?" Jim asked after Laporte told him about the lead prosecutor in Dekker's case.

"I'm planning to meet him this Saturday." Laporte rocked back in his office chair.

"Do you think this will create reasonable doubt at my dad's trial?"

"I don't know. I'm hoping to find evidence that Tom Dekker murdered your mother."

"Please tell my dad I'm coming to Dallas in two weeks. Ask him to call me."

"Okay."

Hollenbeck called Laporte at half past five, and they agreed to meet at the judge's house in an hour.

Hollenbeck's wife, a thin woman in her sixties with long chestnut hair, answered the door when Laporte arrived at his place. Tom Dekker might frame the judge for his wife's murder, the lawyer thought as he followed Hollenbeck out onto the patio.

The judge was tall, potbellied, with thin gray hair combed over his spotted scalp.

"My wife doesn't let me smoke in the house." Hollenbeck sat across the table from Laporte, picked up his cigar from the ashtray, and asked, "Do you mind if I smoke?"

"No."

Hollenbeck didn't remember Owen Dekker's case. Laporte told the judge that Tom Dekker might try to kill him and then gave him Tom Dekker's photograph.

"This picture's fifteen years old," he said. "I'll send you his recent photos when I have them."

Hollenbeck puffed on his cigar. "Thank you for warning me, John. I really appreciate it."

"He might try to frame you for murder. To make you suffer the way his father's been suffering."

Hollenbeck arched an eyebrow. "He probably thinks that his daddy's innocent, that he was framed."

Laporte nodded. "If you decide to go to the police, I suggest you ask them to put Tom Dekker under surveillance for a few weeks. They might catch him the act."

"Okay."

"He might try to kill your wife to set you up for her murder, so ask her to be vigilant."

Hollenbeck frowned. "I will."

Chapter 55

1

Ruskin ran Tom Dekker's name through every investigative database available and couldn't find his current address. He hoped Caroline Dekker or Tom's former stepmother knew something about his whereabouts.

Ruskin's contact at the DMV told him that Caroline Dekker's driver's license had expired thirty-five years ago. She no longer lived at the address in her DMV file. The current resident told the private investigator that she had lived there for five years and that she didn't know Caroline Dekker. Ruskin figured Owen Dekker's sister had left Texas, a long time ago. She might have gotten married and changed her last name.

Ruskin discovered that Caroline had married Bruce Kleparski of Orange County, Florida, thirty-seven years ago and kept his last name after they divorced. There was a fifty-eight-year-old Caroline Kleparski living in West Palm Beach, Florida. Was she Owen Dekker's sister?

Owen Dekker's second wife's Texas driver's license was still valid. She still lived in the house she and Owen Dekker had bought nineteen years ago; she had gotten it in the divorce. Ruskin went to her place on Friday, August 7.

A pleasant-looking woman of about sixty with long blonde hair and wide hips opened the door.

"Good evening, ma'am," Ruskin said.

"Good evening."

"Are you Louise O'Shea?"

Dekker's second wife had gone back to her maiden name, O'Shea, after the divorce.

"Yes. How can I help you?"

"My name's Hugh Ruskin. I'm looking for Tom Dekker. I believe you're his stepmother."

"Why are you looking for him?"

"I'm a private investigator. My client is looking for the father of her child and she believes that Mr. Dekker might be him. It's not about child support. Her son just wants to know who his father is."

"How old is your client's son?"

"Fifteen. Do you know where I can find Tom?"

After a silence, Louise said, "Tom's been missing for the last year and a half."

"Did you file a missing person's report?"

"Yes."

"When did he go missing?"

"In February of last year."

Had something bad happened to Dekker, or had he decided to disappear so the police wouldn't question him about whatever he planned to do to the people who had put his father in prison?

"Do you think he's alive?" Ruskin asked.

"I don't know. If you want to find out if Tom's the father of your client's son, you can take a DNA sample from Tom's dad."

"Do you know his address?"

"He's in prison."

Ruskin wondered if Louise had given him this information because she hated Owen Dekker and wanted everyone to know that he was a lowlife.

"What prison is he in?"

Did Tom Dekker hate Louise for cheating on his father with the man he had murdered? Was he going to punish her?

"The one in Huntsville."

"Do you know any of Tom's friends?"

"No."

"Does Tom have any kids?"

Louise ran a hand through her hair. "Yes. A son. But they never did a paternity test, so we can't be sure Tom's his biological father."

"What's his name?"

"Brent."

"How old is he?"

"Twelve."

"Do you know where he lives?"

"Yes. Let me get my address book."

Louise went inside and came back with a brown leather book.

"He lives in Houston," she said, and gave the private investigator Brent's address.

"What's Brent's mother's name?" Ruskin asked.

"Erika Milliken. Are you going to ask Tom's father for a DNA sample?"

"I will if I can't get a DNA sample from Tom's son. Does Tom's father have any siblings?"

"He has a sister, Caroline. She lives in Florida."

"Do you have her address?"

"Yes."

Louise told Ruskin Caroline's address, which matched the address of the fifty-eight-year-old Caroline Kleparski in West Palm Beach.

"Do you have her phone number?" Ruskin asked.

"Yes."

After Louise gave him Caroline's number, Ruskin said, "Do you have Tom's cellphone number? The one he had when he went missing."

He hoped Dekker's cellphone provider kept call records for longer than eighteen months (there were carriers that retained call records for five and even seven years).

"Yes." Louise told Ruskin Dekker's number.

"Thank you for your help, Ms. O'Shea."

Ruskin drove three blocks from Louise O'Shea's house, pulled over, then grabbed his tablet and searched a missing persons website for Tom Dekker.

Dekker had really been reported missing. He had last been seen on February 15 of last year.

How the hell are we going to find him?

Ruskin closed the browser and opened the spreadsheet containing the jurors' addresses. According to his research, juror number one, Dennis Almanza, had moved to Los Angeles three years ago. Laporte was going to send him a letter today asking him to contact the lawyer as soon as possible. Ruskin punched Almanza's last Dallas area address into the GPS and saw that it was only six miles away. He decided to stop by the place: the current resident might have Almanza's phone number or address or both.

2

Almanza's old apartment was in a complex of three-story buildings in a decent neighborhood. A chubby man in his twenties with a full beard answered the door.

"Hi. I'm looking for Dennis Almanza," Ruskin said. "Is he home?"

"There's no Dennis here."

"Do you know where he lives now?"

"No."

"Do you have his phone number?"

"No."

There were three more jurors who had moved out of the Dallas area: Reece Edgehill (they believed he now lived in Houston), Maria Vasquez (Seattle, Washington), and Benjamin Oglesby (Scottsdale, Arizona). Ruskin decided to visit their last Dallas area addresses in a week.

Twenty minutes later he arrived at the house of juror number two, Celeste Ramos, who still lived at the address provided by the clerk of the court. Celeste was home. She was forty-three, full-breasted, with wavy black hair and olive skin. Ruskin introduced himself, handed her his card, and said, "I need to tell you something important."

"Okay." Celeste looked intrigued.

"You served on a jury seven years ago, didn't you?"

"Yes."

"The defendant's name was Owen Dekker. He was found guilty and sentenced to thirty-five years. Now his son is taking revenge on the people who put him in prison, and that includes the jurors."

Celeste frowned. "Please come in."

They sat on the couch in the living room, and Celeste asked, "Did Dekker's son already kill any of the jurors?"

"He framed the jury foreman, Robert Lochner, for murder. Robert is now in jail awaiting trial."

"I remember him."

"We believe he also framed the lead prosecutor, Paul Marston, for murder. We think he might frame you, too. Have you been questioned by the police in the last few weeks?"

"No. What's the son's name?"

"Tom. Here's his picture." Ruskin pulled Tom Dekker's photograph from his inside pocket and handed it to Celeste. "It was taken fifteen years ago. Do you recognize him?"

Celeste shook her head. "No."

"He may try to set you up for murder or some other serious crime. He may try to kill you. You need to watch your back, Celeste."

"You said he framed the jury foreman for murder. Who was murdered?"

"Robert's wife. Are you married?"

"Yes."

"He may try to frame you for your husband's murder."

"Did you tell the police about him?"

"No. We have no proof that he framed Lochner or Marston."

Celeste looked at Tom Dekker's picture. "Thank you for telling me about this man, Hugh. I'll watch my back. Are you going to warn the other jurors?"

"Yes."

Chapter 56

1

Paul had never seen the guy before. He was dressed in a dark suit, white shirt, and blue tie, and his hair was neatly combed. Paul wondered if he was a lawyer. He didn't think the guy had good news for him, but he was glad to see him anyway: it was nice to take a break from hanging out with murderers, rapists, and robbers.

"Who are you?" Paul asked.

"My name's John Laporte," the man said. "I'm an attorney. I represent Robert Lochner."

Robert Lochner. Paul had no idea who he was.

"I don't know him. Who is he?"

"You took an Alford plea, which means that you don't admit to killing Alison Bowles."

"That's right. I didn't kill her. What do you want from me, Mr. Laporte?"

"Were you framed?"

"Yes. I was framed."

"Do you know who set you up?"

"I think it's one of the people I put in prison when I was a prosecutor."

"Do you have a suspect in mind?"

Did Laporte work for the guy who had framed him? Was it Laporte who had set him up?

"Why do you ask? And who's Robert Lochner?"

"Robert Lochner was set up for his wife's murder. We believe he was framed by the same person who framed you."

Paul's heart began to thump.

Lochner isn't a judge or a prosecutor. Was he a juror?

Lochner hadn't been on the jury that convicted Kowalik.

"Who framed him?" Paul asked.

"We believe it was Owen Dekker. You were the lead prosecutor at his trial. Do you remember his case?"

Paul nodded. Owen Dekker had been tried for murder seven or eight years ago. He had been sentenced to over thirty years, so he must still be in prison.

"Mr. Lochner served on the jury at his trial," Laporte said. "He was the foreman. Dekker framed Mr. Lochner to get even with him. We believe he's going to take revenge on the other jurors and the judge."

"Dekker's still in prison, isn't he?"

"Yes. We think he told his son to avenge him."

"He has a son?"

"Yes. His name's Tom Dekker."

"Do you know his address?"

"He went missing a year and a half ago."

That was a smart move on Tom Dekker's part.

"Do you have his picture?"

"I have his DMV photo." Laporte took out Tom Dekker's photograph and showed it to Paul. "It's fifteen years old. He probably looks different now."

Paul didn't recognize Dekker.

"I've never met him. Does Owen Dekker have any other children?"

"No."

"Does he have any sisters?"

"He has one sister, Caroline Kleparski."

"How old is she?"

"Fifty-eight."

"Tom Dekker has two women helping him. One of them had sex with me to get my semen, which was later planted on Alison Bowles's body. She's in her twenties, she called herself Julie. Does Owen Dekker have any female relatives in their twenties?"

"I'll find out. Do you have her picture?"

"No. The other woman made friends with my wife. She's in her thirties. She called herself Susan. We don't have her picture, either."

"Do you have these women's phone numbers?"

"Yes. They used disposable phones. We checked their phone records and found nothing useful. I'll tell my lawyer to give their numbers to you."

"I assume Susan and Julie disappeared after your arrest?"

Paul nodded. "We need to find them. Maybe we'll be able to get them to turn Dekker in."

"Is Jonah Wallach still your lawyer?"

"Yes. Dekker has a male accomplice. He's Asian, he called himself Edward Zheng. We have his picture, but it's of poor quality."

"How did he help Dekker?"

"The lease of the house where Julie lived was in his name. Do you know what prison Owen Dekker's in?"

"He's in the Huntsville Unit."

"Did Robert get bail?"

"No."

"How did they frame him?"

"They kidnapped Robert's wife and demanded ransom from him. He reported the kidnapping to the police. Then the cops found traces of her blood on his kitchen floor and in the trunk of his car, and he became a suspect."

"Did they find his wife's body?"

"Yes. It was found in a wooded area in southern Dallas two days after the kidnapping."

"When was Robert's wife kidnapped?"

"On June eighth."

"Did you check on the second-chair prosecutor? Did Dekker frame him?"

"We checked on him. He's fine."

"Was Mark Ketteridge my second chair in Dekker's case?"

"Yes."

"Did Dekker frame any other members of the jury?"

"I don't know. We've talked to one of them so far. She's fine."

"Did you check on the judge?"

"Yes. He's fine, too."

"You need to give all this information to my wife and my lawyer. They'll help you look for Dekker."

"Sure."

Paul told Laporte Emma's phone number and the name of the firm where Jonah Wallach worked.

"You can't imagine how grateful I am to you, John," he said. "Thank you. Thank you so much."

Paul wished he could shake Laporte's hand and embrace him. This man saved his life.

"We're going to find Dekker and his accomplices," Laporte said. "We'll get you out of here, Paul."

Chapter 57

1

"When will I see Daddy?" Ollie asked as Emma handed him a glass of orange juice.

Emma's chest tightened. "Soon, honey."

"Is he still in jail?"

"Yes."

Ollie took a sip of his juice and set the glass on the coffee table. "Is he okay?"

"Yes. He's okay and he loves you very much."

"Okay." Ollie's eyes went back to the TV, where Grampa Simpson was telling one of his rambling stories.

Kowalik's apartment had been under surveillance for over a month now, but neither Susan, nor Julie, nor Edward Zheng had shown up yet. They had checked the rest of the numbers in Kowalik's phone records and found that none of them belonged to Susan, Julie, or Edward Zheng. None of the members of the Kowalik jury had been murdered (one of them had died in September of last year, but it was prostate cancer that killed him), imprisoned, or accused of any serious crime. Was Kowalik another dead end?

Had Paul been framed by someone released before June of last year? Maybe it was someone who didn't go to trial?

On July 17, Emma had gone to the hearing where Paul's plea deal was approved, and burst into tears midway through the proceedings. She had cried on the way home and then cried some more before she left to pick up Ollie from school and after he had fallen asleep that night.

The judge could have rejected the prosecution's recommendation and sentenced Paul to life without the possibility of parole, but that hadn't happened; he had accepted the terms of the plea agreement.

Paul was serving his sentence in a maximum security prison in the East Texas town of Livingston called Allan B. Polunsky Unit. The facility housed the state's death row for men; it was a depressing, suffocating place—as well it should be, since it was home to the vilest criminals in Texas, who deserved to suffer. Emma had visited Paul there last Saturday and planned to see him at least once a month until he got out.

She hadn't taken Ollie to the Polunsky Unit yet: she didn't want him to see how dreadful his father's new home was.

"Will he be home by Thanksgiving?" Ollie asked when a commercial came on.

"Maybe."

"I miss him."

"He misses you, too, honey." Emma put her arms around the boy and kissed him on the cheek.

"If they don't let him out, he should escape, like Paddington."

In the movie, Paddington Bear escaped from prison along with a few other inmates.

"Yes." Emma nodded.

"We'll help him escape."

Her phone rang. The number had a Dallas area code.

"Hello," Emma said.

"Can I talk to Emma Marston?" a man asked.

"Who is this?"

"My name's John Laporte. I'm an attorney. Is your husband's name Paul Marston?"

"Yes."

"Was he accused of killing a woman named Alison Bowles?"

"Yes."

Was Laporte Connie Bowles's lawyer? Was she going to sue Paul?

"Can you meet me tonight? It's about Paul."

"What do you want to tell me?"

"I believe I know who set him up."

"Where would you like to meet?" Emma asked, her heart beating fast.

"I can come to your place."

She had never heard of John Laporte. Was he a friend of Wallach's or Hopper's?

"Okay."

"I'll be there in half an hour."

"Okay."

2

Laporte came twenty-five minutes later. He told Emma that his client, Robert Lochner, had been framed for his wife's murder by a man named Tom Dekker because he had been a juror at his father's trial.

"Your husband was the lead prosecutor in the trial," Laporte said. "I have no doubt he was set up by Dekker."

Emma nodded. "I think you're right. You need to tell my husband and his lawyer about Dekker."

Her heart was pounding. They knew now who had framed Paul.

"I talked to Paul this morning. I'll call Jonah Wallach when I get home." Laporte opened his briefcase and pulled out a manila folder. "Here's everything we have on Tom Dekker and his father." Laporte handed the folder to Emma.

"Have you spoken to Tom Dekker?" Emma asked as she leafed through the folder.

"He disappeared a year and a half ago."

"Are you going to look for him?"

"Yes. Your husband said Jonah will help us look for Dekker and his accomplices."

"I'll help you, too. I'll do whatever it takes to get Paul out of prison."

"We're going to find these bastards."

"Paul told you about Susan and Julie?"

"Yes."

"Is Tom Dekker married?"

Emma stared at Tom Dekker's photograph. She didn't recognize him.

"No. And he has no sisters. His father has a sister, but she's fifty-eight years old."

"Did Dekker frame the judge or any of the other jurors?"

"The judge is fine. We've talked to only one juror so far. She's fine. The second-chair prosecutor's fine, too."

"Dekker's not going to confess to the murders. We'll have to figure out how to get Susan or Julie to testify against him. How do you think we could do that?"

"I've given it some thought. We could offer them a reward for information leading to Dekker's conviction. I think five hundred thousand dollars would do the trick. I'm sure the district attorney's office will agree to give Dekker's accomplices immunity if they testify against him."

"You think a reward will work?"

"There's a good chance it will. Money's a powerful motivator."

"How much could Robert raise?"

"Two, three hundred thousand. Could you raise two hundred and fifty thousand?"

"I think so."

If she couldn't raise the full amount on her own, Paul's parents would help her.

"Great." Laporte glanced at his watch. "Thank you for meeting, Emma. I'll keep you posted." He picked up his briefcase and stood up.

"Thank you very much, John. Call me anytime."

Chapter 58

1

Ruskin found that Tom Dekker had never been married and Brent Milliken was his only child. On Saturday, he went to Houston to talk to Erika Milliken, who he assumed used to be Dekker's girlfriend.

A bearded man in his forties, wearing a white T-shirt and blue shorts opened the door of Erika's house.

"Good morning." Ruskin studied the man's face without seeming to do so.

"Good morning."

Ruskin couldn't see any resemblance between the guy and Tom Dekker.

"I'm sorry to bother you so early in the morning. My name's Hugh Ruskin. I'm a private investigator. I'm looking for Erika."

"Why?"

"I want to talk to her about one of her old friends."

"What's the friend's name?"

"Tom Dekker."

The man stepped aside and said, "Come in."

Erika sat in the living room with a laptop on her lap. She was good-looking, slim, with high cheekbones and long auburn hair.

"This guy's a private detective. He wants to talk to you," the bearded man said to Erika, and settled into a leather recliner.

Ruskin introduced himself and said, "I'm looking for Tom Dekker."

He wondered if the bearded guy knew who Tom Dekker was.

Erika put the laptop on the coffee table. "Tom went missing last year."

"When was the last time you heard from him?"

"February of last year."

"Do you still receive child support checks?"

"No."

"Do you think Tom disappeared to get out of paying child support?"

Erika shrugged.

"My client believes that Mr. Dekker is the father of her child. We're looking for him to find out if that's the case."

"What's your client's name?"

A dark-haired boy walked into the room. Ruskin figured he was Erika's son.

"Good morning," the boy said to Ruskin.

"Good morning," Ruskin replied. "How's it going?"

The boy said to Erika, "Mom, can we go to the movies today?"

"Yes, honey," Erika answered.

"Thank you." The boy glanced at Ruskin and left the room.

"Is he Tom's son?" Ruskin asked Erika.

"Yes."

Dekker might keep in touch with his son via the phone or email or Facebook. Ruskin wondered if Erika would let him talk to Brent alone.

Dekker would have instructed his son to tell no one that they were communicating with each other, so Brent would probably keep his mouth shut.

"What's his name?" Ruskin asked.

"Brent."

"Did Tom visit him before he went missing?"

"Yes. Every other month or so."

"Would you be willing to provide me with a sample of your son's DNA? I'd ask Tom's father for a sample of his DNA, but he's in prison."

Erika hesitated. "I don't know. Let me think about it. What's your client's name?"

"I can't tell you her name without her permission. In case you're wondering, it's not someone you know."

"Why is she looking for Tom?"

"Her son wants to know who his father is."

"How old is her son?"

"Fifteen. What do you think might have happened to Tom?"

"Maybe someone killed him and buried his body."

"You think he's dead?"

"Yes."

"Do you know any of his friends?"

"No."

"Thank you for your time, Erika. Please let me know if you decide to provide us with a sample of your son's DNA."

"Okay."

As he walked to his car, Ruskin decided to visit the address where they believed Reece Edgehill, juror number seven, might live. Yesterday, Laporte had sent Edgehill a letter asking him to contact the lawyer. He probably hadn't received it yet.

Ruskin started the engine and messaged Laporte asking if he had heard from Edgehill. When the private investigator was halfway to Edgehill's place, the lawyer replied: "Not yet."

The Houston Reece Edgehill lived in a two-story condo complex called Windsor Park in the northwestern part of the city. Ruskin parked on the street, waited a couple of minutes at the entrance gate, hoping someone would enter or exit, and then climbed over it. He found Edgehill's apartment and pressed the doorbell. There was no answer. He rang the bell again. No answer.

Edgehill was probably at work.

Ruskin took out his notepad, jotted: "Reece, please call me. It's urgent," wrote his phone number and name, and taped the note to the door.

Maybe Edgehill had already been framed and was in jail?

When he walked out of the complex, Ruskin googled "Reece Edgehill arrested" and found no news stories about Edgehill being jailed.

As he approached Interstate 610, Ken Carollo, his friend and former colleague at the Dallas Police Department, called Ruskin and told him that Tom Dekker's cellphone provider had been US Mobile, which kept call records for one year. Dekker's number now belonged to a woman named Victoria Suarez.

Chapter 59

1

On Sunday, Ruskin visited Kevin Huang and Brandon Huber, jurors number four and five. Huang still lived at the address provided by the clerk of the court. He told Ruskin that he hadn't been questioned by the police in the last few months and that he had never met Tom Dekker.

Brandon Huber had moved from Dallas to the suburb of Carrollton. Like Ramos and Huang, Huber hadn't been questioned by the police and had never met Tom Dekker.

It occurred to Ruskin that Tom Dekker might have visited his father in prison under a fake name after he had disappeared. They needed to get a list of people who had visited Owen Dekker after February of last year.

On Monday, Ruskin flew to West Palm Beach.

Caroline Kleparski lived in a one-story house about a mile south of downtown West Palm Beach. Before getting out of his rental car, Ruskin put a pen containing a hidden camera in the breast pocket of his suit jacket. He switched on the camera as he climbed the porch.

A tall, plump woman in her late fifties with graying hair opened the door.

"I'm looking for Caroline Kleparski," Ruskin said.

"That's me."

"My name's Hugh Ruskin. I'm a private investigator. I'm looking for your nephew, Tom Dekker." Ruskin gave Caroline his card.

"Why are you looking for him?"

"My client believes that Tom is the father of her child."

"Tom went missing last year."

"Do you have any idea what might have happened to him?"

Caroline shook her head. "No."

"Were your daughter and Tom close?"

According to birth records, Caroline Kleparski had one child, a daughter named Samantha, who was thirty-six years old. Samantha's age matched Susan's. Was she Susan?

Caroline's daughter had married John Sheldon thirteen years ago and divorced him seven years later. There was one thirty-six-year-old Samantha Sheldon in Florida and she had the same middle name as Caroline's daughter; according to online databases, she lived in Jacksonville. Ruskin had called Ken Carollo this morning and asked him to obtain her photo and address from the Florida Department of Motor Vehicles.

"I don't know," Caroline said.

"Does Samantha still live in Florida?"

"Yes."

"Could you give me her phone number?"

"No. I don't know you well enough."

"How about her address?"

"You can find it without my help. You're a private detective."

Ruskin nodded. "Do you know any of Tom's friends?"

"No. Don't waste your time on Sam. She doesn't know where Tom is. I bet he's dead."

"Thank you for your time, Caroline."

"If you want to find out if Tom's the father of that child, you could test Tom's dad's DNA. He's still alive."

"Tom's father's in prison, isn't he?"

"Yeah. He's innocent, by the way. My brother's in jail for a crime he didn't commit."

2

The next day Ruskin went to visit jurors number six, eight, and nine. Olivia Villanueva, juror number six, wasn't home, and Ruskin taped a note to her front door asking her to call him.

Amalia Calderon, juror number eight, wasn't a suspect in any crime and she had never met Tom Dekker. She remembered both Robert Lochner and Paul Marston.

"Are you sure these guys were framed?" Amalia's husband asked Ruskin.

"You don't have to believe me, Mr. Calderon," Ruskin said. "But you know what they say: better safe than sorry."

Juror number nine, William Stevens, had separated from his wife three weeks ago and now lived with another woman.

"How old is she?" Ruskin asked Stevens's wife, Ashley.

"I don't know. He didn't tell me. Probably half his age."

"Do you have William's address?"

"No."

"Can you give me his phone number?"

"Sure."

Ashley told Ruskin Stevens's number. Then she asked, "Is he in some kind of trouble?" She didn't sound worried at all.

"No."

Ruskin called Stevens, and forty minutes later they met at a coffee shop in North Dallas. Stevens wasn't a suspect in any crime. His girlfriend's name was Helena and she was thirty-one. Stevens had first met her six months ago.

"Can you send me her picture?" Ruskin said.

"What do you need it for?"

"She might be Tom Dekker's accomplice."

Stevens texted Ruskin Helena's photo, and then the private investigator called Emma Marston.

"Hi, Emma. This is Hugh Ruskin. I work for John Laporte."

"Hi, Hugh. My husband's lawyer told me about you."

"I'm going to text you a picture. Tell me if this woman looks like Susan."

He forwarded Helena's photo to Emma.

"It's not Susan," Emma said.

"Okay." Ruskin hung up.

"What did she say?" Stevens asked.

"I need to show Helena's picture to Paul Marston. It might take a while."

"How long?"

"I'll try to do it this Saturday."

General population inmates in the Polunsky Unit were allowed visits only on Saturdays and Sundays.

"Should I stay away from Helena in the meantime?" Stevens asked.

"That's a good idea."

A few minutes after Ruskin got home, his phone rang. It was Ken Carollo.

"I emailed you Samantha Sheldon's picture and address," the cop said.

Chapter 60

1

Laporte was at the gym when Ruskin texted him William Stevens's girlfriend's photo.

"Are you going to show the picture to Paul Marston yourself, or do you want me to do it?" the private investigator asked.

"I want you to do it, Hugh."

"Okay."

Ten minutes later Laporte's phone rang again.

"Hi," a woman said. "Can I talk to John Laporte?"

"Speaking."

"My name's Angelica Vasquez. I'm Maria Vasquez's daughter. You sent her a letter a few days ago."

Maria Vasquez was juror number ten, who had moved to Seattle five years ago.

"Thank you for calling, Angelica," Laporte said. "Did Maria live in Dallas County seven years ago?"

"Yes."

"Did she serve on the jury at a criminal trial seven years ago?"

"Yes."

"Can I talk to her?"

"She died in a car crash a year ago."

Had Dekker murdered Maria Vasquez and made it look like a car crash?

"I'm sorry to hear that. How did it happen?"

"A pickup truck crashed into her car. The pickup truck driver was drunk."

"Is the truck driver in jail?"

"Yes."

"Where did the crash take place?"

"In Seattle. Why did you want my mother to contact you?"

"I'm gathering information about the trial. Again, thank you for calling me, Angelica."

Laporte did an Internet search for the car crash Maria Vasquez had died in and found that it had taken place in September of last year and that the driver of the pickup truck that ran into Maria's vehicle had been sentenced to ten years in prison.

Laporte called Jonah Wallach and told him that they had found juror number ten.

"She died in a car crash a year ago in Seattle."

"Do you think it might have been Dekker's doing?" Wallach asked.

"No. It was a drunk driving accident. The driver that killed her is in jail."

2

Whose picture had Ruskin sent her? Was that woman a relative of Tom Dekker's? Was she his cousin?

Emma opened Ruskin's text and typed a message: "Who is that woman?"

When she tapped Send, her phone rang. The caller ID said Hugh Ruskin.

"I'm going to text you another picture," the private investigator said. "Tell me if you recognize her."

The picture arrived a few moments later. When Emma saw it, her heart sped up.

It was Susan. The photo had been taken at least five years ago.

"Do you recognize her?" Ruskin asked.

"Yes. It's Susan."

"She's Owen Dekker's niece."

Now there was no doubt that Paul had been framed by Owen Dekker's family.

"Do you know where she lives?"

"She lives in Jacksonville. I got her address from the Florida DMV. I'm going to check it out tomorrow."

Tom Dekker might be staying at his cousin's place.

"What's her name?"

"Samantha Sheldon."

"She's Caroline Kleparski's daughter, right?"

"Yes."

Caroline Kleparski believed that her brother was innocent. Did she know that her daughter was helping Tom Dekker avenge his father? Was she helping Tom, too?

"Maybe I should come with you?" Emma said.

"Let me see if she still lives at that address."

"Okay."

Emma called Wallach and told him that Caroline Kleparski's daughter was "Susan."

"I'm sure she knows where Tom Dekker is," she said.

"Let's hope she testifies against him."

She called Laporte a few minutes later.

"Has Hugh told you that we found Susan?" she asked.

"Yes."

"I'm going to start raising money for the reward."

"We'll do the same. Hugh's going to visit Paul this Saturday. He'll tell him that we found Susan."

Chapter 61

1

Reece unlocked the door to his apartment, stepped aside, and let Laurie enter first. In the living room, he kissed her and said, "I'll take a shower."

They had had a few drinks at a downtown bar and were tipsy. Reece's eyes shone with lust; he couldn't wait to have sex with Laurie.

"Okay." Laurie (Reece knew her as Rebecca) grabbed the remote from the coffee table and switched on the TV.

Reece went into the bathroom, and a minute later Laurie heard him turn on the shower.

Everything was going according to plan.

They had thought of framing Reece Edgehill, juror number seven, for murder but then decided to change things up a bit. She opened Reece's laptop, which sat on the coffee table, and typed in the password (she had watched Reece enter it twice before; it was simple and easy to remember: montana). The desktop appeared on the screen. Laurie took a thumb drive from her pocket, plugged it into the laptop, and then opened the file browser. The thumb drive contained fifty-one child porn pictures, five child porn videos (unfortunately, they had been unable to find more), as well as a computer virus that was going to cause Reece's laptop to freeze, thus making him take it to a repair shop. Laurie copied the folder with the child porn files (it was named "Young") to the My Documents folder and then closed the laptop.

There were many cases when repair shop technicians found child porn on their customers' computers and contacted the police, who then arrested the owners of the devices for child porn possession. They hoped the guy fixing Reece's laptop would stumble upon the child porn files planted by Laurie.

Even if Reece took a plea deal, he would get at least five years in prison, and he would have to register as a sex offender for life. His life would be completely ruined. But he should be glad he wasn't going to spend decades in jail, like Paul Marston, Robert Lochner, and Dennis Almanza.

When she heard the shower stop, Laurie took off her shirt and jeans.

She had first had sex with Reece three weeks ago, while she was still sleeping with Dennis Almanza. He wasn't good looking, but he had a decent body, which made sex with him tolerable.

Tom didn't mind her having sex with Edgehill, Almanza, and Marston. It was actually him who had suggested that she seduce the men.

"Baby, you're so hot," Reece said as he came in. He was wearing only a towel around his waist. "You want to do it here or in the bedroom?"

"The bedroom." Laurie kissed him on the lips and then pulled off his towel.

Chapter 62

1

"Thank you for coming, Detective," Laporte said.

"You're welcome." Ferland looked at Robert, who was sitting next to his lawyer.

"I know who set me up," Robert said.

"Who was it?" the detective asked in a disinterested tone.

Robert told Ferland about Owen and Tom Dekker and Paul Marston.

"Talk to Paul Marston, if you don't believe my client," Laporte said. "He's a former assistant district attorney. He used to be one of you. He's trustworthy."

Ferland leaned back in his chair and folded his arms across his chest. "Has he been tried yet?"

"He took an Alford plea."

"So he's a convicted felon."

"He was framed by Tom Dekker."

Robert said, "Tom Dekker has an accomplice, his cousin. Her name's Samantha Sheldon. She helped Dekker frame Marston. You need to look into her."

"Do you have any evidence that Dekker framed Marston or you?"

"You need to find Tom Dekker, Detective. He's murdered at least two people, and he's going to kill again."

"I guess you don't have any evidence."

Laporte said, "Dekker might kill the judge that presided over his trial, and if that happens, I'll tell your boss that I warned you about him, but you ignored me."

Ferland stared at him for a moment. "What's the judge's name?"

"Andrew Hollenbeck."

"Who was the lead detective on Marston's case?"

"Adam Korbin. Don't question Owen Dekker about this. He'll tell his son that the cops are on to him."

"You said I need to find Tom Dekker. Is he in hiding?"

"Yes."

2

Ruskin arrived in Jacksonville at one p.m. He picked up a rental car at the airport, bought a box of energy bars and a case of bottled water at a convenience store, and then drove to Samantha Sheldon's place. Tom Dekker's cousin lived in an apartment complex west of the St. Johns River called Pinebrook Pointe. When Ruskin got there, he found that Samantha's building couldn't be seen from the street.

He rang Samantha's doorbell. There was no answer. Ruskin figured she might be at work. He stuck a small piece of paper between the door and the jamb and then placed a motion-activated spy camera (it was hidden inside a fake rock) about ten feet from the staircase leading to Samantha's apartment. The camera allowed you to view footage from anywhere in the world over the Internet. Every Wi-Fi network in Samantha's building was password protected, but that was no problem: the camera could connect to the World Wide Web via a SIM card.

Two hours passed before someone climbed the staircase. It was a woman in her thirties, who didn't look like Samantha Sheldon. Ruskin waited half an hour and went back to Samantha's apartment. Again no one was home. The piece of paper was still where he had put it.

At six o'clock a man in his thirties ascended the staircase. Ruskin checked Samantha's place twenty minutes later. No one was home, and the piece of paper was still between the door and the jamb.

Ruskin drove to a nearby hotel and got a room. He returned to Samantha's apartment at nine. No one answered the door, the piece of paper was still in its original place.

Was Samantha with Tom Dekker?

Ruskin went back to the hotel. When he watched the surveillance footage the next morning, he saw that no one had gone up the staircase to Samantha's apartment while he was asleep.

At one-thirty, Ruskin received an email from his friend Ed Rivenbark, who worked at the Correctional Institutions Division of the Texas Department of Criminal Justice. In his message Rivenbark informed Ruskin that two people had visited

Owen Dekker in prison after February of last year—his sister and his second ex-wife (perhaps she still had feelings for him). Caroline Kleparski had visited Dekker three times: on March 16 and December 21 of last year and July 18 of this year; and Louise O'Shea twice: on June 15 of last year and May 23 of this year. The last time Tom Dekker had visited his father was on December 4 of the year before last. Ruskin forwarded the email to Laporte.

Samantha Sheldon was on Owen Dekker's approved visitor list; she had last visited him two years ago. She might visit Owen again this year, to update him on their revenge campaign, for example. She would probably call the prison before leaving for Huntsville to confirm that Owen had visitation privileges.

Ruskin dialed Rivenbark's number. His friend picked up on the second ring.

"Thank you for the information, Ed," Ruskin said.

"You're welcome, buddy."

"Can you do me another favor?"

"Sure."

"I think this guy's niece is going to visit him soon. She'll probably call the unit the day before the visit. Can you ask the guys in Huntsville to let you know when she calls them?"

"Yes. I'll call you as soon as I hear from them. What's the niece's name?"

"Samantha Sheldon. Thank you, man."

Ruskin checked Samantha's place again at six p.m. No one was home, and the piece of paper was still stuck between the door and the jamb. Ruskin rang the bell of the apartment across from Samantha's. A young woman opened the door.

"Hi. I'm looking for your neighbor." He pointed at Samantha's door. "When was the last time you saw her?"

"Maybe a few weeks ago."

"I'm looking for Samantha. Your neighbor's name's Samantha, right?"

"I think so."

"Thank you very much."

Ruskin called Laporte and asked how long he wanted him to wait for Samantha Sheldon.

"I think she's with Dekker," he said.

"How long does the camera's battery last?"

"At least a month on standby."

"Leave the camera and come back to Dallas."

"Okay."

Chapter 63

1

Reece never opened email attachments from strangers, so when his laptop froze, he figured it had caught a virus from one of the porn sites he had visited (most likely from the bestiality ones. He wasn't into bestiality, by the way; he was just curious, and there was nothing wrong with that).

Reece took his laptop to a computer repair shop named Hi-Tek Solutions, where the clerk ran a diagnostic test and told him to call tomorrow.

When Reece phoned the shop the next afternoon, the clerk told him that his laptop had been fixed. Reece breathed a sigh of relief.

He arrived at the shop at a quarter to seven.

"I'm here to pick up my laptop." Reece put the receipt on the counter.

The clerk grabbed the receipt, looked at it, and said, "Just a moment."

He disappeared through the door behind the counter and came back with Reece's laptop half a minute later.

"I want to test it," Reece said as the clerk set the laptop on the counter.

"Sure." The clerk opened the laptop and turned it on.

Reece ran some of his most often used programs, then closed them and shut down his laptop.

"Thank you very much, bro." He paid the bill and left the shop.

2

Benjamin Oglesby called Laporte at two that afternoon.

"Did you live in Dallas County seven years ago?" Laporte asked him.

"Yes."

"Did you serve on the jury at Owen Dekker's trial seven years ago?"

"I did serve on a jury seven years ago, but I don't remember who was on trial."

"Did you find the defendant guilty?"

"Yes."

Laporte told Oglesby about Tom Dekker and emailed him Dekker's and Samantha Sheldon's photos.

Oglesby wasn't a suspect in any crime and hadn't been questioned by the police in the last few months.

"If you see Tom Dekker or Samantha Sheldon, please call me," Laporte said.

"Okay. Thank you, Mr. Laporte."

"Have a nice day."

Laporte hung up and then sent Wallach a message saying that they had found juror number twelve.

Ruskin had spoken with Olivia Villanueva and Lawrence Turley, jurors number six and eleven, this morning (neither of them was a suspect in any crime), so they now had only two jurors left to warn: juror number one, Dennis Almanza, and juror number seven, Reece Edgehill.

Why hadn't Almanza and Edgehill responded yet? Had they been arrested?

Laporte opened Google and did a search for "Reece Edgehill arrested Houston." No relevant results were found. A search for "Reece Edgehill arrested" yielded no relevant results, either.

He got a lot of hits when he googled "Dennis Almanza arrested Los Angeles." He clicked on a Los Angeles Times story titled "Man charged with murder of 27-year-old woman." The article reported that a thirty-three-year-old Los Angeles resident named Dennis Almanza had been charged with the murder of Stephanie Jarvis, also a Los Angeles resident. The murder had taken place on July 25, and Almanza had been arrested three days later.

The Dennis Almanza who had served on the Owen Dekker jury was thirty-three, too.

"Oh my God," Laporte muttered as he stared at Almanza's photo in the LA Times article.

3

On Saturday, Ruskin drove to the Polunsky Unit and showed Paul Marston Helena's photograph. Marston didn't recognize her. Ruskin didn't tell him about the Los Angeles Dennis Almanza because Laporte wanted to make sure the guy was the right Dennis Almanza.

Before heading back to Dallas, the private investigator called William Stevens and delivered the good news that Helena wasn't Tom Dekker's accomplice.

Chapter 64

1

The police gave Hausler a sample of the semen found on Stephanie Jarvis's body a week after he made the request. The second DNA test produced the same results as the one done by the state crime lab: the semen belonged to Dennis.

Lisa had never returned Hausler's calls, which baffled Dennis to no end. She knew he was in jail and needed her help, so why wasn't she calling his lawyer back? Hausler had contacted every hospital in Los Angeles, Orange, and Riverside Counties; none of them had a patient named Lisa Wilson. Was she in a hospital in another part of California? Or maybe she didn't want to help him? Why didn't she want to help him? He had always treated her well, they had never had an argument.

Every time Dennis called Lisa, it went straight to voice mail. Was her cell always off? Had she blocked the jail's number?

When Dennis walked into the visitation room on Monday, August 17, he was hoping to see Lisa beyond the glass partition, but instead he found a man he'd never met before waiting for him there.

"Good morning, Dennis," the man said.

"Good morning."

"My name's John Laporte. I'm an attorney."

"I already have a lawyer."

"You've been charged with murder. You claim you're innocent."

"I am innocent."

"Were you set up?"

Dennis nodded. "I think so. That's the only explanation I can think of."

"What evidence do they have against you?"

"They found my semen on the victim's body. It's possible that whoever killed her found one of my used condoms in my garbage and planted the semen that was in it on her."

"Do you have any idea who might have framed you?"

"No."

"I think I know who set you up and how they obtained your semen."

Dennis raised his eyebrows. "Who was it?"

"Did you serve on a criminal jury in Dallas seven years ago?"

"Yes."

"Was the defendant's name Owen Dekker?"

"I think so."

"You were framed by his son, Tom."

It made sense. A son had taken revenge on one of the people who had sent his father to prison.

"Am I the only juror he framed?"

"No. He also framed Robert Lochner, he was the foreman. Mr. Lochner is my client."

"Was Robert framed for murder, too?"

"Yes. Tom Dekker also framed the lead prosecutor, Paul Marston."

"Also for murder?"

"Yes."

"You said you know how they got my semen."

"Do you have a girlfriend?"

"Yes."

"When did you first meet her?"

"About four months ago."

"What's her name?"

"Lisa."

"How old is she?"

"Twenty-six."

"Were you with her when the murder took place?"

"Yes."

"Did your lawyer try to contact her?"

"Yes. She never returned his calls."

Did Laporte think Lisa had helped Tom Dekker get his semen?

Was Lisa Tom Dekker's accomplice? Was that why she hadn't returned Hausler's calls?

"I believe Lisa provided Dekker with your semen." Laporte pulled out a photograph and showed it to Dennis. "Does she look like Lisa?"

It was Lisa's idea for him to send his DNA sample to My Family Tree.

She *was* Tom Dekker's accomplice.

"No."

Lisa had planted Stephanie Jarvis's blood on his shoe. She must have done it when she was at his place on the evening of July 26, the day after the murder (he hadn't seen her after July 26).

"Do you have Lisa's picture?"

Lisa thought she wasn't photogenic (at least that was what she told Dennis), so she didn't like being photographed. Dennis had only one picture of her, which he had taken without her knowing.

"Yes."

"Is it on your phone?"

"It's on my phone and my laptop."

The police had his cellphone, but his laptop was in his apartment.

"Did you post it on Facebook or anywhere else?"

"No. You can get it from my laptop. It's in my apartment. I'll give you the password."

"Okay."

Dennis told Laporte his laptop password and where Lisa's photo was stored.

"I texted the picture to my friend Brian Stokes a while ago," he said. "He might still have it."

Dennis gave Laporte Brian Stokes's address.

"Who has the key to your apartment?" Laporte asked.

"My parents. They're in Dallas. I'll ask them to mail the key to you."

"Have you ever been to Lisa's place?"

"No."

"Do you know her address?"

"No."

"What's her phone number?"

She had probably used a burner phone to communicate with him.

Dennis gave Laporte Lisa's number and then said, "Please tell my lawyer everything you told me."

"Sure. We're going to help you, Dennis."

"Thank you, John. Thank you so much."

2

Laporte called Wallach and told him that the Los Angeles Dennis Almanza was juror number one.

"It appears Julie was his girlfriend," he said. "She gave Dekker Dennis's semen, which he planted on the victim's body."

"Does Dennis have her picture?"

"Yes."

Then Laporte called Jeremy Hausler, and they agreed to meet at Hausler's office. He stopped by Brian Stokes's apartment, but no one answered the door.

After Laporte told him about the Dekkers' revenge campaign, Hausler asked him to be his co-counsel on Almanza's case, and the lawyer agreed.

"If you need any help with Robert Lochner's case, let me know," Hausler said.

While Laporte was talking with Hausler, Almanza's mother called him and asked where he wanted her to send the key to her son's apartment. Laporte told her to mail it to his hotel.

He checked Stokes's place again at six p.m. Almanza's friend was home.

"Dennis is innocent," Stokes said as he scrolled through the texts he'd received from Almanza. "Someone set him up."

He held up his phone, showing Laporte a photo of a young woman. The picture had been taken in a park. "Here it is. Do you want me to forward it to you?"

"Yes, please."

Chapter 65

1

Paul was lying in bed trying to fall asleep when he suddenly realized that one of the people who had visited him in the Dallas County jail had eyes similar to Tom Dekker's.

The guy's name was John Colter, he was a volunteer for the Innocence Initiative of Texas. Colter looked to be Dekker's age. He had a beard and mustache. Paul tried to picture Dekker with a beard and mustache.

Was John Colter Tom Dekker? Had Dekker come to gloat?

The bastard might visit him in the Polunsky Unit someday.

Paul reached under the mattress and pulled out an envelope containing photographs of Emma, Ollie, and Tom Dekker. He opened the envelope, took out Dekker's picture, and peered at his face.

It had been two months since Colter's visit, so he could be wrong about his eyes, but he didn't think so.

The next morning Paul called Wallach.

"I think Tom Dekker visited me two months ago in the county jail," he said. "He told me he was a volunteer for the Innocence Initiative of Texas. He called himself John Colter. Please call the Innocence Initiative and ask if they have a volunteer by that name."

"Okay. Do you want me to ask the jail for the security footage from the visitation room?"

"Yes."

2

Wallach looked up the Innocence Initiative of Texas on the Internet and found that their website's Contact Us page had an email address, but no phone number. The organization's office was located in Fort Worth. He sent the Innocence Initiative an email in which he introduced himself and asked if they had a volunteer named John Colter. Then he called the county jail and spoke to the guy in charge of security cameras, who told him that visitation room surveillance footage was stored for only thirty days.

Two hours later Wallach received a reply from the Innocence Initiative of Texas. They informed him that they did have a volunteer by the name of John Colter. Wallach emailed back asking for Colter's contact information, and the Innocence Initiative responded that they couldn't provide it for him.

At two p.m. Wallach entered the modest office of the Innocence Initiative of Texas in Fort Worth.

"I need to talk to the person in charge of volunteers," he told the receptionist.

"Just a moment." The receptionist left and came back a minute later with a short middle-aged woman wearing rimless glasses.

"Hi, I'm Kathryn Galecki," the woman said to Wallach, smiling.

"My name's Jonah Wallach."

"You emailed us today, didn't you?"

"Yes."

"Let's go to my office."

When they went into Galecki's office, she said, "You need the contact information of one of our volunteers, right?"

"Yes. His name's John Colter."

Galecki settled into her chair. "Why do you need his contact information?"

"Two months ago a man claiming to be a volunteer for your organization visited my client in jail. He said his name was John Colter. We believe he was involved in framing my client for murder."

"What's your client's name?"

"Paul Marston."

"Is he a lawyer?"

"Yes."

"He worked on some of our cases. Excellent lawyer. Was he convicted?"

"He took an Alford plea. Did you send Colter to visit Paul?"

"Let me see." Galecki turned to her computer and started hitting keys. Half a minute later she said, "No, we didn't send him."

"I need to talk to Colter. Maybe it wasn't him who visited Paul."

"What would you do it if it was him?"

"I'd ask him if he was involved in framing Paul."

Galecki glanced at the computer monitor. "We only have his email address and phone number."

"That's okay."

"How was Paul framed?"

"A murdered woman's blood was planted in the trunk of his car."

"And you think Colter might have planted it?"

"Yes. John Colter might not be his real name."

Galecki picked up a small notepad and pen and said, "Okay. I'll give you his contact information."

She wrote Colter's phone number and email address down on the notepad, tore off the sheet, and handed it to Wallach. "Call me after you talk to him."

"Sure."

As he rode the elevator down, Wallach dialed John Colter's number and his call went straight to voice mail. He left Colter a message asking him to call; he said it was about Paul Marston. Then Wallach sent Colter an email saying that he needed to talk to him about Paul Marston.

Chapter 66

1

Reece's text read: "Hey, wanna hang out this Friday?"

He had sent it two hours ago. If he was in jail, he wouldn't have been able to message her.

It had been a week since she had planted child porn files on Reece Edgehill's laptop and infected it with a virus. Why wasn't Reece in jail?

Perhaps he had been released on bail.

If Reece had been charged with child porn possession, he would have been severely depressed and sex would have been the last thing on his mind.

Why wasn't he charged with child porn possession? Did the technician not see the child porn files?

Maybe Reece hadn't taken his laptop to a repair shop yet. Maybe the virus hadn't worked. Or maybe Reece hadn't picked up his laptop from the shop yet.

Laurie texted back to Reece: "Sure," then pulled out her second disposable phone and called Tom.

"What's up, baby?" Tom said.

"Reece texted me two hours ago. He wants to hang out this Friday. I think the technician didn't see the files."

"Okay. We're going to plan B."

"Okay. Bye, honey."

"Bye, baby." Tom hung up.

Their plan B was to frame Reece Edgehill for murder.

Perhaps the universe wanted Reece to spend thirty years in prison and not five.

Laurie had no sympathy for Reece. The son of a bitch had had no sympathy for Owen Dekker, an innocent man who had happened to be in the wrong place at the wrong time. The case against Tom's father had been very weak, yet Reece had voted to convict him, along with eleven other morons. It only took one juror to prevent a guilty verdict. Reece could have been that juror, he could have saved Owen, but he hadn't. Robert Lochner could have saved Owen, Dennis Almanza could have saved him.

But they hadn't. Every single person on that jury deserved to be punished.

They had no doubt that Owen Dekker was innocent. He had had no motive to kill that man. The police had said that Owen had murdered him because he had slept with his wife, but the truth was that the guy had never had sex with Louise Dekker. He had made advances to her, but Louise had turned him down, and then he had started spreading rumors that he had slept with her.

The police had been right about only one thing: Owen had been at the victim's house around the time of the murder. But the man had already been dead when Owen got there (he hadn't called the police because he was afraid they would pin the crime on him, which they did). Owen believed that the murder had been committed by a burglar.

There was a popular saying: It's better that ten guilty go free than one innocent be convicted. Tom had a theory about why jurors did not, and would not, follow this wonderful doctrine.

A guilty verdict pleases thousands, if not millions, of people, who think that evil has been punished. On the other hand, when someone is acquitted, only a handful of folks are usually happy: the guy who went free and his family and friends. Humans tend to want to please others, so jurors prefer the option that results in the highest number of satisfied people.

2

On Tuesday, Laporte visited Dennis Almanza again to show him the photo he had gotten from Brian Stokes. Almanza confirmed that it was Lisa's picture.

On Wednesday, Wallach went to the Polunsky Unit and told Paul Marston about Dennis Almanza. When Marston saw Lisa's photo, his eyes widened, and he said, "Yes, it's Julie."

Laporte emailed Julie's photo to Judge Hollenbeck, Mark Ketteridge, and the jurors and asked them to contact him if they saw her. He received the key to Almanza's apartment that same day, and he gave it to Hausler.

Chapter 67

1

On Thursday, August 20, Ruskin went to Houston to look for a debtor of one of his agency's clients. After he found the guy and served him with a summons, he drove to Reece Edgehill's place: juror number seven still hadn't contacted them. This time he entered through the exit gate after a car drove out.

His note was gone. No one answered when Ruskin rang the doorbell.

He left another note asking Edgehill to call him and then found the Windsor Park homeowners association office. An employee named Aubrey asked if she could help him, and Ruskin told her that he was trying to reach one of their residents.

"His name's Reece Edgehill. He lives in apartment one-twenty-seven. Could you give me his phone number?"

Aubrey consulted her computer and asked, "Why are you trying to reach him?"

"I have important information for him."

"Just a moment." Aubrey rose from her desk and walked into the manager's office. She came out about a minute later, followed by a short dark-haired woman in her fifties.

"Hi, I'm Jane," the dark-haired woman said to Ruskin. "I'm the manager."

"My name's Hugh Ruskin."

"Are you Mr. Edgehill's friend?"

"I'm a private investigator. I have important information for Mr. Edgehill."

"I'm afraid we can't give you his phone number."

"It's an urgent matter. I need to talk to him today."

"I can call him and ask him to call you."

"Okay." Ruskin took out his business card and handed it to Jane. "Thank you very much."

He drove to Samantha Sheldon's apartment and found that the piece of paper he had stuck between the door and the jamb was still there.

Ruskin went back to Edgehill's place at seven p.m., but again no one was home.

2

Laurie and Reece had dinner at an Outback Steakhouse that Friday evening. Reece kept refilling her glass with wine, probably worried that she wouldn't have sex with him if she was sober. They stayed at the restaurant until nine and then went to Reece's place.

Reece's laptop sat on the coffee table in the living room. Laurie logged into it while Reece was in the shower, and found that the virus had been removed. Reece had had his laptop fixed, which meant that the virus had worked. The next time they planted child porn on a juror's computer, they would have to make the files very easy to stumble upon. Laurie deleted the folder with the child porn files and closed the laptop.

"Have you ever had a threesome?" Laurie asked as Reece pulled off her panties in the bedroom.

"No. Have you?" Reece looked at her with keen interest.

Laurie shook her head. "Do you know any women who'd be interested in a threesome?"

"Do you want me to ask?"

"Yes. But not tonight. Let's do it tomorrow."

Reece grinned. "Okay. Have you ever had sex with a woman?"

"Yes."

That was true: she had fooled around with a lesbian classmate when she was in college. It had been fun and she had liked it, but she hadn't loved it.

"Nice." Reece leaned over Laurie and sucked her nipple into his mouth.

Chapter 68

1

"Did they find Dekker's cousin?" Paul asked.

Emma shook her head. "Not yet."

"Did they check Julie's phone records?"

"Yes. It's a disposable phone. She used it only to talk to Dennis."

Lisa/Julie's cellphone had been activated on April 24. It had been off since July 29, the day after Almanza's arrest.

"How much money have you and Robert raised so far?"

"Five hundred thousand. Laporte thinks it'll be enough."

Emma had taken out a loan of a hundred and fifty thousand dollars using their house as collateral. Paul's parents had raised a hundred thousand. Robert Lochner was going to contribute two hundred and fifty thousand.

Paul looked at her for a long moment, then said, "Thank you for not leaving me, Emma. I love you so much."

"I love you, too, honey."

In the beginning, you thought Paul was a murderer, didn't you?

A pang of guilt pierced Emma.

Had Tom Dekker ever doubted his father's innocence?

Laporte had told Emma that Isaac Hemphill, the victim in Dekker's case, had been murdered in his house. The killer had hit him on the head with an ashtray and then stabbed him in the chest. The case against Owen Dekker had been based on two pieces of evidence: hours before the murder Owen left Hemphill a voice mail threatening to kill him if he ever talked to his wife again; a witness saw Owen leave Hemphill's house around the time of the murder. Owen had had no alibi.

It had probably been easy for Owen to convince his son that he was innocent. He might have told Tom that the witness had been wrong, or that the victim had already been dead when he entered the house.

How would she have voted if she had been on the Dekker jury? If those two pieces of evidence had been all they had had against Dekker, she would probably have voted not guilty. It was better to let ten guilty go free than to punish one innocent.

What if Owen Dekker was innocent? The police had alleged that Owen had made Hemphill's murder look like a burglary gone wrong. Maybe Isaac Hemphill had really been killed by a burglar?

"I think we'll find Dekker's cousin soon," Paul said. "Maybe within a few weeks."

He could be right. Samantha Sheldon would return to her apartment in Jacksonville sooner or later, and when she did, Emma would be one of the first to know: Ruskin had given her access to the video feed from the hidden camera monitoring the staircase to Sheldon's apartment, and she checked the footage several times a day.

"I hope we catch her and Dekker in the act."

"That would be great."

Chapter 69

1

Laurie was sitting in a café in West Houston when Reece called her.

"Where are you?" Reece asked.

"I'm at the coffee shop."

Laurie glanced at her watch. It was five past nine. When had Reece woken up? Was she the first person he had called after he woke up?

"When did you leave my apartment?"

"Around eleven."

"Eleven p.m.?"

"Yes. Is Heidi still at your place?"

Heidi was the woman who had joined Laurie and Reece in a threesome last night. She was in her early thirties, with a cute face and a good body. She was dead now.

"No. Did you let anyone in after I fell asleep?"

"No. Is everything okay?"

"Yes."

"Did Heidi steal something?"

"No. Everything's fine. Bye." Reece hung up.

Laurie pulled out her other disposable phone and called Samantha, who was at a coffee shop two miles from Reece's place.

"Call the police," Laurie said.

"Okay."

Samantha threw her cup in the trash can by the door, walked out of the coffee shop, and went to the supermarket across the street. The store had surveillance cameras, so she was wearing dark sunglasses to hide her face. She dialed 911 from a payphone outside the supermarket and told the operator that someone had been stabbed in her neighbor's apartment. She changed her voice a little, just in case.

"There's blood near his door," Samantha said. "Please send the police to check."

She told the operator Reece's name and address.

"Please hurry. Maybe someone was murdered in there."

"I'll send someone right away."

"Thank you."

They figured that drops of blood near Reece Edgehill's apartment door would give the police probable cause to enter his residence (they doubted Reece would let the cops in voluntarily), but it was possible that the responding officers would leave him alone. If Reece wasn't arrested today, they would make an anonymous call to the police tomorrow or the day after and tell them he had murdered Heidi.

Reece had two options: he could either call the cops and tell them about Heidi's murder or get rid of her body and not contact the police. He might succeed in removing the body from his apartment, but no matter how thoroughly he cleaned his place, the cops would surely find traces of Heidi's blood there.

Samantha returned to the coffee shop and called Tom. He told her he would pick her up after he picked up Laurie.

2

Reece woke up on the couch in the living room, wearing only his boxers. The sun was shining outside. As he sat up, he saw Heidi lying on the floor between the coffee table and the television set. She was naked and covered with blood.

Reece sprang up, his heart hammering. Heidi's throat had been slashed, there were two stab wounds in her abdomen.

Who had killed her?

Reece shuffled over to the body and stared at it.

What the hell happened last night?

The tequila bottle was empty.

Had he gotten drunk and blacked out? He had never blacked out before.

Who had murdered Heidi?

Where was Rebecca? Was she dead, too?

"Rebecca," he called out.

No answer.

The kitchen was empty. A kitchen knife lay on the counter by the sink. It looked like one of Reece's. He didn't remember putting it there. Had it been used to kill Heidi?

Reece went into the bedroom. It was empty, he saw no bloodstains. His and Heidi's clothes lay on the floor beside the bed. Reece opened the closet. Rebecca wasn't there.

"Rebecca, where are you?"

She wasn't in the bathroom, either.

Reece poured a glass of tap water in the kitchen and drank half of it.

Where was Rebecca? Had Heidi's killer taken her?

Had she left before Heidi was murdered?

He picked up the knife and examined it. The knife was clean. He would throw it away, just in case.

He needed to inspect the furniture and the walls in the living room: there might be bloodstains on them.

Who had murdered Heidi?

Did I kill her?

Could he have forgotten killing Heidi? Could it be a weird case of amnesia?

Had Rebecca killed Heidi?

Why would she do it?

Reece pulled out a chair and sat down at the kitchen table.

What should he do?

Should he call the police? They would pin Heidi's murder on him, no doubt about it. How would he prove that he hadn't killed her?

No one would believe that Rebecca or someone else had murdered Heidi.

I could get rid of her body.

He could put the corpse in a trunk and then dump it on the outskirts of Houston. He didn't have a trunk, but he could buy one. The condo complex had no security cameras, so there would be no footage of him moving the trunk out of his apartment.

Heidi might have told someone that she was going to his place.

The police might question him about Heidi, but they had no reason to suspect that he had murdered her.

What if a cop pulls me over and asks me to open the trunk? It's unlikely, but possible.

What if someone sees me dumping the body?

His DNA might be on Heidi's body.

He would wash the corpse.

He might have had sex with Heidi without a condom and left his DNA inside her. He would wash Heidi's vagina.

Heidi's car. He would have to move it a few miles away from the condo complex.

Heidi drove a gray Honda Accord. Hopefully, she had parked it not far from the entrance.

What if she had gotten a new car?

Reece went into the bedroom, took the keys from the pocket of Heidi's jeans, and was relieved to see a well-used Honda key fob on the key ring.

He would have to replace the carpet in the living room.

Reece sat down on the bed.

He couldn't get rid of the body now. He had to wait until it was dark.

He should call Phil and ask for advice. Phil Pardue was a criminal lawyer. They had been friends for five years and Reece trusted him.

But first he needed to call Rebecca.

Reece dialed Rebecca's number, and she answered. She didn't know Heidi was dead. She sounded calm; she didn't seem to be in any danger.

Reece drank some more water and then called Pardue.

"Hi, Reece," Pardue said.

"Hi, Phil. Are you busy?"

"No."

"If I hire you as my lawyer, anything I tell you will be protected by the attorney-client privilege, right?"

"The attorney-client privilege protects communications made to obtain legal advice. Do you want to ask me for legal advice?"

"Yes."

"Then everything you tell me will be confidential."

"I'm hiring you as my lawyer, Phil."

"Okay. So what's the problem?"

"Someone... Someone was killed in my apartment last night. I have no idea who did it. It wasn't me."

"Who was killed?"

"Someone I know."

"Is it a man or a woman?"

"A woman."

"How was she killed?"

"Stabbed to death."

"Don't touch the body. Don't touch anything."

"Okay."

"You have to call the police."

"They're going to arrest me. They're going to pin this on me."

"You have to call them, Reece."

"What should I tell them?"

"Don't talk to them until I get there."

"How long will it take you to get here?"

"About twenty-five minutes."

"I'll call the police when you get here."

"Okay."

Ten minutes later Reece's doorbell rang. He wondered how Pardue had managed to get here so quickly.

Maybe it wasn't Pardue.

When he looked through the peephole, Reece saw a cop. He felt his stomach drop. Why was the cop here?

Did Pardue call the police?

The doorbell rang again, and then the cop said, "This is the police. Open the door."

He was not required to open the door.

The cop could break it down.

Why would he break it down? He didn't have a warrant.

The cop banged on the door and shouted, "This is the police! Open the door!"

He could open the door and tell the policeman to leave. The cop wouldn't see Heidi's body because Reece had moved it to the corner of the room.

Reece unlocked the door and opened it. "How can I help you?"

The cop was pointing his gun at Reece. His partner stood at the top of the staircase, his pistol also aimed at Reece.

"Show me your hands," the cop ordered.

Reece opened the door wider and raised his hands to shoulder level, palms out.

"I'm Officer Beverson with the Houston Police Department. Is this your apartment?"

"Yes."

"What's your name?"

"Reece Edgehill." Reece swallowed hard.

"Are you alone?"

"Yes."

Beverson peered inside. "Can we come in?"

"Why?"

"There's blood near your door. Was someone stabbed in your apartment?"

Reece looked down and saw that there were small red stains on and near the doormat.

Was it Heidi's blood?

"It's not blood," he said.

"Can we come in, Mr. Edgehill? Just to make sure everything's okay."

The cops' pistols were still pointed at Reece.

"No," Reece said. "You can't come in. Please leave."

"We have probable cause, sir. We don't need your permission."

"My lawyer will be here in a few minutes. I'll let you in when he gets here."

"Please step outside, sir."

"Okay, I'll do it. But I'm not giving you permission to enter my apartment."

"Don't step on the blood."

Without putting his shoes on, Reece stepped out of his apartment and closed the door. Beverson patted him down with one hand and then asked, "When did you call your lawyer?"

"Fifteen minutes ago."

Beverson's partner took his radio off his belt and requested backup.

"What happened?" Beverson asked Reece. "Did someone get hurt?"

"Nothing happened."

"Then why did you call the lawyer?"

"We're friends. I invited him for a drink."

"Whose blood is this?"

"It's not blood."

"Is there someone else in your apartment?"

"No."

A middle-aged woman passing by stopped to gawk at Reece and the cops.

"We'll have a warrant within an hour."

"Okay."

Two more police officers showed up a few minutes later. Beverson explained the situation to them, and then they examined the red stains near Reece's door.

"Are you sure your lawyer's coming?" Beverson asked Reece.

"Yes."

"What's his name?"

"Phil Pardue."

Would he get bail? Would he be able to afford it?

Was he facing the death penalty?

"Reece!"

He looked past Beverson and saw Pardue hurrying toward the staircase to his apartment.

"Is that your lawyer?" Beverson asked Reece.

"Yes."

"I'm Mr. Edgehill's attorney," Pardue announced as he climbed the steps.

"I'm Officer Beverson with the Houston Police Department," Beverson told the lawyer. "Mr. Edgehill said he would let us into his apartment when you got here."

Pardue asked Reece, "Did you call the police?"

"No."

"Who called them?"

"I don't know."

Beverson said to Pardue, "There's blood near the door. Don't step on it."

Pardue glanced at the red stains. "Okay."

"Should I let them in?" Reece asked him.

Pardue nodded. "Yes. Don't say anything to them."

His heart thundering in his chest, Reece opened the door and said to Beverson, "You can come in."

Chapter 70

1

Wallach had just gotten off the phone with Victor Hopper, who had told the lawyer that he was leaving for Houston, when his cell rang.

"Hello," Wallach said.

"Hi. Is this Jonah Wallach?" a man said.

"Yes."

"This is John Colter. You left me a message a few days ago. I'm sorry I didn't call you back sooner. I just checked my messages."

"Thank you for returning my call, Mr. Colter. How are you doing?"

"I'm fine."

"I'm Paul Marston's attorney. He told me you visited him in the Dallas County jail two months ago."

"Yes, I visited Paul. I feel so sorry for him. I think he's innocent."

"He said that you offered to help him prove his innocence."

"Yeah."

"Could we meet for coffee today or tomorrow? I want to talk to you about Paul's case."

"I'm out of town right now. I'll be back in three weeks."

"I'll give you a call in three weeks."

"Okay."

Was Colter Tom Dekker? Would the guy meet him in three weeks?

2

It was one in the afternoon when Laurie, Samantha, and Tom arrived in Dallas. They bought two pizzas and a bottle of red wine to celebrate framing Reece Edgehill. After eating two slices of pizza, Samantha stepped out onto the porch and called her mother.

"Hi, Mom," Samantha said.

"Hi, honey. How are you?"

"I'm fine. And you?"

"I'm fine, too."

"How's your back?"

"It's all right. Sarah and I are going to Vegas in three weeks. Do you want to come with us?"

"I'll think about it."

"We're going to stay at Treasure Island. It's a great hotel."

"I'll let you know in a week."

"Okay. A private investigator came to my house two weeks ago."

"What did he want?"

"He's looking for Tom."

"Uncle Owen's Tom?"

"Yes."

"Why is he looking for him?"

"His client thinks that Tom might be the father of her child. He asked me for your address and phone number. He thinks you might know where Tom is."

"Did you tell him Tom's missing?"

"Yes."

"Did you give him my address and number?"

"No."

"What's his name?"

"Hugh Ruskin."

"Did he tell you his client's name?"

"No. I wonder if it really is Tom's child. By the way, when are you going to give me a grandchild, Sam? You're not getting any younger, you know."

"Soon, Mom. I promise."

"Don't wait too long."

"I have to go, Mom."

"Okay. Bye, honey."

"Bye."

Samantha went back inside and asked Tom, "Do you have any other children besides Brent?"

"No," Tom said. "Why?"

"A private investigator is looking for you. He talked to my mom two weeks ago. He told her his client thinks that you might be the father of her child."

"What's his client's name?"

"He didn't tell my mom her name."

"Is it a boy or a girl?"

"I think he works for one of the guys we set up. I think one of them figured it out."

"Figured what out?" Laurie asked.

"That I set him up." Tom frowned.

"The trial was seven years ago," Laurie said. "You have to be Sherlock Holmes to figure it out."

Tom said, "They're probably going to warn the other jurors."

Samantha nodded. "Yeah."

"I guess we'll have to pause for a few months. Maybe a year."

They had framed three jurors and one juror had died in a car crash, so they had eight jurors left to punish.

Tom was upset that he had to postpone framing his next target, but on the other hand, he was glad that Marston, Lochner, Almanza, and Edgehill knew or would soon know *why* they had been set up.

"A year is better," Samantha said.

"What's the private investigator's name?" Tom asked.

"Hugh Ruskin."

Two months ago, he had visited Paul Marston in jail under the name of John Colter. Now Marston's lawyer wanted to meet "John Colter."

Had Marston figured out that John Colter might be Tom Dekker? Did Ruskin work for Marston?

"I think it's Marston who figured it out," Tom said.

He went into the bedroom, took a new burner phone from his bag, activated it, and called his friend Charlie Chao. Chao lived in Fort Worth and was a small-time criminal. Tom had paid him a thousand dollars to sign the lease of the house where Paul Marston and Laurie's trysts took place. Chao hadn't asked why he had to use a fake driver's license and what Tom needed the house for.

"Did anyone ask you about that house?" Tom said.

"No."

"If anyone asks you about it, tell them it wasn't you."

"Sure."

When he hung up, Samantha asked him, "Are you going to call Eva?"

Eva was an acquaintance of Tom's, who lived in the Dallas suburb of Irving. She was the woman Emma Marston had seen get into the trunk of what she thought was her husband's car (he had kidnapped Alison Bowles four hours before Samantha and Emma started tailing him). Tom had told her that the kidnapping was a prank.

"No," Tom said. "They'll never figure out that the kidnapping was staged."

Chapter 71

1

"How did you know Heidi?" Pardue asked.

"She was a friend of mine." Reece took a swig of water.

They were in an attorney conference room of Houston Central Jail. It had been five hours since Reece's arrest.

Homicide detectives had wanted to question him, but he had invoked his right to remain silent and refused to talk to them.

"Did you have sex with her last night?"

"I don't remember. Maybe. We were going to have a threesome."

"Who was the third person?"

"A friend of mine. Her name's Rebecca."

"You have no idea who killed Heidi?"

"None. We had some drinks, and I must have gotten drunk and passed out. When I woke up this morning, Heidi was dead. I have no idea what happened, but I know I didn't kill her."

"Was Rebecca at your apartment when you woke up?"

"No. She left around eleven last night."

"Did you talk to her today?"

"Yes. But I didn't tell her that Heidi's dead."

"How long did you know Heidi?"

"About three years."

"Did you ever date her?"

"Not really. We kept it casual."

"Did you have sex with Rebecca last night?"

"I don't remember."

"Did you ever date Rebecca?"

Reece shook his head. "We keep it casual."

"How long have you known her?"

"About a month."

"What time did you pass out?"

"I don't know. Probably before eleven."

"You passed out before Rebecca left?"

"Yes."

"What time did Heidi and Rebecca come to your place last night?"

"Heidi came around nine and Rebecca around half past eight."

"Who do you think killed Heidi?"

"I think she let someone in after Rebecca left, and that guy killed her. It was probably someone she knew."

"What about Rebecca? Could she be the killer?"

"I don't think so. Why would she kill Heidi?"

"What's Rebecca's last name?"

"I think it's Madison."

"Do you know her address?"

"No."

"What's her phone number?"

Reece told Pardue Rebecca's number and then asked, "Do you know what time Heidi was killed?"

"They say she died between eleven p.m. and midnight."

"Should I tell the cops about Rebecca?"

"Let me do all the talking, Reece. Don't say a word to anyone."

"Are you going to tell them about Rebecca?"

"Yes."

"Are you going to tell them that we were going to have a threesome?"

"No."

2

Pardue called Rebecca and left a message asking her to call him. The next morning he told the lead investigator in Edgehill's case, Detective Patrick Craven, that Reece had passed out before Heidi was killed and that Rebecca Madison had been at Reece's place on the night of the murder.

"She might have killed Heidi out of jealousy," the lawyer said.

Pardue also told Craven that Heidi might have let her killer into the apartment and that she might have known him or her.

Four hours later Craven called Pardue.

"We checked Heidi Monger's phone records," the detective said. "She didn't receive or make any calls after she got to Edgehill's place. She didn't text anyone, either."

"So?"

"You said she might have let her killer in. She didn't contact anyone and no one contacted her after she arrived at Edgehill's apartment. How did the killer know where she was?"

"She might have told the killer where she was going before she left for Mr. Edgehill's apartment. Also, it's possible that the killer was a stranger."

Chapter 72

1

The judge set Reece's bail at fifty thousand dollars. He put up his condo as collateral and was released later that day. He stopped at a cell phone store and bought a new phone with a new number: his old cell had been seized by the police as evidence. His apartment was taped off as a crime scene, so he checked into a motel about two miles from his place. He took a shower and then called Pardue to give him his new phone number.

"They found your semen on Heidi's body," the lawyer told him. "One of your kitchen knives has traces of her blood on it. They believe it's the murder weapon."

"Do they consider Rebecca a suspect?"

"I don't know. By the way, I can't reach her. She's not returning my calls."

Why wasn't Rebecca calling Pardue back?

Maybe she was the killer?

Reece called Rebecca and left a message saying he had gotten a new phone number and asking her to call him.

On Tuesday afternoon, Pardue called Reece and asked him to come to his office. Reece wondered what this was about. Had Pardue figured out a way to prove his innocence?

When he entered Pardue's office, Reece saw a man sitting in a chair in front of the lawyer's desk. He was wearing a dark suit and tie. There was a briefcase on the floor beside him.

"This is John Laporte," Pardue told Reece. "He's an attorney from Dallas."

"Nice to meet you, John." Reece shook Laporte's hand.

"Did you serve on a criminal jury in Dallas County seven years ago?" Pardue asked Reece.

"Yes."

Laporte said, "I believe you were framed, Reece."

"Framed?"

"And I know who did it."

"Who framed me?"

"The son of the man the jury you were on convicted seven years ago. His name's Tom Dekker. He framed three other people before you: two jurors and the lead prosecutor."

Laporte took two photographs from his briefcase and put them in front of Reece. "Do you recognize either of these women?"

One of the women was Rebecca; Reece didn't recognize the other one.

Reece pointed at Rebecca's picture. "I know her. She's a friend of mine. Her name's Rebecca."

"She's Tom Dekker's partner. She helped him frame one of the jurors and the prosecutor."

"Do you know where she lives?"

"No."

"Did they let the three people Dekker had framed out of prison?"

"No. We have no proof they were set up."

Reece pointed at the second photo. "Is she Dekker's partner, too?"

"Yes. Two weeks ago I wrote you a letter asking you to contact me. Did you receive it?"

"Yeah, I received it. I wish I'd called you." Reece sighed.

Laporte took another photograph from his briefcase and handed it to Reece. "This is Tom Dekker. The picture's fifteen years old. Have you ever met him?"

"No."

Chapter 73

1

As she waited for Owen, Samantha wondered how many other innocent people were in the Huntsville Unit besides her uncle. She had read that according to estimates, at least two percent of prisoners in the United States were innocent. There were about fifteen hundred inmates in this prison. Two percent of fifteen hundred was thirty. Did these innocent people want revenge against those who had put them behind bars? Samantha was sure at least some of them did.

Owen came in, sat across from Samantha, and lifted the phone.

"Hi, Sam," he said, smiling.

"Hi, Owen. How are you doing?"

"I'm fine. How are you?"

"Fine."

"I'm so glad to see you, Sam. How's your mom?"

"She's fine. She says hello."

"Great." Owen smiled. "How's Tom?"

Owen didn't know that Tom was officially missing (Samantha had asked her mother and Louise, who had no idea about Tom's revenge plan, not to tell Owen that his son had gone missing). When he last visited Owen, Tom had told him that he wouldn't be able to visit him for a long time.

"He's fine."

"Does he plan to visit me this year?"

"I don't know."

"How's your job?"

"Good. Remember Paul Marston? He was the prosecutor at your trial."

"Yeah."

"He went to prison for murder."

Their conversation might be monitored, so Samantha couldn't tell Owen that they had framed Marston. He should have no trouble figuring it out. A few days before the trial began, Owen had asked Tom to punish the prosecutor and the jurors if he was convicted (he didn't want the judge to be punished because it wouldn't be the judge's fault if he was found guilty). Tom had promised to fulfill Owen's wish and said that he might set them up, so they would know what it was like to be in prison for a crime you didn't commit. Owen had loved the idea.

Owen raised his eyebrows. "Wow! When?"

"Last month."

"Who did he kill?"

"Some young woman. He got a life sentence."

"Wow! He seemed like a decent fellow." A little smile touched Owen's lips.

She would tell Owen about Lochner, Almanza, and Edgehill the next time she visited him or when he called her.

"How's your health?" Samantha asked.

"Fine."

"Is your blood pressure okay?"

"Yes. I called Caroline last Wednesday. She said she's going to Vegas next month. I miss Vegas."

"I may go with her."

"Have you ever been to the buffet at Wynn?"

"No."

"You have to try it. Louise says their food is amazing."

"I'll try it."

"Louise was here in May. She looks great."

Samantha nodded.

She liked Louise. Louise had defended Owen and never abandoned him (it was Owen who had suggested that they divorce). She still hadn't remarried, although it had been six years since the divorce.

Samantha felt sorry for her: Louise was infertile and had no children of her own.

Speaking of children, her mother was right; she needed to have a baby soon. If her boyfriend didn't want to have a child, she would use a sperm bank.

"Her niece got into Princeton," Owen said.

"That's wonderful."

"She's going to study psychology."

2

Samantha promised to visit Owen again in November, then hung up the phone and headed for the door. When she came out of the visitation room, a prison guard walked up to her and said, "Are you Samantha Sheldon?"

"Yes."

"I need you to come with me."

"What's this about?"

"They have a few questions for you."

"Who?"

"Please follow me."

Marston must have told the police that he had been set up by Tom.

They had nothing to worry about. The police had no evidence that Tom had framed anyone.

Did the cops think she was Tom's accomplice?

They might follow her after she left the prison, so when she arrived in Dallas, instead of going to Tom's place, she would get a motel room (she would stay there for only one night because she was leaving for Jacksonville tomorrow).

Chapter 74

1

The door opened, and Samantha Sheldon entered the room. A moment later her eyes met Emma's. Samantha's face didn't change.

The guard closed the door behind Tom Dekker's cousin.

"Hi, Susan," Emma said.

"Please take a seat, Ms. Sheldon." Laporte pointed to the chairs on the other side of the table.

"Who are you?" Samantha asked.

"I'm your friend Emma," Emma said. "Don't you remember me?"

"No. And my name isn't Susan."

"You look just like my friend Susan."

"Who are you?" Samantha asked Laporte.

"I'm John Laporte. I'm Robert Lochner's attorney. You know Robert, don't you?"

"No. What's this about?" Samantha looked around the interview room.

"Do you know where Tom Dekker is?" Laporte asked.

"No. He went missing a year and a half ago."

"Tom framed Robert Lochner for murder.

Samantha raised her eyebrows. "Are you sure it was Tom?"

"Yes."

"I know nothing about that."

"Please take a seat."

Samantha pulled out a chair and sat down.

"Tom framed Robert because he sat on the jury at Tom's father's trial," Laporte said. "He also framed Emma's husband, Paul Marston. Paul was the lead prosecutor at Owen Dekker's trial."

"I think you're mistaken. Tom's a good man. He'd never do something like that."

"You helped Tom frame Paul. You also helped him frame Reece Edgehill, who was a juror at your uncle's trial. Remember Reece?"

Samantha scowled. "Are you insane?" she said indignantly. "I didn't help Tom frame anyone."

"We have proof." Laporte took a tablet from his briefcase, opened a video file, and put it in front of Samantha.

On the screen Samantha Sheldon and Tom Dekker were standing at the door to Edgehill's apartment. The video was shot by a thermometer-shaped spy camera Victor Hopper had placed on one of the posts supporting the overhang above Edgehill's door two days before Heidi Monger's murder.

Lisa/Julie opened the door and let Samantha and Tom in.

"This is the door to Reece Edgehill's apartment," Laporte said. "The video was shot on the night of Heidi Monger's murder."

Laporte skipped to the part where Samantha, Tom, and Lisa/Julie came out of Edgehill's apartment, and paused the video when Tom closed the door.

Samantha shifted in her chair. "What do you think this video proves?"

"It proves that you were involved in Heidi Monger's murder."

"I don't think it proves that."

"We'll see. The question is, did you actively participate in killing Heidi Monger?"

"Tom didn't kill anyone."

"Who's the woman who opened the door? Is she Tom's girlfriend?"

"I don't know."

Emma said, "There's a reward for information leading to Tom Dekker's arrest and conviction. It's five hundred thousand dollars. This money could be yours, Samantha."

"Tom didn't kill anyone."

"You're facing a life sentence, Samantha. You should make a deal with the police. They'll give you immunity if you turn Tom in."

Laporte said, "You won't get immunity if Tom's other partner makes a deal first."

"If you think this video won't convince the jury that you helped Tom kill Heidi, you're wrong," Emma said. "Remember what happened to your uncle. Sometimes even weak evidence leads to a conviction."

The door opened, and Samantha turned around. Detective Patrick Craven came in, held up his badge, and said, "Good morning, Ms. Sheldon. I'm Detective Craven with the Houston Police Department."

Craven had been watching their conversation on the closed-circuit monitor in the observation room next door.

Samantha stood up. "I'd like to go home."

"You're not going anywhere, Ms. Sheldon." Craven pulled out a pair of handcuffs. "You're under arrest."

"For what?"

"For the murder of Heidi Monger."

Samantha put her hands behind her back, and the detective cuffed them.

"I want a lawyer," Samantha said.

Chapter 75

1

Samantha took Craven and his partner, Detective Pablo Navida, to her car, and Craven did a quick search of the vehicle. The glove box contained a rental agreement with Samantha's name on it; she had rented the car in Dallas yesterday. Craven found two cellphones in Samantha's bag, both of which were locked. When he asked Samantha to unlock them, she said that she had forgotten the passcodes.

"If you're innocent, you have nothing to worry about," Craven said.

"I'll unlock them when I remember the passcodes."

Craven opened the car's GPS history and wrote down the last ten destinations, hoping one of them was Tom Dekker's address. He texted the addresses to Detective Beau Ferland and asked him to check them out.

When they got into the detectives' car, Craven said to Samantha, "Laporte was right. You won't get immunity if Tom's other accomplice makes a deal first. It won't take us long to track her and Tom down. A few days at most."

He pulled the SIM card from one of Samantha's phones, put it in his cell, and looked up the phone number associated with the SIM card in the settings. There were no contacts stored on the SIM card. He repeated the procedure with Samantha's second phone (its SIM card had no contacts on it, either), then called Detective Delgado of the Houston Police Department's Homicide Division and asked him to obtain phone records for the two numbers for the last three months. Craven was going to try to track Tom down through his cellphone; he was sure his number was in Samantha's phone records.

The drive to Houston took an hour and ten minutes. As Craven escorted Samantha to the booking room, his phone rang. It was Ferland.

"We got Dekker and his second accomplice," Ferland said.

"What's her name?"

"Laurie Harcourt."

"I'll send someone to pick them up. Thank you very much, Beau."

Craven hung up and said to Samantha, "Your cousin and Laurie have just been arrested. Make a deal before Laurie does, Samantha."

2

Three years ago, Laurie's beautiful five-year-old son had been killed before her eyes.

Ethan was crossing a street on his bicycle when an SUV ran him over. Laurie had screamed her boy's name just before it happened, hoping he would hear her and stop. The driver didn't hit the brakes before he struck Ethan; he was probably checking his fucking phone. The bastard's name was Louis Carrera, he lived a block away from Laurie.

"You killed my son, you fucking motherfucker!" she yelled at Carrera after calling 911. "You killed my boy!" She wanted to rip this piece of shit apart.

Laurie and Tom had been dating for a year at the time.

Carrera received a two-year sentence and was released after serving nine months. Laurie didn't think her son's killer deserved to live. An eye for an eye, a life for a life. She asked Tom if he would kill Carrera for her, and he said yes without hesitation. A month after Carrera got out of prison, Tom had stabbed him to death in an alley not far from his home.

Laurie remembered how delighted she had been when Tom told her that Carrera was dead. Those who said that revenge was not the answer were idiots. There was nothing sweeter than revenge. Everyone was happy when Osama bin Laden was killed, weren't they?

Tom had always been there for her. He was the love of her life. She couldn't betray him.

"There's a reward for information leading to Tom Dekker's arrest and conviction," Craven said. "It's five hundred thousand dollars."

Five hundred thousand grand was a lot of money.

Would Samantha sell them out for half a million dollars?

For half a million dollars and immunity.

Samantha might have already started cooperating with the police: it might have been her who had told them where Tom lived.

"Who's offering it?" Anna Gibson, Laurie's lawyer, asked.

"Paul Marston and Robert Lochner."

Laurie had played a big part in framing Paul Marston: she had provided Tom with Marston's semen, which he placed on Alison Bowles's body (a week before Alison's murder, she had kept the condom after having sex with Marston). Her part in setting Robert Lochner up was minor: when they were in his house on the day of his wife's kidnapping, she had drawn Tamara Lochner's blood with a syringe, sprinkled it on the kitchen floor, and then wiped it off with a rag.

Detective Navida said, "If Samantha Sheldon makes a deal first, she'll get immunity and the reward, and you'll go to jail for a very long time, Laurie."

"We're trying to help you, Laurie," Craven said.

"You're not helping anyone by not cooperating with us," Navida said. "Tom's going to jail whether you testify against him or not. You can't save him, but you can save yourself."

"You don't want to spend the best years of your life in prison, do you?" Craven said.

"What did Samantha tell you?" Laurie asked.

Craven smiled. "A lot."

"Did Samantha actively participate in killing any of Tom's victims?" Navida asked.

Neither Samantha nor Laurie had taken part in killing any of Tom's victims. When he told them about his revenge plan, Tom had said that he would do all the killing himself.

"I want to talk to Anna." Laurie said.

"Sure."

The detectives stood up and left the interview room.

"I think you should make a deal," Gibson said.

"I can't do it. I love Tom."

"They're right, Laurie. Tom's going to jail whether you testify against him or not. You have to make a deal. Today."

She could buy a nice house with the reward money.

"If I make a deal, what will happen to Samantha?"

Would Tom forgive her if she cooperated with the police?

Laurie was sure that he would eventually. He would understand that it was the optimal course of action.

"She'll probably go to jail."

"For how long?"

"I don't know. I'm sure she'll eventually cooperate with the police, too."

Laurie took a deep breath. "Okay. I'll make a deal. But I won't testify that Tom killed that woman in California unless the Los Angeles prosecutors give me immunity."

"Sure."

Chapter 76

1

All charges against Robert Lochner, Dennis Almanza, and Reece Edgehill were dropped. The Los Angeles County District Attorney agreed to give Laurie immunity from prosecution in the Stephanie Jarvis case.

Two weeks after her arrest, Samantha Sheldon agreed to cooperate in exchange for a reduced sentence. In late October, Tom Dekker took a plea bargain to avoid the death penalty. He admitted to murdering Alison Bowles, Tamara Lochner, Stephanie Jarvis, and Heidi Monger. He got life without the possibility of parole. Samantha was sentenced to eight years. Both Tom and Samantha stated that the revenge plan was Tom's idea and his father had no knowledge of it.

On November 6, the Texas Court of Criminal Appeals overturned Paul Marston's conviction. A week later, five hundred thousand dollars was wired into Laurie Harcourt's bank account.

On December 6, Laurie announced a fifty-thousand-dollar reward for information leading to the arrest and conviction of the real killer of Isaac Hemphill.

THE END

SAMPLE CHAPTERS FROM

DEAD GIRLS

When Holly finds a phone with pictures of murdered women on it on the bus to Miami, she realizes that one of the passengers is a serial killer. A game of cat and mouse begins after the owner of the cell sends Holly a message saying that he wants his phone back.

Holly's shocked to find out that the killer knows her name and address. She races against time as she and her fellow passenger Nick Hayden try to figure out the identity of the owner of the phone. When he murders a young woman during one of the stops, Holly fears he'll kill her before the end of the day.

Chapter 1

1

A jolt of terror shot through Brooke when she peeked into the picnic pavilion over the foundation wall. Maggie was lying on the floor and the jogger was stabbing her in the chest with a knife. Brooke ducked down and covered her mouth to hold back a scream.

When Maggie had left to get a water bottle from her car, Brooke had decided to hide and scare her (they were in their twenties, but they didn't consider themselves too old for pranks like that). Maggie was accompanied by a man in a blue jogging suit when she came back, and Brooke wondered if he was flirting with her. Maggie and the jogger went into the pavilion, and moments later Brooke heard someone grunting. Then she heard a thud.

Are they making out? she had wondered, and peeked into the pavilion.

What should I do?

Her heart was pounding like a jackhammer, her stomach was knotted up.

If this is a dream, I want to wake up now.

"Nice," the jogger said in a low voice. "Very nice." A pause. "You're cute."

Brooke scanned the woods, praying that someone would emerge from the trees.

If she ran for help, the jogger would see her and chase after her. She wasn't fast, so she didn't think she'd be able to outrun him. When he caught her, he would stab her to death.

There were no other people in sight, so even if someone heard her screams for help, she would probably be dead before they came to her rescue.

A squirrel scampered up a nearby oak and vanished.

It was quiet in the pavilion.

What's he doing?

Brooke squatted, pressed her back against the wall, and looked up. The killer might see her if he came close to this side of the pavilion.

She breathed as quietly as she could, ready to bolt as soon as the jogger's forehead appeared above her.

What should I do when he leaves?

She should follow him and try to prevent him from getting away.

She heard footsteps on the other side of the pavilion.

Did he leave?

She counted to fifteen, then peeked around the corner of the foundation and saw the killer walking down the trail toward the parking lot. When he disappeared behind the trees, Brooke took out her phone and rushed into the pavilion.

She gasped at the sight of Maggie. Her friend lay faceup on the concrete floor covered in blood, her dead eyes staring at the ceiling, her mouth open in a silent scream.

"Maggie," Brooke called.

Maggie didn't answer.

She's dead.

Blinking away tears, Brooke dialed 911.

Don't waste time, Brooke. Follow the killer.

"Nine one one, what's your emergency?" the operator said as Brooke pulled the car keys from the pocket of Maggie's jeans.

"My friend's been stabbed in the Arbor Hills Nature Preserve," Brooke replied, running out of the pavilion. "She's in the pavilion near Arbor Vista Drive. I'm following the man who stabbed her. Please send the ambulance and the police. She's dying, please hurry!"

It would take the cops at least five minutes to get here. The killer might be gone by then.

What if she couldn't find anyone to help her stop the killer from getting away?

"What's your name, ma'am?"

"Brooke Osterman."

"What's your friend's name?"

"Maggie Culver."

"Where are you right now?"

"I'm running toward the parking lot on Arbor Vista Drive."

"Please stop following the man who stabbed your friend and find a safe place to hide."

"Send the ambulance and the police."

"They're on their way."

"Please don't hang up."

"Okay."

When Brooke ran out of the woods, she saw the killer approaching the parking lot. She slowed down to a trot so he wouldn't get suspicious.

Was he going to his car?

There were no other people nearby. She could find someone to help her in the main parking lot off Parker Road, but it was five hundred feet away and she didn't want to let the killer out of her sight.

She slipped behind the wheel of Maggie's Mazda and told the 911 operator, "He's in the parking lot on Arbor Vista Drive. Tell the police to go to the parking lot on Arbor Vista Drive."

When the killer opened the driver's door of his black BMW, Brooke started the engine and told the 911 operator, "He's driving a black BMW."

She had to stop the killer from leaving the lot.

Brooke backed out of the parking slot and headed toward the black BMW.

"How far are the cops?" she asked the 911 operator.

"They should be there any minute."

Brooke stopped right behind the BMW as it pulled out of the parking space. The killer had no time to brake and banged into the side of the Mazda, rocking it hard.

If he tried to drive away, she would ram his car. If he tried to get away on foot, she would run him over.

She pocketed her phone as the killer climbed out of the BMW. He walked over to her door and said, "Are you blind?"

Brooke rolled her window down a couple of inches. "I'm sorry. I stepped on the brake instead of the gas. I'm very sorry. Let me get my insurance information."

It appeared the killer didn't know that the Mazda belonged to the woman he had just murdered.

She opened the glove compartment and began to rummage in it, pretending to look for her insurance card.

"I don't need your insurance information," the killer said. "Just move your car, please."

"No, no. I don't want to get in trouble."

Half a minute later, the killer said, "Just give me your number. You can give me your insurance information by phone."

"Can you give me your insurance information?"

"Just move the car."

"Who's going to pay for the damage to my car?"

"This accident's your fault."

She heard a siren approaching.

"I'm not an expert," Brooke said. "I don't know whose fault it is."

"I'll give you two thousand dollars. Now move your car."

"Two thousand isn't enough. I have to replace both doors."

A police cruiser pulled into the parking lot, siren wailing, lights flashing.

"Did you call the police?" the killer asked, looking at the cruiser.

"No. Someone else did."

As the cops drove up to them, Brooke climbed out of the Mazda and waved.

"They're going to tell you the accident's your fault," the killer said.

The police car stopped and two officers got out with their guns drawn.

"My name's Brooke," Brooke said as she stepped away from the Mazda.

An ambulance came screaming down Arbor Vista Drive and turned into the lot.

Brooke pointed to the killer and said, "This man murdered my friend. Please arrest him."

Chapter 2

1

This is who I'll kill first.

She was a slim olive-skinned cutie, probably in her twenties, with long brown hair, big breasts, and a perky butt, wearing a purple tank top and tight blue jeans. The ID tag on her plastic suitcase said that her name was Veronica Mendez. Osiris had overheard that she was headed to Houston.

Veronica was his type. She was Castor's type, too.

Castor is going to enjoy raping her.

The phone number on the ID tag had a Dallas area code, so Osiris assumed that Veronica lived in the Dallas area. Was she going to Houston to visit her mama and papa? To see her hot boyfriend, who probably had tattoos all over his body (Osiris had no tattoos—not because he didn't like them, but because he didn't want to have identification marks)?

Veronica was traveling alone, which made her a good target. Was anyone meeting her at the Houston bus station?

The bus made only one stop between Dallas and Houston—in a tiny town called Buffalo, with a population of about 2,000—so they had two choices: they could snatch Veronica either in Buffalo or in Houston. Because there was a good chance someone was meeting Veronica at the Houston station, Osiris favored the former option.

He opened the camera app on his phone, surreptitiously took Veronica's picture, and then emailed it to Castor.

It was ten minutes to twelve. Osiris was waiting in line to get on the bus, two people ahead of Veronica, his small duffel bag slung over his shoulder. He occasionally glanced at the woman, who was staring at her cellphone, unaware that she had gotten on a serial killer's radar.

The bus was scheduled to depart at 12:05 p.m. and arrive in Buffalo at 1:40 p.m. It left Buffalo at 1:55 p.m. He and Castor would have fifteen minutes to abduct Veronica, which was enough because they knew what they were doing.

Osiris was thinking of sitting next to Veronica on the bus and building a rapport with her so it would be easier to lure her into their trap.

His phone vibrated, announcing an incoming text. The message was from Castor, and it read: "Nice."

2

Holly Williams handed her ticket to the bus driver fifteen minutes before she found a serial killer's cellphone with pictures of murdered women on it.

It was going to be a long trip, possibly the longest bus trip she would ever take.

Her destination was Miami, and she would arrive there the day after tomorrow at 1:15 in the morning, thirty-six hours from now. Holly liked traveling by bus—it was cheap and gave you a chance to see the scenery—but she couldn't imagine enjoying a thirty-six-hour bus ride. To date, her longest bus trip was eight and a half hours, from Houston to New Orleans.

Holly Williams was twenty-nine, tall, slender, with blue eyes and shoulder-length curly blond hair. She worked in the marketing department of a real estate development company in Dallas, and she loved her job.

After the driver, a lean middle-aged man with gray hair, checked her ticket, Holly gave her suitcase to a baggage handler and climbed into the bus.

Thirty-six hours. How do people endure long bus journeys?

They must be exhausted as hell and close to going insane at the end of the trip.

Holly loved Miami. It was a beautiful and fun place with hot guys, great nightlife, and amazing beaches. They called it the Magic City, and Holly thought it was an apt nickname. She had been to Miami four times, and each time she had flown there and back to Dallas. Why had she decided to take a bus this time? It was a long story.

"Is anyone sitting there?" Holly asked the man in the aisle seat in the seventh row on the right side of the bus, pointing to the seat next to him.

"No." The man shook his head. He was in his thirties, athletic, with a short beard and mustache, and wore a black T-shirt and blue jeans. A tattoo of a dagger decorated his right forearm.

"Can I sit there?"

The man smiled. "Sure." He stepped out into the aisle.

"Thank you." Holly slid into the window seat and put her canvas messenger bag on the floor. "I'm Holly. What's your name?"

"Nick."

Holly pulled a bottle of water from her bag and took a sip.

"Where are you headed?" Nick asked.

"Miami. You?"

"Same place as you."

Holly put the bottle in the bag and pushed it under her seat.

"Want to hear a joke?" Nick said.

"Yes."

"What's the difference between crocodiles and alligators?"

"What is it?"

"One will see you in a while and the other will see you later."

Holly smiled.

About five minutes later the bus door swung closed and the air conditioning came on.

"Good afternoon, ladies and gentlemen," the driver said. "My name's Bill and I'll be your driver today."

Bill told the passengers that they would be stopping in Buffalo and that the estimated time of arrival in Houston was four-fifteen. He asked them to use headphones and keep the volume low when listening to music, and said that they weren't allowed to smoke, drink alcohol, or use drugs aboard the bus.

3

At seven minutes past noon, the bus pulled out of the terminal and turned right onto Commerce Street. Holly took the charger from her pocket, plugged it into an outlet on the back of the seats in front of her, and connected it to her phone. Nick reached into his duffel bag and brought out a book called Napalm & Silly Putty, by George Carlin.

Holly stared out the window until the bus merged onto Interstate 45, then turned to Nick and asked, "Is it a good book?"

"Yeah. I love George Carlin. He was hilarious. Have you seen any of his specials?"

"Yes."

"Which one?"

"The one where he talks about the big club."

"It's a big club and you ain't in it." Nick smiled.

"I wish I'd brought a book with me."

"What kind of books do you like to read?"

"Science fiction and thrillers."

"If you get bored, you can take a nap."

"That's the plan. I brought an inflatable neck pillow. It's really comfortable. Did you bring a pillow?"

Nick shook his head. "No."

Holly opened a browser on her phone and searched for "Miami weather."

Nick asked, "Have you been to Miami before?"

"Yes."

"Do you have family there?"

"No." Holly closed the browser. "It will rain in Miami on Wednesday."

"Rains usually last only half an hour there."

"I love Florida weather. I'd move there if they didn't have hurricanes."

"Have you ever been in a hurricane?"

"No. Have you?"

"Yeah. Once, about twenty years ago. It wasn't that bad."

"Where? In Florida?"

"No, in North Carolina."

"I've heard North Carolina is a beautiful place."

"Yeah, it's nice."

Holly looked out the window and saw they were passing a wastewater treatment plant.

"What's the longest bus ride you've ever taken?" she asked as she took her earphones from her pocket.

"I took a bus to Chicago two years ago. That's the longest bus ride I've taken before this trip."

Holly plugged her earphones into her phone. "How long was it?"

"Over twenty hours."

"I like buses. And I like trains, too."

"They're safer than planes. If your bus or train crashes, odds are you'll survive. If your plane crashes, your chances of survival are slim to none."

"Yeah." Holly nodded. "Remember that Malaysian plane that disappeared a few years ago? I wonder what happened to it."

"I read that four people missed that flight. If I missed a plane that crashed, I'd buy a lottery ticket the next day."

"Do you think those people were saved by their guardian angels?"

Nick nodded. "Yes."

"Me, too."

Holly placed her earphones in her ears, opened the music player on her cell, and put on Just the Way You Are by Bruno Mars. When the song ended, she touched Nick's arm and said, "Excuse me, Nick."

Nick lifted his eyes from his book and looked at her.

"I need to go to the restroom." She smiled apologetically.

"Sure." Nick got up and stepped out into the aisle.

Dead Girls is available now on Amazon.com.

Made in the USA
Monee, IL
24 September 2020